FICTIONAL-ish

NATALINA REIS

————————HOT TREE PUBLISHING————————

LIST OF BOOKS

M/F STAND-ALONES
Her Real Man
Loved You Always
Blind Magic
Fictional-ish

M/M STAND-ALONES
Lavender Fields
Infinite Blue

THE JEWEL CHRONICLES
Desert Jewel
Snow Jewel
Rebel Jewel

Fictional-ish © 2019 by Natalina Reis

Fictional-ish is a work of fiction. All names, characters, events and places found therein are either from the author's imagination or used fictitiously. Any similarity to persons alive or dead, actual events, locations, or organizations is entirely coincidental and not intended by the author.

For information, contact the publisher, Hot Tree Publishing.

WWW.HOTTREEPUBLISHING.COM

EDITING: Hot Tree Editing

FORMATTING: RMGraphX

COVER DESIGNER: Soxsational Cover Art

ISBN: 978-1-925853-42-1

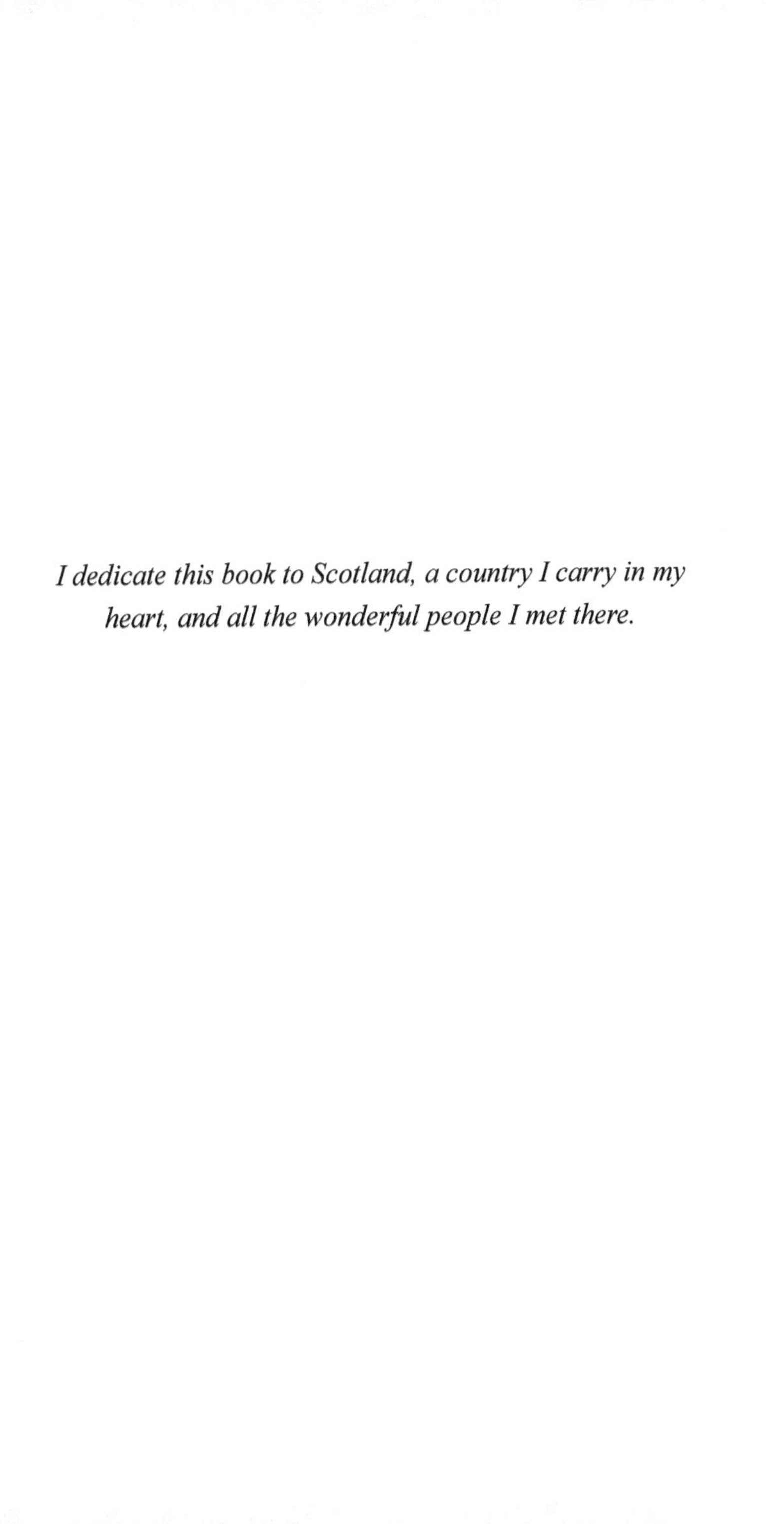

I dedicate this book to Scotland, a country I carry in my heart, and all the wonderful people I met there.

CHAPTER ONE
Wedding Hell

Kyle

"I fucking hate surprises, Livie!"

My groomsman—woman?—knew that. When most kids loved opening gifts to find out what was inside, I was always the one oddball who spent an inordinate amount of time sneaking into closets and underneath beds to take a peek at my gifts before they were wrapped. Not out of a sense of real curiosity but because I honestly did not want to be surprised. I didn't want my face to betray what I felt as I unwrapped them. So, I practiced my expression of delight for even those disappointing or just outright awful presents, because when it came down to it, I didn't want to disappoint anyone kind enough to buy me a gift.

When Livie spirited me out of the house that evening with the promise of a huge surprise, I cringed. I was sure it was some kind of bachelor party, but I was immediately horrified by the possibility I was going to hate it and thus crush my goofy but lovable best friend's well-intentioned heart. Livie was my better half. Always had been. I often wondered what would happen if she moved away. Or if *I* moved away. Livie was my sounding board, my go-to for anything I couldn't trust others with. We'd been through thick and thin and still stuck together in the end. I loved my freckled friend, and the last thing I wanted to do was hurt her feelings by hating whatever surprise she and my other misguided groomsmen had come up with.

"Will you stop fretting and move a little faster?" Livie was practically pushing me in front of her as I dragged my feet toward the door of an old, nondescript building I had never seen. She had driven us there with her usual reckless enthusiasm and evaded all my questions almost as efficiently as she avoided crashing into the other unsuspecting drivers on the road.

"You almost killed me on the way here." Not far from the truth. My stomach was still a bit unsettled from her usual driving antics. "And now it seems you want to finish the job by murdering me in some abandoned warehouse."

My head shot forward as she swatted the back of my neck. "If I wanted to kill you, I'd have done it a long time ago." She shoved me forward again. "Let's go, Kyle. I promise you'll like it." I hated it when people said that.

Livie had been acting strangely even for her. Ever since I had told her about my impending nuptials with her childhood enemy, her usual exuberant behaviour had been somewhat subdued. Which in itself was worrisome. I got it. At least, I thought I did. She and Mia were like two Betta fish sharing the same bowl—they took no prisoners. The fact I was marrying Mia could not have been easy to swallow and, to give her due credit, Livie had taken the news like a champ. But I knew that inside she was boiling. Livie had always been the kind to cover up pain with a smile, but I had long ago learned to see through those deceptive happy layers and sarcastic bite—she was not a happy camper.

The front door was unlocked, and we walked into a dark corridor that led us to—nowhere, it seemed. "Are you sure we're in the right place? There's nothing here but dust."

With a giant push, she shoved me through the wall—well, it was really a door I hadn't seen—into a bright room. I blinked for a second as I heard the yells and hoots from a small crowd of friends.

"Welcome to the bachelor party to end all parties." Livie's declaration made me shiver in apprehension. Oh shit. What had she planned now?

Once my eyes got used to the bright lights, I scanned the room around me. It was set up like an old British pub, with a dark wood bar that ran most of the front-facing wall, a few scattered wooden tables and chairs, and art nouveau lamps hanging from the ceiling and jutting out from the walls. Hell, I'd never guess from the looks of the outside that the inside was such a jewel of boozy architecture.

"I knew you'd like the old-world feel of this place." Livie knew me too well.

"It's fucking brilliant." It was. The whole atmosphere made me believe I had just stepped out of time and place. "Where did you find this place?"

She snorted. "I know people."

"Bullshit. You googled it, didn't you?" She was a true black belt of the Google search. We sat down side by side on a couple of the bar stools while my other friends gathered around us. "I don't care how you did it. I love it."

Livie jumped from the stool as soon as her butt hit the seat. "But this is just a small part of your surprise, my friend." Opening her arms wide, she made a production of looking around her like an actor on stage. "The committee and I have carefully planned an evening of sensual delights for our poor friend who will soon be deprived of the world at large." The small crowd whispered in fake awe.

"You speak as if I'm about to face a firing squad." Which was quite effective at rattling me just enough that my stomach filled with rocks.

"You're marrying the queen of the bitches." Never one to mince words when it came to my fiancée, Livie opened her gorgeous blue eyes and wrinkled her freckled nose. "Of course you're a dead man walking. So your friends decided to give you a night to remember. Are you ready?"

I shook my head and chuckled. "Quit the theatricals, Olivia Marie," I said, doing my best impression of her mom, the only woman capable of semi-controlling my best friend.

A big bang echoed through the pub, and a door opened behind the counter. Liam and Ben came through it, dramatically carrying a huge tray over their heads. They stumbled to the counter and almost dropped their burden. The tray slammed a bit too hard on the counter in front of me, a spray of liquid splashing up in the air.

"I present you your last meal." Livie stretched on her tiptoes so she could better look over the tall counter. "Your favourite food in the whole wide world."

She was exaggerating a bit, but not by much. The tray was packed with piles of chips covered in an obscene amount of chicken salt right next to a collection of sausage sizzles, oozing sauce, and fried onions from every angle. My salivary glands went into overdrive.

Livie stopped me from making a swipe at the tray. "But wait! What would be the perfect drink to go with all that wonderful food?" Another one of my friends emerged from the kitchen with a bucket full of beer.

We all attacked the food and the drinks with great enthusiasm. The sausages were sinfully delicious, and the beer washed it all down in a wave of coolness and bitterness. I must have downed at least three beers before I decided I probably should stop, considering my ride, who didn't drink often, was more drunk than the Drunken Scotsman. Surprised, but more than just a little amused, I watched as she stumbled all the way from the other side of the bar toward me, crashing into chairs and tables and spilling more than half of her beer on a couple unfortunate friends who were in her way.

"The fucking stripper cancelled on us." Her words spilled out of her mouth thick and slurred. I took the beer out of her hand and placed it on the counter behind me. She waved a hand above her head and licked her lips. "But no problem. Livie is here."

I chuckled and held her hands in mine. "What are you

going to do? Strip for me?"

She stopped moving for a moment and then let out a loud, reverberating burp. "Yes, that's what I must do—I'll strip." She pulled her hands away from me and began unbuttoning her shirt.

"Fuck. Are you crazy, Liv?" No, but she was totally wasted. I grabbed her hand and pulled it away from the buttons of her shirt. "You most definitely will not strip in front of all these guys." I had lowered my voice to an almost whisper and waved the other guys away from us.

She bent forward until her forehead was leaning against my chest. "But you'll be disappointed that the sexy stripper didn't show you her girls. And you're marrying that bitch, and—" She went quiet and still, and for a moment I thought she had fallen asleep, but she lifted her face to me. "I hate that you're marrying stupid Miss Perky." She suddenly sounded like her old teenage self, crying on my shoulder about something horrible Mia had done to her.

I brushed my hand over her head and kissed her forehead. "You knew I'd get married someday, Liv. What difference does it make that it's to Mia?" It was a rhetorical question. I knew exactly what was bothering her but couldn't do anything about it.

A little sob made her hiccup. "But she's a bitch. I hate her." She lowered her face to my chest again and sobbed a few more times. "And what about me, Kyle? What about me?"

I drew her closer to me, baffled by the pain in her voice. "What about you? You're my best friend and always will be.

That won't change just because I'm marrying Mia." I hoped.

With her mascara running down her freckled cheeks, Livie looked up at me again. "But you'll never love me like I love you."

She must have drunk more than I thought. "Of course I love you, fool. You're my best friend."

"No, no, no…." She pounded on my chest softly and then slipped a hand behind my neck and pulled my face toward her. "You don't understand. I love you. I've always loved you." And she kissed me.

The touch of her lips sent my mind spiralling out of control. We'd been friends for so long, and she picked *that* moment to tell me she felt that way? It was a sloppy kiss that tasted and smelled like stale beer. A kiss that filled me with guilt. I had crushed on her so hard when we were teenagers and never thought she felt the same. How had I missed it?

Bad timing. Terrible timing.

Livie went slack in my arms. A little snore told me she had fallen asleep, her nose smooched up against my chin as her lips slipped away from mine.

What am I going to do about this?

The only thing I could do—make sure I never mentioned this moment to her and hope she couldn't remember it in the morning. As much as I loved Livie, *we* couldn't happen. I was *in love* with her nemesis and getting married the next day. Livie had to move on.

***

Livie

There was a sickly smell of lilacs in the air as all the guests walked slowly but purposely to their seats. I sat in the back, avoiding the time I would have to stand by my best friend and watch him marry the queen of bitches. I hated weddings in general, but this one in particular. The simple thought of Mia walking down that aisle in her perfect, way-too-expensive white gown made me want to puke. Mia was not my favourite person in the world. In fact, there were so many people I would name ahead of her should I ever decide to make a list of my favourite people that she would need an airplane and a GPS to find number one. Truth be told, I hated her guts. It was nothing new either. We had been BEFs—best enemies forever—since we were in primary school.

The fact that we had grown up side by side did not change or influence the way we felt about each other. Mia, however, had always been really good at making others believe we were friends. My mother, who was one of her mum's friends, believed to this day we were like bread and butter, Vegemite and toast, mac and cheese… one didn't go without the other. We both knew though that we were more like water and oil, or fire and TNT.

Throughout our years in primary school and then high school, we brought the term frenemy to a whole new level. Miss Perky—as I decided to name her during the later school years, not so much because of her temperament but rather because her nipples always seem to stick out of every blouse she wore—thrived on conniving new and more creative ways to humiliate me in front of the whole school and I—in a much more subtle way but not any more saintly—did my worst to make her sound like a brainless idiot. We spent most of those incredibly useless years in a tug-of-war where neither she nor I ever really won. That was, until now.

Sitting in that gloomy church with the nauseating smell of flowers hanging from every pew tickling my nose and my gag reflex, I had to admit she had me licked. Finally. Yes, she had won. Big time. In a few minutes, she would be walking down that pretentious red carpet into the arms of the guy I had loved since primary school. Kyle, the boy who had made a name for himself stuffing live worms down every girl's shirt in grade three. I had been his first victim. When that squirmy, slimy, wiggly creature slid down my childish chest into the waist of my skirt, I nearly died. Not because I was scared of worms, but because I had no idea at the time what exactly was crawling inside my shirt. Instead of screaming like a banshee, I got Kyle in all kinds of trouble with the teacher and later the principal. Strangely enough, I took his mischief as a sign he liked me, and I was more than excited to join his bug-related trickery for the rest of our primary career.

As we grew up, it didn't take me long to realize I liked watching him, that slow burn in my gut sending little shivers up my legs and arms every time my eyes met his. The electrical shocks caused by a simple brush of the fingers or his knee against mine when we sat side by side eating ice cream at the Pink Parlour bar. Even though Kyle had never actually shown any interest in me outside the friends-forever arena, I was pretty certain he was just waiting for the right time. So imagine my surprise—and total and utter dismay—when I got a call from my BEF announcing her engagement to my boy. WTF?

Fast forward to today and this horribly tacky church where my hope for ever-after happiness would be getting married to the one person I hated the most in the world. My heart was crushed and my dreams burnt to the ground. There was no tomorrow.

My cell phone vibrated, and a quick glance at the screen told me it was Kyle. What did he want? Maybe he had seen the error of his ways and wanted to tell me the wedding was off.

"What's going on?" I asked him, my fingers crossed in desperate supplication to Lady Luck.

"Can you come up here?" *Here* was the little sacristy room upstairs where he had been getting his shit together with his father and best man. Whatever the shit was that grooms had to do right before the wedding—possibly pray for mercy or for an earthquake to stop the ceremony.

"What's wrong?" I asked, my heart filling with a new hope.

"I need your help." He needed my help. This was it. He wanted a way out of this freaky union, and I was just the woman for the job.

Despite my stiletto heels, I flew up the stairs and knocked loudly on the wooden door to the sacristy. Kyle appeared behind the door, a frown on his face, dishevelled and half dressed, his shirt unbuttoned with the tails flapping around his pants.

He grabbed my hands and pulled me inside, closing the door behind me. "I need help."

"Getting out of the church unnoticed?" I said, a little beam of madness touching my brain. "We could sneak you out the back, I guess."

"Stop messing with me," he said, half laughing. "I need help with this freaking shirt and bow tie."

A little disappointed, I gave him the once-over. "You look like hell."

"Yeah, well nothing has gone right this morning," he said, sweeping his fingers through his short black hair. "First, I get out of the shower, slip on a puddle, and end up in the ER being fitted for a boot," he says, pulling up his pants leg to show me an orthopaedic boot. "Then my best man gets the flu and can't leave his bathroom. Now this fucking shirt will not button and the bow tie is a mess."

I reached out for the bow tie hanging from his neck. "I don't know what you did to this thing, but it's hopeless," I said, giving up on trying to tie the damaged accessory that looked like it had gone through a shredder.

Kyle threw his hands up in the air. "Hell, what else is going to happen? My father is on his way to pick up the rings from my sick best man, and he might not make it back on time. What else can go wrong?"

He really shouldn't have asked me this. Because something came over me, and stepping closer to him, I grabbed him by the open collar of his shirt, pulled his face to mine, and said, "If you'll give me a minute, I think I can make this worse."

I never got the chance to show him exactly how I was going to make it a whole lot worse because someone knocked frantically at the door. Reluctantly, I let him go and opened the door. It was one of the bridesmaids, her headband askew and her strapless dress looking dangerously close to slipping off her impressive bosom.

"What's wrong?" Kyle asked, his face betraying the anxiety he felt.

"It's Mia," she said, the words coming out of her mouth as little gasps while she tried to catch her breath from running up the steep stairs. "There was an accident."

Kyle crossed the short space between them, reaching for her shoulders but dropping his hands and clenching them into fists instead. He took a deep breath. Her headband flew off her head completely, falling right by my feet, and her once well-coiffed hair looked a lot like the dust bunnies I often found under my couch.

"What accident?" Kyle screamed. "Is Mia okay? What happened?"

The unfortunate messenger tried to free herself from Kyle's insistent gaze in vain. "Sh-she's f-fine," she stuttered. "It was her dress."

Kyle stared at the dishevelled girl, his head cocked to the side in what I used to call his whatcha-talking-about look.

I came to his rescue. "What do you mean, it's her dress? What happened?"

The bridesmaid, looking relieved that she was no longer the target of his killer glare, took a few more steps inside the room and sat on a nearby stool. "Little Malory, her niece, was walking around with a glass of fruit punch and tripped… all over Mia's dress."

Restraining the fit of mad laughter begging to be released, I turned my back on her, covering my mouth with my hand.

"So her dress is ruined," Kyle said. "Somehow it doesn't surprise me, what with the way things have been going today. Didn't her mum say she had one in the closet that fit her perfectly?"

Yeah, if I remembered correctly—and I was pretty sure I did—her mother had offered to let her wear this amazing vintage dress that fit her like a glove—why did all the bitches have amazingly fit bodies? But the bridezilla had opted for spending a few thousand dollars on a spanking-new ostentatious dress instead.

"Mia won't hear of it," the bedraggled bridesmaid said, attempting to comb back her disaster hair with her hand. "She saw the accident as a signal that the vibes are not right today."

Kyle's eyes had grown to the size and shape of small saucers—an amazing feat considering the almond shape of his Asian eyes. "Is she breaking off our engagement? Is that what you're saying, Chloe?" Did I hear a tone of joyful expectation in his voice?

The girl jumped to her feet, stepping on the edge of her dress. A loud ripping sound sliced through the air as she struggled to straighten. "No, no, no," she said, looking forlornly at her now torn gown. "Just postponing it. She says she's getting really bad vibes from this whole thing. She told her dad to cancel the wedding for now. When I left the house, he was making some calls."

"Is she crazy?" Kyle exclaimed, his arms shooting upwards. "Do you know how expensive that's going to be?"

"Her father said he would do whatever his baby wanted," Chloe said, shrugging. "You know how he is."

Just as my heart was jumping for joy in my chest and I could feel my butt and my feet begging me for a little victory dance, I noticed my friend had dropped on the nearest chair, his forehead practically on his knees, his hands clasped behind his head.

"It's just a little setback, Kyle," I said, forcing myself to be there to comfort him.

His head popped up and his beautiful black eyes locked with mine. "Little? Setback?" he said, spitting out the words. "This is my wedding day too, you know. I had enough trouble working myself up to this, and now I have to do it all over again."

I was just about to ask him what he meant by that when he turned to Chloe, who was still fussing over the torn hem of her dress. "Why didn't she talk to me before she made that decision?"

In unison, Chloe and I both gave him the are-you-kidding-me look. Mia was entitled, spoiled, and all around the most self-centred person I had ever met, and everybody knew that. Surely, *he* knew that as well.

He dropped his head back to his knees. "Tell her I will

call her as soon as I no longer want to strangle her with my own two hands," he said, his voice muffled by his pants.

Chloe's eyebrows shot up into deep arches. "Do you really want me to tell her that?"

"Just tell her he will call," I said, gently guiding her to the door, my hand on her shoulder blade. "Thank you for bringing the news. You may want to stop in the bathroom and fix your hair." *Unless you want birds to nest there.*

We were left alone, Kyle and I. I wasn't sure what to do or say. Just a few minutes ago I had been ready to let it all out and confess my love for him in hopes of stopping the wedding. Somehow, now that the ceremony was a no-go after all, I was rethinking my insane decision. As much as I despised Mia, this man was my friend and I didn't derive any joy from seeing him destroyed and hurting.

I pulled up another chair and sat beside him, my hand drawing invisible circles on his back. "Sorry, Kyle," I said. "This must be really upsetting to you, but look on the bright side...."

Raising his head, he looked at me. "Bright side? There is a bright side to this mess?"

There was a huge bright side for me at least. Obviously, this didn't mean anything to him. "Well, you get some more time to reconsider marrying this crazy bitch." It came out with absolutely no thought or hesitation. I bit my tongue. As true as that was, it was not the right thing to say.

To my surprise, the corner of his lips lifted in a half smile. "Leave it to you to make me laugh," he said, a little chuckle escaping him. "I guess it won't hurt to wait a little longer. The wedding was her idea after all."

I perked up. "It was? You didn't ask her?"

"I did, but she was the one determined to have this big show of a wedding," he said, his back now straight, my hand caught between him and the back of the chair. My fingers began tingling, and not because of the loss of circulation. I could feel his strong back muscles beneath my twitchy digits, a feeling that was quickly spreading through my body into inappropriate places—we were in a church, after all. "I was happy having a short, quick civil ceremony. You know I suck at anything formal."

It was true. He had always been the easy-going, *whatever* person in my life. My grounding force. The one who could always bring me down from my bouts of frantic anxiety and ridiculous excitement.

"Why did you give in then?" I asked, certain areas of my body quickly catching on fire. *Get a grip, woman!* I managed to wiggle my hand from behind his back and hopefully stop the wave of heat coursing through my veins.

Kyle gave me the look—you know, the one that calls you crazy without actually saying the words? "Have you met Mia?" he asked, his eyebrows arched high on his forehead. "What Mia wants, she gets. End of story."

"Well… so maybe this little break is a good thing and it will give you the chance to re-evaluate your relationship and what you really want," I said, hope flooding my heart. "In the meantime, how does an unhealthy dose of chicken salt-covered chips sound?"

My mum was right—as much as I hated to admit it. The

way to a man's heart really was through his stomach. Kyle immediately brightened at the mere mention of cheap and delicious fast food.

"Let me get this monkey suit off," he said. "There's a great place just down the road."

CHAPTER TWO
Love Lost

Livie

In my dreams he always came to me dressed in a perfectly cut suit, his big, strong hands checking the cufflinks just like James Bond in every spy movie ever made. His long and confident stride brought him close enough to me that I could feel his warm breath on my face. With his hand he reached out and encircled my waist, pulling me closer to him before seeking my lips with his.

In reality, Kyle came out of his room in a pair of dirty joggers, scratching his dishevelled hair. The phone had rung while we were talking and he'd left for a few minutes to go answer it. Now, he slogged his way to the chair next to mine in the living room and plopped himself on it as if his muscles had turned to mush. His lips opened wide in a long, wide yawn that allowed me to see farther into his throat than I ever wished to. But that shadow of a beard across his handsome face and the way his black, silky hair stuck out every which way made me want to kiss him anyway. Only I couldn't. He still belonged to my nemesis. At least for now.

I was plotting. There were a million insane ideas percolating in my brain. To not take advantage of this respite—Mia putting off the wedding—would be even crazier than my plan to win him over to my side. There had to be a way of making him see how well the two of us fit together. How perfect I was for him and him for me. To just come out and tell him wouldn't work. At least that's what I told my crazed brain. It couldn't be that direct, that simple. Subtlety was not my middle name, however, and the more I planned, the crazier the ideas got.

"Where have you gone, Livie?" I heard him ask. I stared at him uncomprehendingly. "I was asking you something, and you were just staring out into space."

"Sorry. Spaced out for a second." Plotting, always plotting. "What's up?"

I had stopped by his apartment to make sure he was all right. Even though I couldn't understand it, he had taken the wedding disaster hard and had been sulking for almost a week now. My worries proved to be justified when he opened the door to a filthy, messy place. He might not be the tidiest person on earth, but the pigsty inside his house was totally out of character.

He combed his hair with his long fingers and smiled. "That was Mia." What was he smiling about? Hadn't the bitch left him at the altar just a week before? "She called to apologize. We're getting married after all."

If I hadn't been sitting, I would have fallen on my butt.

It took me a few tries to find my voice. "What do you mean, the wedding is on? She left you high and dry. Why would you want to marry her after all that?"

Kyle laughed, resting his head on the back of the couch. "Liv, I love Mia and she loves me. Why would I let something like a postponed wedding get in the way of our happiness?"

I stuttered again and had to cough to clear my throat. There was a gigantic knot stuck between my lungs and my vocal chords. "She cancelled the wedding over a dirty dress. Who does that?"

The smile died on his lips, and he straightened his back. "Liv, you know I love you. We've been friends forever, but I can't let you talk about my fiancée like that." I couldn't believe what I was hearing. "We love each other and want to be husband and wife. You have to accept that and put whatever the issues between the two of you behind you if we are to stay best friends."

"Are you really threatening to break up our friendship over this?" I was beside myself, even if a tiny voice in the back of my head kept telling me to shut up and accept what I obviously couldn't change. "She's a freaking bitch, and she will make you miserable."

Kyle raised his hand in front of my face. "Stop, Liv, please. I don't want to be mad at you." His lips were a tight, thin line on his gorgeous face. "Please, just be happy for me. This is what I want. Mia and I are good for each other. She's not the girl you knew anymore. Neither are you. We've all grown and moved on."

My heart had dropped into my stomach and was on fire, burning into a charred chunk of coal. It was over. All my hopes, crazy dreams, and even crazier plans had been crushed to a powder. This was really it. Kyle, the man I had loved since we were kids, was going to marry the only woman I could truly say I hated. I knew she would make him unhappy. Once the novelty was over, she'd be back to her true self and crush my friend's heart and soul.

As wrong as it sounded, I had to accept it. I didn't have to like it, but I had to suck it up and be happy for Kyle. Except I couldn't. I really couldn't. I knew Mia too well. There was no way she really loved Kyle. He was nothing but a toy for her to play with for a while and then discard like she had done with so many before him. Mia loved no one but herself. I wanted to be there for him, but I didn't think I could.

"I'm sorry, Kyle." Tears burned their way into my eyes. "I can't just roll with it. I love you too much, and I know Mia doesn't." Had I just said the three-letter word?

"I love you too, Liv, and that won't change because I'm married. I promise. I will still be your best friend. How can you doubt that?"

I'd had it. Jumping to my feet, I tightened my hands into fists and braced them against my hips. Both my face and my eyes burned as tears blurred my vision. "You just don't get it, do you, Kyle?" Inside I was yelling, but my voice came out a whisper. "I don't want to be just your best friend anymore. I want more."

Kyle tilted his head, a confused look in his eyes.

"What do you mean?"

"I love you. Love with a capital L. Like a woman loves a man." The tears rolled freely down my cheeks and collected into pools in the corners of my lips. "I don't want to be your groomsman. I want to be your bride and be loved by you forever."

Stunned, Kyle didn't move or speak, blinking rapidly. I didn't know what I expected him to do, but that was not it. Expecting him to hug me and comfort me was unreasonable, but I still wanted him to.

When he didn't do anything, I let out a little sob and grabbed my purse. "I get it—you're in love with Mia's curves and perfect complexion, with who she wants you to think she is. I can't be there to watch it, Kyle. I love you too much." He made a move to take my hand, but I backed away from him. "I hope she makes you happy. I do. But I won't be around to see it."

Before he could do anything, I turned and ran out the door, clutching my stomach as nausea and dizziness overwhelmed me. Mia had won again.

***

"What's the frown for?" Liam had suddenly appeared out of nowhere and was staring at me as if surveying a strange painting, eyes all screwed and forehead raisin-wrinkled.

I caught myself and smiled. "No frown. See?" I pointed at my mouth. "Only smiles. I'm the happiest man in town." I was, with one notable exception: my best friend wouldn't be here to share my big day. I had tried to call her a million times and convince her everything would work out in the end. I had a whole speech prepared, but she never answered my calls.

"Are you ready, man?" Liam gave me another suspicious look while I straightened the bow on my tux, wishing Livie was there to help me.

Today was my wedding day. Finally. Using her mysterious powers, Mia had been able to reschedule the whole thing in just a little over a week. Miracle Mia, I started calling her. I supposed the fact her family was loaded could have had a big role in the miracle, but still….

"Ready as I'll ever be," I said. The wedding had turned out to be a huge production even after I had asked Mia if we could maybe have a simpler affair, but she had her mind set on this fabulous wedding, and I couldn't say no to the woman I loved.

Liam was my best man and looked unusually well put-together. He was a jeans and T-shirt type of guy, and I didn't think I had ever seen him in a tuxedo. I almost didn't recognize him when he came in through the church door in the classic black tux, a shiny silk bow tie around his neck. "Hey, my best mate is being put in shackles," he had said. "The least that I can do is get dressed up for it."

My hands shook as I took my place at the altar next to Liam. The church was packed with guests, an ocean of colours mingling with the many flower arrangements decorating the aisle and the pews. There was an intense, sweet scent of lilacs hanging in the air that tickled my nose to the point I had to scratch it. The violinist began playing the wedding march, and I turned to the back of the church where my bride emerged, arm in arm with her father, and began her progress down the red-carpeted aisle.

I couldn't take my eyes off her. Mia was extraordinarily beautiful. From her perfectly coiffed hair to her delicious curvy body, she was exquisite. With her first wedding gown ruined, she had bought a new one that fitted her even better, the mermaid shape of the skirt hugging her round hips and the lace-edged décolletage emphasizing her voluptuous breasts. Desire stirred inside me, hot and out of control. I couldn't wait to get to the hotel where we were spending our first married night. Mia had been insistent about keeping the pretence we hadn't slept together since our reconciliation. "I'm in the eye of the public, and I don't want any wagging tongues to mess up our day," she had said. I'd agreed, but my body was not happy with the decision. I wanted to run my fingers and lips over her skin, taste the sweetness of her on my tongue, and get lost inside of her. Mia was creative in the bedroom, and making love to her was the most exciting thing I had ever done. I couldn't wait to explore further.

When she finally reached the altar, her father dropped her arm and offered her hand to me with a smile. I liked her dad, so I hoped my face did not betray the rather lascivious thoughts I was having. As her hand touched mine, I stopped shaking. This was really happening.

The rest of the ceremony was a blur. I remembered saying the ritual *I dos,* and the hot, sensual kiss Mia gave me at the end, but everything else was enveloped in fog. We left the church under a tempest of rice and rose petals and practically threw ourselves into the white limousine waiting in front to take us to where the reception was to take place, forty minutes or so away. As soon as the doors were closed and the car began rolling away, Mia reached under her dress and pulled down her panties. My groin caught on fire. Was she really going to make love to me right inside the moving limo?

"What are you doing?" I asked stupidly, unable to form a coherent thought.

Mia lifted the tight mermaid bottom of the dress until it was wrapped around her waist, exposing her naked self to me. I threw a quick glance at the privacy screen between the driver and us to make sure it was closed, and took off my jacket, dropping it unceremoniously on the floor of the car. The bow tie and the shirt went next, immediately followed by my pants and briefs. I was so ready, it hurt. This was the effect Mia had on me every time.

She had propped herself against one of the doors and opened her legs invitingly. The desire to bury myself in her right away was overwhelming, but she lifted her hand between us before I could place myself over her sexy body.

"I don't think so, sweetheart," she said, shaking her finger. "You pleasure me first. Then I'll let you fuck me."

I heard a grunt and was surprised to find out it came from me. I wanted her so badly right then, but I would do what she asked. Wasn't that what love was? Give and take?

I stretched the best I could on the seat, awkwardly bending and sticking my bare butt against the tinted window so I could taste her. Mia grabbed the back of my head as soon as my tongue met her warm folds and pressed me against her. It was hard to breathe in that position, but she was enjoying my ministrations, so I continued to use my tongue until she yelled out, her fingers knotting in my hair, fingernails scraping my scalp, pressing me so close I thought I was going to suffocate.

"Was that good for you, sweetheart?" I asked as soon as she let go of me.

The throbbing in my nether bits was unbearable. I needed her. As if reading my mind, Mia wrapped her hand around my arousal and stroked me before leading me inside her. I almost came as soon as my length slid between her folds, but she was not done with me yet. Her hands came around to my back and grabbed my buttocks, squeezing and kneading them, pulling me closer and closer to her. Her legs came around me too, crossing at my waist while she gyrated and ground me deeper inside of her until I could no longer control it. Every muscle in my body clenched and then let go, releasing into the best climax I had ever experienced. My body twitched for a while on top of her, spent and sated.

"Get off me, Kyle." Mia pushed me away. "We need to freshen up. We'll be at the venue in a few."

I wanted to lie down beside her and run my hands over her sexy body until I fell asleep. Instead, I sat up and collected my clothes to get ready to endure a long, crowded party I didn't want to be at. "Could we just skip the reception and go straight to the hotel?" I asked. "There are a few things I'd love to try on you." I winked at her as I pulled my pants on.

Mia stopped for moment and stared at me, a small frown on her lips. "Don't be ridiculous. They're expecting us. After all, we are the guests of honour." Her tone left no room for discussion. Further lovemaking wouldn't happen until much, much later after a long and tiring reception. "Besides, I want to show my new husband off. My friends wouldn't believe I was actually marrying Livie's man. I want to make sure I can rub you in their silly faces."

A bitter taste rose to my tongue. What did she mean? Surely she was joking around. Mia had a strange sense of humour sometimes. I shook my head and finished buttoning the white shirt. Whatever she had meant, we loved each other, and that was all that mattered.

* * *

Livie

Hard to believe that life went on as usual. Despite the turmoil and pain inside me, the earth still turned on its axis and new days dawned. Blurry-eyed and reluctant to get up, I lingered in bed a few extra minutes, my face buried in the pillow, unwanted thoughts running through my head. How dared the world continue to move forward when I could barely get out of bed in the morning?

Finding strength I didn't think I had, I dragged myself out of bed, took a shower, and dressed up. I still needed to pay rent. The weather outside was beautiful, a typical day for the end of winter in the southern hemisphere—cool with a ghost of warmth around the edges. The sun was a round, fiery orb in the blue skies, and the sight of such beauty made me cry. I wiped my tears with the back of my hand, irritated that I couldn't control my emotions. Over a man! Growing up I couldn't understand when other girls cried their eyes out after they broke up with a boyfriend, and now I was just as pitiful as those girls. But no, it wasn't the same. They had broken up with someone they barely knew but thought they loved. I'd broken up with a friend I'd loved all my life. How did I walk away from that without deep wounds?

Work at least distracted me. Being around anything to do with books was always good therapy for me. I was in charge of acquisitions for several bookstores owned by the company I worked for. I often buried myself in books in search of those I thought would sell. In the process, I had found many amazing authors who would go otherwise undiscovered. I loved working for a corporation that strove to be different from others. While other bookstores had a tendency to snub independent authors, ours always supported them, proudly displaying them up front where no one could miss them.

"You look like shit." My boss, Jackson, didn't believe in subtlety. He was standing by my desk, staring down at me and grimacing. "What the hell happened?"

I'd had an especially turbulent night, my mind drowning in memories of the times Kyle and I had been inseparable.

I had thought we'd be like that forever. So many times I had wondered whether he felt the same way I felt about him. All those good memories had turned into melancholy and kept me up at night and in a daze throughout the day.

"Nothing, I had a bad night, that's all." I avoided his eyes but could still feel his piercing scrutiny. Jackson was a good guy and great boss. Not many CEOs cared about their staff as he did, but sometimes that quality turned into an annoying trait when he became way too curious about my personal life. "I'll be fine. Do you need something?"

"You have the worst dark circles under your eyes. Are you sure you're not sick?" He never gave up. Ever. "I can give you the day off if you need to see a doctor, Livie."

"I'm okay." The words shot out with a lot more irritation than what I meant to. "Sorry. I'm all right, Jackson, really. What do you need?"

He looked at the papers he held in his hands as if suddenly remembering them. "Yes, if you had a bit of time to go over this list. I can't make heads or tails of it, and I have a meeting out of town in a few hours." He peered at me again, squinting. "If you're not up to it, I can ask Lucy instead."

No, this would be the perfect distraction—mindless, boring work. "I'll do it." He thanked me and turned to leave, but not before throwing another worried glance at me. "I'm okay, I promise. Go to your meeting and stop fussing about me."

The rest of the day was a blur of titles and checklists, rote tasks that effectively took my mind from the dangerous and dark place it had been for the past couple weeks. Kyle was married now. Even though I had avoided social media, once in a while, I would catch sight of a wedding picture and my heart bled all over again. Seeing the smile I loved so deeply hurt too much now. Watching him looking at Mia, resplendent in her designer wedding gown, with such adoration in his eyes was heartbreaking. Why couldn't he look at me like that instead?

Common friends couldn't help but slip news of the newly married couple every so often; they were still enjoying the warm and white sands of the Maldives, their honeymoon pictures showing how happy they both were. Everyone was whispering about Mia's change for the better, all for the love of one good man. Bullshit! I didn't believe it for a second. I knew her too well, but Kyle loved her, and what was it people said? *Love conquers all.*

I wanted him to be happy but away from me, somewhere I wouldn't have to listen to anecdotes about their lives or come across pictures of their bliss. I needed to go somewhere far away where I could bury my head in the sand and pretend I'd never met Kyle. Except I couldn't. Where would I go? I could barely afford a vacation somewhere in Australia, much less go anywhere for a long period of time.

I left the building with my back straight and determined to put the whole sorry incident behind me. Feeling better, I grabbed a coffee from the Starbucks across the street and walked purposely down to the train station. The sea of commuters pressed around me as we all rushed to board the train, and I almost tripped over someone's feet.

There was not one available seat in sight, so I held on to the overhead bar and braced myself against the jerky moves of the carriage. When the doors opened at my stop, I propelled myself toward them, helped by the throng of people behind me. It wasn't until the train was moving away, leaving me behind on the station platform, that I realized I had dropped the book I'd had in my hand. I watched the train vanish down the line, tears dancing in my eyes and an indescribable sadness exploding inside of me. I would never again see the words inscribed on the inside cover, written in a familiar sloppy script, that said, "Love you forever, my friend." How appropriate that I would lose the last book Kyle had given me.

* * *

Kyle

Married life was not as smooth as I'd expected. Our honeymoon in the Maldives had been a whole month of sensual bliss. Mia was insatiable in bed, so much so that for the first time in my life—and quite a surprise it was—I was looking forward to a quiet night on the couch, reading a book and drinking coffee. When I suggested it, Mia laughed hysterically and proceeded to undress me for yet another exciting but exhausting lovemaking session. I began questioning my sanity and my masculinity. What man would complain about having too much sex? Maybe I was coming down with something. Tropical climates sometimes had weird effects on those who were not used to them, or maybe I had been stung by an insect and had some kind of flu-like condition. Whatever it was, I was happy we were back in good old Australia where spring was colouring everything in sight and I could go back to my job. My editor, Samuel, had left me messages asking me to accept a few assignments. I was ready to tackle as many as I could, so I had called him back as soon as I was in town and accepted the jobs.

"What are you doing, Kyle?" Mia was getting ready for a day at the spa with her friends. I didn't know much about spas, but it seemed counterproductive to prim yourself up beforehand. Yet that's what my wife had been doing for the past hour—putting on makeup, doing her hair to within an inch of perfection, shaving her legs, and a number of other things I didn't know the name to.

"Working," I answered, stealing a glance at her. She was perfect, and as soon as my eyes landed on her body, my hormones went into overdrive. *Damn! Behave.* "I'm writing a couple of articles for Samuel."

"That weird guy from the magazine?" Everything seemed weird to Mia if it didn't meet her strict expectations of physical beauty, a trait I had just begun to notice. Nobody's perfect, right? We all had our flaws, and Mia was not any different. I nodded, lowering my eyes to the keyboard again. "Why do you insist on working? I told you before, I have enough money to keep us both in the lap of luxury forever. Why don't you go to the spa and treat yourself to a man-grooming day?"

Nothing against guys who attended to their looks, but the suggestion left a sour taste in my mouth. Was she suggesting I was not groomed enough? I grumbled a reply, and she slipped her arms into the silky coat she had bought the day before.

"Whatever! Just be ready to attend to my needs when I get home, darling," Mia said, bending down and tilting my chin up to plant a kiss on my lips. Her words vibrated on my skin as she whispered, "I'll be ready for some nooky, sweetheart."

Despite my will not to respond to her promise of sensual pleasure later that day, my body had other ideas. I latched my lips around hers, already swollen with desire. Her tongue stroked mine for a second before pulling out. I thought I groaned in disappointment. Mia gave me a knowing look and left. I could hear her laughing behind the closed door. Damn, and double damn, now I was so aroused I couldn't focus on my work. For a moment I contemplated taking a warm shower and attending to the problem myself, but if I did, would I be able to perform to her requirements when she came back? In the end, I did take a shower—a very cold, very shrivelling type of shower.

CHAPTER THREE
Scotland Bound

Livie

"Are you crazy?" My mum was not known for subtlety. She was also one of the few women left on the planet who wore giant rollers at night. She looked like a weird cartoonish character as she followed me around the house. Gesturing frantically, a telltale sign of her Italian ancestry, she almost crashed into my back when I suddenly stopped by the bed.

"Mum, I'm going and that's that." I dropped the pile of sweaters I was carrying into the suitcase on top of the bed. "It's an amazing opportunity, a dream come true. Nothing you can tell me will change my mind."

"But Scotland? Why so far? Couldn't you just open a bookstore here in good old Australia?" I turned around to pick up some more clothes, and Mum blocked me in a move that would put a rugby player to shame. "It's because of Kyle, isn't it?"

I evaded her and managed to reach the dresser. "I couldn't care less what Kyle does or does not do. If he chooses to ruin his life by marrying that bitch, it's his prerogative. Life goes on." Even if my heart was crushed into a powder and blown into the winds. "He made his choice. Now I'm making mine."

Mum was not going to give up easily. "But you've been best friends since you were little. And what happened between you and Mia? You were such good friends." How could she be so clueless?

In anger, I turned around so fast I almost knocked her off her feet. "Don't be daft, Mum. Mia and I have never, ever been friends. Ever." I enunciated each sound for effect. "I've hated her with a passion from the moment I first met her, and the sentiment is totally mutual." My mum blinked and stumbled backward just enough for me to realize how shocked she was. "She's been trying to outdo me forever, and she has won this war—she got Kyle. If he's dumb enough to marry her, then they deserve each other."

With pain and frustration boiling in my chest, I plopped myself on the edge of the bed and burst out crying. *Damn!* This was the last thing I wanted to do. But the tears wouldn't be denied. They kept forcing their way out until they poured like a salty waterfall over my cheeks.

My mother sat next to me and slid an arm over my shoulders. "I'm so sorry, honey. I had no idea." She patted my back with her usual awkwardness. She had never been very good in situations like this, one of the reasons I didn't usually confide in her. "What's wrong with Mia? She always seemed like a nice girl."

I swore I heard a bone crack when I snapped up my head.

"She's a psychotic, manipulative bitch who will do anything to get her way. Everybody knows that except her parents, Kyle, and apparently you and Dad." She blinked in dismay. "I'm going to Scotland, Mum. There is nothing left for me here." I realized I was being cruel to her. After all, I was leaving my parents behind, but at that moment I was also furious at them. How could they both be so blind to believe that devil's spawn was my friend? It would have been funny if it wasn't so tragically sad.

Mum dropped her hands on her lap and looked at me with suspiciously shiny eyes. "I really am sorry, Olivia Marie. Dad and I will support you in whatever you decide, no matter how sad we are to see you move so far away." She wiped a stray tear with the back of her hand. "We love you, you know that."

Guilt filled me with its poisonous gases, and I threw myself into her arms. "Sorry, Mum. I'll miss you too. But look at it from the positive side." I was the queen of the silver linings, even though I was having a hard time finding one in my current situation. "Dad has always wanted to take you to see where his family came from in Scotland. Now you can. I'll be your personal tour guide and hotel."

Crisis averted—at least for now—I finished packing my bags while my mum removed her rollers and did her hair. I had already shipped a lot of my household goods to Montrose, the little town in Scotland where I would be setting up my store. My dad had offered to drive me to the airport in the morning, but I had decided it would be easier for everyone if I spent the night at a hotel next to the airport and left from there. No goodbyes, no tears.

My father was in the living room, making himself scarce while I was having my emotional breakdown with Mum. Neither of my parents had ever been too proficient at emotional support. They were great parents but a little lacking in this area. Faced with some kind of emotional crisis, neither had a clear idea of what to do. The Italian in my mother tried to solve every sentimental ailment with food, and my dad stayed out of it altogether. By the time I sat in the back seat of my father's car, my mum had handed me a huge box full of cannoli and lamingtons "for the trip."

I wasn't looking forward to living so far from my parents. In spite of their failings, I loved them and would miss them terribly. But I was a grown woman, and when my boss had offered me this opportunity, I could not turn it down.

"We need people we can trust to spearhead this new business venture in Europe," Jackson had told me. The conference room was practically empty except for the two of us and a large plate of Tim Tams. Jackson had a weakness for the biscuits, and they always appeared like magic whenever he was around. "We're starting by opening branches in England and in Scotland, and we will open stores in France and Germany soon."

Jackson was the CEO of a large cooperation that specialized in innovative businesses. All that meant was they came up with new ideas to revitalize already existing businesses. Their most recent venture was a return to old, quaint bookstores. Trying to steer away from the gigantic book moguls around the world, my company was opening small bookstores with equally tiny coffee shops that reflected the feel and charm of the small towns of yesterday.

"Selena has volunteered to take over the one in England." Crumbs peppered his white shirt, and I had to fight the urge to swipe a hand over it to clean his mess. "How would you like to be my man—woman—in Scotland?"

I almost choked on my own Tim Tam. "What? What do you mean?" The new business focused on individuality rather than the uniformity of most large chains in the world today. If successful, this could be the next big thing. It had never occurred to me I'd be offered the opportunity to manage one.

"You've told me before how much you've always wanted to own a bookstore. You'd be perfect for this." Jackson's lips were stained brown, but he seemed oblivious to the fact. I brushed a finger across my lips, hoping he would take the hint. He didn't. "What do you say? Do you want it or not? We'll set you up, take care of immigration issues, and all you have to do is pack."

There was an extra bonus to this proposal that even Jackson was not aware of—it would take me away from Kyle and his unhealthy relationship with my BEF, one I had no wish to witness. It had only taken me a few days to decide and accept the position. If it weren't for the fact my heart was bleeding from Kyle's betrayal, I would be thrilled with the opportunity. As it was, my excitement was severely dampened by my invasive thoughts and feelings, which stubbornly veered off to Kyle every chance they got.

After I said goodbye to my parents in the lobby of the

hotel, I returned to my room, wiping away the determined tears I didn't seem capable of stopping. I turned on the TV, hoping the background noise would keep my brain occupied enough I didn't have the chance to think of my parents or Kyle.

A soft knock on the door startled me awake. *Shit. I must have fallen asleep.* I wiped the thin string of drool stretching from the corner of my mouth to my chin and brushed my hair with my fingers. Who could that be? Did my parents forget something? Nobody knew I was at that hotel other than them.

Curious, I shuffled to the door, kicking the one shoe I still had on to the corner of the room. A quick peek into the peephole and my stomach dropped. My hands flew to cover my mouth as if to hold in a scream. *Kyle! What is he doing here?* How did he even know I was there? Mum, of course. She'd always had a soft spot for him, but then again, who could blame her? Kyle was a charmer, the sweet boy next door who was the picture perfect of innocence and wholesomeness.

I took a few steps backward, not sure of what to do next. Should I open the door and see what he wanted? Or should I pretend I wasn't in the room and ignore him? He knocked again. And again. I stepped forward and got friendly with the door, forehead against it and hands starfished on either side of my head.

"What do you want, Kyle?" At first, my voice came out so soft, I was sure he hadn't heard it. I spoke louder. "What the hell do you want now?"

His voice, which always made my heart flutter and sing, reached me through the door, muffled and strained. "I need to talk to you, Livie. You can't leave without talking to me."

Who did he think he was? I could do whatever I wanted. After all, wasn't he doing the same thing? "Go back to your wife, Kyle. That's where you belong." My voice caught on the last word.

"Don't be like that, Liv. I need to talk to you." Despite my anger, I felt the sudden urge to open the door and draw him into my arms, such was the pain in his voice.

No, no way. Don't be stupid.

"Please, Liv. Let me explain."

"What's to talk about? Didn't you go back to your wife even though she left you at the altar?" Silence. I slammed my palm against the door. "Well, didn't you?"

"Yes." It was a tiny word, but it carried my life with it— my hopes, my heart, my dreams. Tears burned in my eyes, but damned if I would let him see me cry.

"Then there's nothing to talk about, Kyle." My voice was so much calmer than I felt, anger and bitterness churning away inside my chest. "Go away and forget I exist. I'll do the same."

Turning around and half running, I threw myself on top of the bed, covering my head with the pillow so I couldn't hear him calling me, insisting on talking to me. I was done with him… or at least that's what I told myself as my heart wept inside of me.

***

I stood by the door, numbness taking over my senses as I realized she wasn't coming back to open it. My world was collapsing around me, shattering into a million tiny pieces, and I was helpless against it. Losing Livie was like losing a limb. We had grown up together, two peas in a pod. I couldn't imagine a life without her. Worse even, I couldn't bear knowing she was mad at me for marrying Mia. I loved my wife, and until the day of the bachelor party, I'd had no idea of Livie's feelings toward me. Even then I thought it might have been the beer talking. Was it possible to hate oneself for being in love with the wrong person? No, not the wrong person. What was I thinking? Mia was the right person for me, even though our union meant the loss of my friend. Confusion flooded all my senses as I rested my forehead against the door and took a deep breath, trying to regain some feeling. I did. And it hurt like hell.

After making myself leave with the full and painful knowledge that my best friend was leaving the country and me behind, I stopped outside in the parking lot to take stock. My heart was still beating, albeit too fast for comfort, and my lungs were taking air, however shallowly. I wasn't going to die because of this, but that knowledge didn't make it any less painful. I loved my best friend, so much that the mere thought of her smile made my heart swell like a balloon, threatening to push through the bones and flesh of my chest. But I had no choice. I loved Mia, my wife. Nothing was going to make me regret that, not even my freckled, blue-eyed friend. Despite what Livie thought, I had not made a mistake. I hadn't.

Resigned but far from satisfied, I drove back home, my head buzzing with unsettling thoughts and a deep, red-hot dagger of regret driven through my heart.

CHAPTER FOUR
A Cup of Fiction

Livie

"Ironmonger? What the hell is that?" I was standing in front of what was to be my home for the next few years, my hand propped over my eyes to protect me from the brightness of the sun, and staring at the store that occupied the whole first floor of the building.

Jenny giggled, obviously amused at my lack of knowledge of Scottish vernacular. She had been laughing almost nonstop since I arrived at her doorstep the night before with my suitcases in hand. "That's a hardware store. You know, tools and things for the house."

I'd only just arrived and was already convinced that the Scots were a funny lot, which would explain my dad's quirks, since he was a first-generation Aussie. Their accent was hard to decipher but yet pleasing to the ear, and while very guarded in demeanour, they were super-friendly all the same.

"My flat is over a hardware store?" I stared at my

friendly hostess, who sported a huge smile on her face. She was tiny and cute, with wild, curly ginger hair framing a heart-shaped rosy face. "Won't it be noisy?"

"Nuh, there's a landing between your flat and the store." She took a few steps toward a green door next to the store's big window and opened it. "Yours is the only flat in the building. It will be perfectly quiet. Well, the pub across the street might get a bit noisy on weekends, but other than that, quiet as a church."

I followed her into the darkness of the lobby and up the winding stairs. "How old is this building?" It had obviously gone through some recent remodelling, but the stairs and the whole facade were definitely old.

We arrived at another green door, which I guess led into my flat. "Oh, a couple hundred years maybe. Early nineteenth century, I think." Being around such old buildings was going to take some getting used to for this Aussie city girl.

Jenny opened the door to reveal another landing, this time carpeted, facing a short flight of stairs. "What the hell? Stairs inside my flat?" I put the suitcases down to give my arms a rest. That was a lot of steps to climb every time I came home.

She closed the door behind us and pointed to our right. "Here's the kitchen." Bloody hell, if there wasn't a fully equipped modern kitchen hiding around the corner! "The rest of the living area is up these steps." My mouth refused to close as I followed my new, and only, Scottish friend into what was to be my place.

The flat was beautiful and, however small, so much bigger than what I had expected. I was pleased.

"This is awesome, Jenny. Thank you." I was not sure whether she would think a hug too much of a personal space intrusion, so I smiled instead.

"I'm glad you like it." She clapped her hands and brought them to her lips. "Right. I'll leave you to it. There are sheets on the bed, extra blankets in the closet, pots and pans in the kitchen, some food in the refrigerator, and towels in the bathroom. Whenever you're ready, I can take you shopping for more. In the meantime, why don't we grab something to eat after you have a chance to settle?" She gave me her phone number—the house still had a landline—and left.

For the next couple hours, I unpacked, wandered around, mentally plotting how to make this gorgeous flat my own, and then took a quick shower. The shower itself proved complicated as I tried to figure out how to turn on the hot water and then almost fell over the toilet stepping out of the bathtub. *Freakishly tiny bathroom!*

With my wet hair still tucked into a towel, I punched in the numbers for Jenny. She picked up right away. We would meet in twenty minutes at the pub across the way for a quick lunch, and then she would take me to the bookstore.

I couldn't wait to see my new store. My first store ever—well, not exactly mine but close enough. I had dreamed about it since I was a little girl, bookworm that I was, spending more time with my fictional friends than with the real ones. Adding a coffee shop to it was the icing on the cake. Caffeine and books. What could be better? The skeleton of the store, so to speak, was already done by the company people—architects and decorators had carved what would be my dream come true from an old building in downtown Montrose and added the usual and expected touches. The twist in this venture was that I had the freedom to change it to fit my vision and make it mine-ish. All financed by my boss.

I slipped into a pair of soft jeans and a white sweater and wondered whether I'd need a jacket. While summer was still full blast in Australia, this part of the world was soldiering through what Jenny called the worst winter in memory. At the last minute, I decided to err on the side of caution and donned my winter coat even though I was only going across the street to the Witch's Heid. *Funny name for a pub.*

Jenny was waiting for me just inside the front door. "Not the best place in town, but I figured it would do for a quick bite." She looped her arm in mine and led me to a corner table. I sat on the small bench in the niche by the window, and she sat across from me on a rickety wooden chair. "The stovies are very good here and just the perfect food for this cold weather." Jenny waved a server to our table. "You in?"

It just happened that I actually knew what stovies were—a belly-filling concoction of potatoes and meat. My father often spoke of them in a wistful, slightly melancholic voice, remembering his Scottish grandmother who would stuff her grandchildren with it. I'd never eaten it since there was nobody from the old country around as I grew up and my father had never been able to reproduce his grandmother's cooking—or any cooking at all, for that matter.

We ordered stovies and a couple of lagers. I hoped I liked both the dish and the drink since I was insanely hungry and thirsty. My grumbling stomach reminded me I had not eaten a full meal since Heathrow during the layover between flights. I had snacked on a couple crumpets that morning smothered in butter as Jenny tried to convince me instant coffee was as good as fresh brewed. It wasn't.

"Have you thought of what you want to call the bookstore?" Another twist of this venture was the manager got to pick the store name. Individuality was the name of the game.

"How does A Cup of Fiction sound?" I had spent many an hour thinking of a name, the perfect distraction to take my mind off my recent heartbreak.

Jenny clapped her hands and squealed. "I love it. I'm so excited about this. This town hasn't seen a proper bookstore in a while."

The server came back with two steaming bowls of stovies and two beers. My mouth watered as soon as the warm scent reached my nostrils. I didn't know whether it was my hunger or the actual food, but nothing had smelled that heavenly in a long while. Forgetting my manners, I dug in with the fierceness of a starved sailor after spending weeks on maggoty tack. The hot potato and meat mixture melted in my mouth and slid slowly and satisfyingly down my throat. I may have moaned a bit.

"Better than sex." At least, better than the sex I had been getting for the past few months, which amounted to zero. I had lost all interest in dating. I was still too much in love with my traitor best friend to even consider kissing another guy, much less engage in more intimate activities. *I'm done with love. I am!* I might try sex again later, but love was persona non grata in my book.

Jenny giggled again, taking dainty bites from her fork. "Nothing like the comfort of stovies on a cold day." I nodded, shovelling giant portions of food into my mouth. "Let's go to the store after this so you can decide what you want to do before the opening."

"Did the books arrive?" I had to force myself to swallow a huge bite so I could speak. "Last time I talked to you, you told me there were a few on back order."

I took a swig of the beer, which was lighter than what I was used to and went down easily. A bit too easily. I had to watch it or I'd be drunk in no time.

Jenny followed suit, licking the foam from her bright pink lips before speaking. "Yes, the last box came in two days ago. I haven't been able to put it all on the shelves, but book-wise we are ready."

My corporation was gambling on the idea of a fiction-only chain. I adored fiction, so I loved the idea, but no one really knew what that meant in terms of sales. The whole venture could bust. For me, the concept of being surrounded by all kinds of fiction and nothing but fiction was heaven on earth. I just hoped there were many others out there who were of the same mind.

After lunch, we wrapped ourselves in our coats and walked down the street. The temperature had fallen several degrees, and I thanked myself for having brought a coat even though I had forgotten my gloves. The bookstore was on High Street in the same spot another one had been for the past fifty years. The owners had retired and sold the place. I hadn't been here before, but I had followed the whole project from my office in Australia even before I was offered the position. The building was old, like most of the buildings in town, and it had not been renovated or upgraded for almost as many years as the store had been open. My boss had invested quite a bit of money to make sure the place was not only up to modern standards of safety and comfort, but also that it looked well-taken care of—a place where a bookworm like me would feel right at home. Now, it was up to me to decide on the finishing touches, those that would make the place one of a kind.

We didn't have long to go. The whole coastal town was tiny, it seemed, lined along one main street that branched out into a myriad of other side streets. The building where the bookstore was located was about halfway down High Street, in a corner between the main road and a side street. The large display window frames had been painted white to match the windows of the flats above it and sandwiched the front door. Inside, a neutral-coloured rug welcomed weary feet into a shelf-lined world. Every wall of the two public rooms had floor-to-ceiling wooden shelves, filled with books and book-themed props. Here and there, to break the space into smaller, cosier niches, there were freestanding, chest-high bookshelves. The rest of the space was sprinkled with small bistro-type tables and wooden chairs, a couple of comfy, overstuffed armchairs, and a longish wooden counter that doubled as register at one end and coffee counter at the other. Behind it, a tiny but well-equipped kitchen ran the back wall, complete with coffee machine and a sandwich-press.

"Oh, Jenny. It's lovely." I opened my arms and twirled around, admiring the whole place. "I love it." I swept a hand over the powder-blue tabletops and the faded pink backs of the chairs. A few more touches and it would be perfect. "Where can we get some cheap vintage accessories?"

"I'm glad you asked," Jenny said, looping her arm into mine and pulling me toward the door. "Ever heard of Oxfam?"

I let her guide me down the street again with the promise of thrift shopping, and while she chatted away beside me, arm in arm like two conspirators, my mind wandered to Australia for a moment—and the beloved face of my best friend. I wished he was here to share this with me. Nobody else in the world understood and knew me better than he did. I missed him something fierce, and for a second, I entertained the idea of forgiving his betrayal and giving him a call.

No! You won't do any such thing.

Our friendship was over. He was married to my BEF and gone from my life forever. End of story.

"I don't get it, Kyle. I just don't get it." Liam had that outraged look he had been displaying ever since I got married. It was a mixture of disbelief, confusion, and anger. It would have been comical if I wasn't feeling the very same feelings myself.

Why do I keep doing this to myself? Was I turning into some kind of masochist who got off on pain and loss? There were so many questions flying around in my head at any given time of day or night, but there was always only one answer. *I love Mia. I have to give my marriage a chance.*

"Dude, what you do with your life is your business, but as your friend I have to say something." Liam took a long drink from the beer bottle and wiped his mouth with the back of his hand. "Why would you stay with that spoiled princess? What kind of hold does she have on your balls, mate? Is she really so good in bed you can't envision a life without her? Because I know love is not part of that equation. She treats you like a dog on a leash."

Yes, Mia was amazing in bed. Unfortunately. That's what kept me going back to her in the beginning of our relationship. We hadn't started as a couple. Not really. In the beginning it was all very casual. I'd meet her for drinks and we would end up entangled in my bed or hers. Nothing was promised, no words of emotional attachment ever exchanged. But then everything changed. Sex was not enough for me any longer. My everyday interactions with Livie had me craving a deeper connection. Before Mia, I had briefly entertained romantic thoughts about Livie. Every time I turned around, she was dating some guy I immediately took an irrational dislike to, and my heart was crushed. No, pureed to a messy, nondescript pulp. A bleeding heart could make a man do some pretty stupid stuff. Unfortunately, I was not immune to the stupidity bug. But deep down I knew, Livie was my friend. Period.

"You let go a true friend and picked Mia instead? I remember how you used to pine over Livie. What happened to that?" My friend had been watching too many romantic comedies with his girlfriend. I chuckled humourlessly. "Come on, dude. Tell me the truth. What is this woman holding over your head?"

I loved her, that's what. Or at least I thought I did. Lately I'd been having doubts. After only three months of married bliss, the bliss was severely lacking. The sex was still amazing, but I had found myself avoiding it more often than not. Mia was turning out to be not so much the sweet woman I thought she was and more the spoiled, selfish, even mean one Livie always claimed her to be. Besides our interaction in bed, there wasn't much of a connection between us. She wanted to spend her days in spas and her nights at clubs and society events. I wanted to sit at home together and watch a movie or cuddle on the couch with a book. But gossip was her worst trait. Not a day went by without her bad-mouthing someone undeserving of such judgment. Nobody seemed to measure up to her. Not even me. Especially me. If I had to rank her priorities on a totem pole, I would be the lonely guy at the bottom, just below the cat.

"Let's change the subject." I did not want to dwell on this.

It was too painful and made me feel like a total idiot on top of everything else. "It is what it is and leave it at that." He raised his eyebrow. "Besides, Livie went to Scotland. By now she has a red-haired, kilted boyfriend and doesn't have the time to even think of me."

If I could ever choose a superpower, it would be that of turning back time and undoing something that at the time seemed so insignificant, but ended up changing my whole life. For the worse. I would go straight to that day and un-ask Mia to marry me. I'd walk away the fastest my legs would carry me and never talk to her again. But I didn't. Allowing her beauty to cloud my judgment, I tied myself to a woman who was not who she seemed to be. I still hoped I was judging her too harshly and that any day now she'd prove me wrong. I was not, however, holding my breath.

* * *

Livie

"Don't ever say I don't take good care of you." Jenny's Scottish accent was now so familiar to my ears, I didn't even hear it anymore. She handed me a huge to-go cup. "A large latte from the Coffee Pot especially brewed for you."

I smiled and took the cup from her. She spoiled me rotten. "Thank you, love. I don't know what I'd do without you." The coffee was hot and smooth, bringing life and heat back to all my extremities as it slid down my throat. "Holy shit, this tastes amazing. Did Morag brew this? She's like a coffee goddess." I giggled, taking another sip. "Nobody saw you, right?" It just wouldn't look good if people caught me drinking coffee from another coffee shop.

Jenny unwrapped her scarf and threw her coat and gloves on top of a chair behind the counter. She shook her head. "I was stealthier than a spy. Don't forget you are interviewing today."

"Crap! I hate doing that." I had been trying to hire a second employee, one of the immigration requirements in Scotland. In order for me to be able to live and run a business in the country, I had to have two locals as full-time employees. So far, I only had Jenny. I had interviewed a couple of people who did not look promising, and I had someone else coming later that morning. "Can't you do it for me?"

"You're the boss, lass. Not me." Jenny busied herself straightening up around the store, effectively leaving the burden of job interviews solidly in my lap.

I stole a glance at the wall clock. I had only a few minutes left before the candidate arrived. "Jenny, hold the fort for a few. I'm going to use the bathroom." Not waiting for the protest I was expecting, I almost ran to the bathroom in the back of the store. Jenny hmphed behind me, and I laughed. "I'll be back before he gets here. I promise."

By the time I returned, Jenny was involved in a conversation with a dark-haired man who towered over my friend by at least a foot. I stopped to study him. Was he the new candidate? He looked a bit too old for a job that paid very little and lacked the kind of lustre a more mature person would prefer. So maybe a customer then.

"Here's the boss," Jenny said suddenly. The man turned around to face me, and I forced a smile onto my lips. He was handsome. Strikingly so. "This is Mr Callum Miller, Olivia."

I offered my hand. "Hello. Welcome to A Cup of Fiction, Mr Miller." I smiled again, still unsure of who he was.

"Call me Cal, please." He had a pleasant, soft voice and the typical strong accent of that part of Scotland. He held my hand in a firm grasp and shook it. "Pleased to meet you, Ms Dunn."

Feeling a bit flushed, I looked up at him and asked, "What can I do to help you, Cal? Anything in particular you're looking for?"

To my surprise, he laughed. "Och aye, a job for a start." He was my job interview? "If it's still open, of course."

"I'm so sorry. For some reason, I was expecting a uni student or something." Did he realize this job paid peanuts? "Please, come and sit down." I led him to a table and invited him to sit down across from me. Jenny was staring at us, an amused smile on her lips. She would pay for it later.

"The job is still open, then." I nodded. "You're wondering why a grown man would want a job like this." It was not a question. I nodded again. "First, I love books. Second, I like low-stress jobs." His eyes were pale blue like a summer sky. Mesmerizing. "But the real reason is I want to find out how to run one of these places and see whether it will be worth risking my life savings to buy a store somewhere in Aberdeen."

"Competition." A chuckle escaped my lips. "Corporate espionage, then?"

"I guess we could call it that." He laughed again. "Have I just totally ruined my chances at getting the job?"

"Oh, I don't know. I'm kind of intrigued by the whole thing." I turned around to Jenny, who was actively eavesdropping from the counter. "What do you think, Jenny? Should we hire a spy?"

Jenny took a few steps in our direction. "I dinnae ken. It might be fun." She winked at the handsome Scot. "I'd hire him. But I'm not the boss."

I took him to the back office and interviewed him for a while. He was not only handsome but also seemed to have all the right answers to my questions. With each passing minute, he was looking more like the perfect employee— well-read, enthusiastic, handy around the coffee machine, and with vast experience in book retail.

"How did I do?" he asked as soon as he was finished answering my last question. "Do I get the job, or do I have to go home and weep?"

I made a big production of pretending I was thinking, a hand cupping my chin and *hmm*ing under my breath. "Well, I suppose it wouldn't hurt to give you a try." Cal slapped the tabletop enthusiastically. "But I reserve the right to fire you if it doesn't work out."

"Deal." He extended his hand toward me, and I shook it, his palm soft and warm against mine. "When do I start?"

After some paperwork, we indulged in coffee and some

of the rowies that Mrs Bailey from the corner bakery baked for our coffee shop every morning and talked for a while. Jenny joined us off and on when the store was empty, and they both worked together to totally baffle me with a demonstration of Doric, the local dialect. I had a sneaky suspicion they were pulling my leg, but they swore up and down that it was a bona fide Scottish dialect.

When Cal finally left, I was stunned. For the first time since I arrived in Scotland, I had spent a couple of hours without once thinking of Kyle. I was relaxed and couldn't wipe what I was sure was a silly smile from my face. Maybe my heart was finally on the mend. Or maybe Scotland's fabled mystique was working its magic on me. I wasn't complaining.

We closed the store at six as always and headed to the pub for a bite to eat. Eating out was becoming a bad habit. Laziness had taken over me, and the simple thought of having to cook gave me the hives. Sooner or later I had to go grocery shopping and start eating at home, but for now, I was grateful for the comfort food of local pubs.

"What did you think of Cal?" I asked Jenny on our way up the street. The edges of my coat were flying behind me like the wings of crazed cranes, so I pulled them closer to me and held them in place. The wind blowing from the ocean was frigid and made my breath come out in thick white puffs. I shivered.

Jenny blew on her gloved hands and rubbed them together. "He was handsome, the cheeky bastard." That he was. Masculine beauty in the flesh. Well-defined jaw covered in a light stubble framing the most kiss-worthy lips I had seen in a while. His quick wit didn't hurt either. One of the things I liked best about Kyle was the fact he was funny and had a great sense of humour.

Shit! I was doing so good not thinking about him.

"He was pretty taken by you, boss." Jenny bumped me with her elbow and laughed. "Cal and Livie sitting in a tree—"

"Stop that, Jenny. You sound like a ten-year-old." But I laughed anyway.

The air inside the pub was thick with the heat from a larger than usual crowd. "Bachelor party," Jenny announced, clapping her hands in delight. "We might get a few pints for free."

Grabbing hold of my elbow, Jenny led me through the sea of people with the expertise of a weathered sea captain. "Excuse me. Pardon. Coming through. Bloody hell!" I followed her, laughing under my breath as she talked her way to the bar. "Can't a girl get a pint anymore?" she yelled at the barkeeper. "And put it on their tab."

Pint in hand, Jenny weaved her way through the crowd again with me in tow and found a free table by the window. "You're a true miracle worker, girl." I was in awe.

"You just have to keep positive, that's all." She poured some of the beer into my glass. "I learned that in yoga. Believe it and ye can achieve it." She burst out laughing at her own words and almost spilled half of the beer on the table. "What a crock of shite."

It took a while for the waitress to bring us our dinners,

but we did eventually get them. The noise of the room had reached alarming levels, and we could only hear each other if we screamed, so we remained quiet for most of the meal, not that it stopped Jenny from making jokes. If everything else failed, she was proficient at making just the right gestures or facial expressions to convey the meaning of her joke without uttering a single word.

On our way out, we paid for dinner and emerged into the cold evening once again. Despite the icy wind, a small crowd of people gathered just outside the pub door smoking. I was so distracted by the huddle of frozen smokers that I bumped into someone.

"Oh shit, I'm so sorry." Powder blue eyes met mine. "Cal? What are you doing here?"

The dashing Callum Miller, dressed in a long, light brown, woollen coat, smiled at me. "Ms Dunn, what a surprise. I'm here to wish my mate good luck. He's getting hitched very soon. You?"

"Just out for dinner and heading home now." Someone had lit a furnace inside me. "Nice seeing you again."

"Yes, you too. I'll see you tomorrow at work." Cal waved with a smile and walked around us.

It was then I noticed the beautiful blonde woman attached to his arm. Jenny must have too because she gave me the WTF look I had quickly recognized as her trademark. We both stared after the tall couple as they walked in the building. I couldn't decide whether to be disappointed or happy that my new employee was already taken.

"Eejit!" Jenny exclaimed. "When he could just as easily

have dated you instead." I shook my head, amused—even if a tiny bit dejected—and turned around to cross the street to my flat. "Men never know what's good for them."

And just like that, memories of Kyle and his boy-next-door face flooded my mind and my heart, leaving me gasping for air. I missed him so much.

CHAPTER FIVE
Planning an Escape

Kyle

"What are you reading?" Mia was curled on the couch, her face all scrunched up as she scanned the pages of a book. I had never seen her read a book with such enthusiasm or emotion. Mia was not much of a reader, unless you counted her beauty and gossip magazines as reading.

"Fabulous romance," she said, looking up at me. Her thick lashes framed her pretty blue eyes. At some point, I had been turned on by her bedroom eyes, but that was long gone now. "But so sad. The guy she was married to left her after only a few months." My stomach clenched. "You'd never do that to me, would you?"

I was thinking about it a lot lately. Our marriage was a total flop. Mia did not love me; that had been obvious for months now. In fact, I didn't think she liked me even a little bit. Anytime she had the chance, she made sure to make me feel like the biggest idiot on earth. Or the worst husband. Or both. I ground my teeth and a sour taste assaulted my mouth.

"Did I tell you?" Mia swung her long, sexy legs over the edge of the couch and threw the book on the floor, not interested anymore. "My father was able to secure tickets for the gala next week. You'll have to buy a new tuxedo. You already wore the one you have twice."

The mere mention of another outing where she paraded me like a competition poodle to all her society friends while whispering demeaning comments in my ear made my skin crawl. I jumped to my feet and almost dropped the book I was reading. "I have some errands to run." Lies. Excuses. I had nothing to do today other than ruminate on my bleak future as Mia's husband. "I'm not sure when I'll be back, so don't wait up for me."

I'd been finding frequent excuses to sleep on the couch because I couldn't stomach making love—no, having sex— with her anymore. What had started as love and passion had turned into bitter distaste. If she was willing to put me down every chance she got, I could no longer care for her even as a friend. I was afraid that soon my already soured feelings toward her would further turn into hate. I had never hated anyone my whole life. I cringed at the idea I would start now.

I left the house before she could protest and headed to Liam's place. He had called me earlier and invited me to come and hang out while he was working on some paperwork for his company. Liam worked for the same corporation as Livie. In fact, that's how Liam and I had met a few years back—at an office party when Livie had asked me to tag along. Liam worked in the finance department, a job that totally baffled me as someone who couldn't keep numbers straight. I was all about words. Words made sense to me; they meant so much more than the lines and curls they were made of. Words were magic. Put some together and you had a work of art, something that could break your heart or make you the happiest person on earth. One day I was going to write the great Australian novel.

"How's the witch?" Liam was not a fan of Mia. He invited me in and led me to the kitchen for coffee. "Has she flown away on her broom yet?"

I chuckled and shook my head. "You're talking about my wife." Even as I said it, the words tasted rotten on my tongue. Guilt gnawed on me, vicious and merciless. "She was going on and on about a gala, and I had to get out of there, man."

Liam handed me a mug of steaming coffee and a carton of milk. "Are you ever going to tell me the real reason you're doing this? She loves no one but herself. I don't get it, mate."

I sighed. "I know. Even I sometimes don't get it." I hadn't told anyone. Not sure why—for fear of looking dumb or, worse, being stared at as a cad. I was neither. At least, I hoped I wasn't. The deeper I got myself into this, the harder it was to tell fact from fiction. "She's my wife, what do you want me to do?"

My friend threw me a look framed by raised eyebrows. "You got to be kidding. Is that your excuse?" I nodded, and his mouth fell open. "Dude, get a divorce while you still have your balls attached. She's a fucking bitch, and you know it."

With a deep breath, I changed the subject. "Get me a beer?" I was planning to file for divorce as soon as I could. We weren't doing each other any favours by keeping this charade going any longer, but I had the sneaky suspicion Mia wouldn't agree. I'd keep this under wraps until it was a fait accompli. I had no wish of attracting the attention of the social media gossipers that followed—and were followed by—Mia.

"Get it yourself," Liam said, settling on the chair. "You're deflecting."

"Look at that. The bookkeeper knows big words." Yes, I was deflecting. This was not something I wanted to discuss, even with a good friend like Liam. I waved at the TV. "Turn on the game, mate. We're missing it."

"Holy shit. Forgot." Liam pointed the remote at the television and turned it on. The rugged shapes of rugby players filled the screen, and Liam was successfully distracted from my love life, or lack thereof.

I lowered my eyes to the ground and twisted my hands on the table. My father had always taught me about honesty and responsibility. I wasn't sure I was happy about having learned his lessons way too well. Sometimes I wished I could throw caution to the wind and act like an irresponsible lout.

Liam set his mug down on the table a bit too hard and the coffee spilled over the side. "Fuck. Did you see that? He did not release that ball." Liam stood up and yelled at the TV. "You stupid idiot, didn't you see that?" He looked at me, an outraged frown on his face. "Why aren't they calling a penalty kick?"

I brushed a hand across my mouth and grunted, happy that my friend had forgotten our conversation. We watched the rest of the game together, but my mind was elsewhere. Try as I may to focus on the match, my mind had other ideas—some of which were flying across the world to Scotland.

It seemed that Liam's thoughts were not as much on the game as I'd thought either. "I just don't understand what reason you can possibly have to stay married to a woman who will make you miserable for the rest of your life."

What could I say? I probably deserved it? I had been the one seeking a relationship with Mia, after all. And before that, I had enjoyed her sexual attention to its full extent. I liked to believe I was not the kind of guy to kiss and run. But life with her hadn't been exactly the happy place I'd hoped it would be. Liam reached across the counter and touched my arm, as if trying to snap me out of my trance. "Mate, don't be stupid. End this relationship now while there is still time."

My phone vibrated inside my pocket, startling me. I pulled it out and looked at the caller ID. Samuel. My editor. While I was still moonlighting for other publications, Samuel had me on staff for his magazines. He owned and ran two online magazines—one lifestyle and the other business. I normally wrote for the lifestyle one, but once in a while, I would have a feature in the business one.

I picked up. "Have I missed a deadline?" I wouldn't be too surprised. The way my head kept wandering to Scotland lately, it was totally possible.

"Hey, Kyle." Samuel had a pleasant, soft voice that never seemed to rise over a whisper. "No, nothing like that. I have to talk to you about something."

"Sure. Today?"

"No, come by my office tomorrow, and I'll go over it with you."

"Sure thing, mate." I was getting ready to hang up when I thought of a question. "What exactly is this about?"

"I need you to take Rick's place for a while." Rick was one of Samuel's full-time writers. "He's going on vacation for a couple weeks."

Curiosity tickled me. "Yeah? Where to?"

Samuel muttered an order away from the phone before answering me. "Scotland. He's going to Scotland."

What used to be merely the name of a country now meant so much more for me. Hearing Samuel say those words planted the seed of an idea in my mind—a seed I hoped would change the course of my life.

***

Livie

Waking up in my new room was always a delight. The flat was small, but the room was spacious and bright even if the light of the morning sun hadn't quite made it through the cracks in the curtains. I always allowed myself a few extra minutes in bed, stretching like a cat and enjoying the peace and quiet of a new day.. With a grunt, I rolled myself out of bed and wrapped my shivering body with a fluffy robe. I tiptoed to the kitchen on bare feet and dropped a coffee capsule into my Nespresso machine. The wonderful scent of the coffee reached my nose as I danced around the cold floor. With my mug of hot coffee in my hands, I climbed the short flight of stairs and went to sit by the bay window in my room, my favourite place in the house. A narrow, padded bench hugged the whole length of the windowsill. I picked up the book I had discarded there the night before and propped my legs up on the bench as I leaned against the wall. I had about ten minutes before I had to jump in the shower and get ready for work. My plan was to fully enjoy my coffee and my book, but as soon as I opened it the phone rang.

"Get your cute little arse here right away," Jenny sang from the other end of the line. "You're late."

"I am not!" I stole a look at my laptop, open on the bedside table, and almost fell off the bench. "Shit. It's nine." I jumped to my feet, nearly spilling the coffee all over the rug. "Shit, shit, and double shit." Stumbling over the boots I had left in the middle of the floor, I opened the closet door and began frantically fishing for something to wear. Anything would do. "I'll be there very soon. Can you hold the fort?"

"Of course, silly. Cal just got here." There was some

mumbling I couldn't understand. "The boss is late, Cal. We're going to have some fun. Laters, Livie." *I am going to kill her.* Right after I got dressed and ready.

In the almost six months the bookstore had been open, I had never once been late. By the time I arrived at the shop, a few of the regulars were already loitering around, some reading books from the shelves, others enjoying a cup of coffee and a rowie. I wasn't sure how put-together I looked since I barely had time to look in the mirror. I brushed a hand over my hair, hoping I looked halfway decent. Cal may have had a girlfriend, but that didn't mean I was comfortable looking like a frumpy bum in front of him.

"Well, good of you to join us, Ms Dunn." Cal's face opened into a generous smile. "We thought you had decided to take the day off."

I shrugged my coat off and into a chair behind the counter. "The stupid alarm went off at the wrong time." Picking up a couple of dirty cups from the counter, I bounced over to the sink. "I hate being late. Anything important happen?"

Unbeknown to me, Cal had stepped closer, and I almost crashed into him when I turned around. His arms went to my shoulders and lingered there. We were so close I could feel the warmth of his body on mine. "There was one call—some reporter is coming next week to interview us for a magazine article." He leaned over slightly. "You smell amazing."

Heat rose from my neck to my face. I gulped. "Reporter? For what?" My body was misbehaving again.

His hand slid down my arm and shivers assailed me.

"Something about a series they are working on about new business ideas. They want to shadow us for a while." The heat from his hand on my elbow was doing strange—and yet delightful—things to my senses. "We should go out for dinner one of these days." His whisper took me by surprise, and I searched for something to say to no avail. I had been struck dumb. "I take that as a yes? Tomorrow after work?"

I nodded frantically, still totally incapable of uttering words, and he left me, a wicked smile playing on his luscious lips. I silently chided myself for being such an idiot and returned to the dirty dishes. Better to take a few minutes with my back to the rest of the world—or at least the store's patrons—until my face stopped burning and I had regained the power of speech. Cal was a fine male specimen.

"Would love a cuppa, love." I turned around to find Mrs McGraig and her wonderful toothless smile staring at me. "That young lad is something, isn't he? He could charm the knickers off any girl in town, I'm sure."

My face burned even more fiercely. Had she seen and heard my short conversation with Cal? She signalled toward the shop windows with her chin, and I followed it with my eyes. Outside, there were two or three girls with their faces glued to the glass, staring at Cal who was engaged in conversation with one of the customers. I chuckled.

"Silly lasses, sometimes they stay there for almost an hour, pretending they're interested in your pretty book display," Mrs McGraig said, turning her face slightly toward the windows. "But who can blame them? If I was twenty years younger, I may be doing the same. That Callum is a handsome man, isn't he?"

I couldn't deny it. "Yes, he is." I stole a glimpse at his tall frame and sighed. What was I thinking? I had just broken up with the love of my life—if you could actually break up from a never-happened relationship—and Cal had a girlfriend. It was not like I was hoping that something would happen, was I? I shook my head, laying all the blame on my irrational and misbehaving girly parts, and turned around to brew Mrs McGraig's Earl Grey. "Are you in the mood for a rowie?"

"Aye, ye know I cannae say no to one of Bailey's rowies." I grabbed the tongs and dropped one of the buttery pastries in a small saucer. "So, lass, how come you don't have a special lad in your life? You're a bonnie lass. And successful."

Sliding the plate over the counter to her, I laughed softly. "Men are more trouble than they are worth." *Liar! If Kyle hadn't gone back to his witchy girlfriend, I would be in his arms as we speak.* "I like being single." *Stop it already. You're lying to yourself.* Not that I minded being single. I just didn't like being single from Kyle.

"There's certainly nothing wrong with that, lass," the older woman continued. "But it's nice to have someone to cuddle with at night."

The yearning for Kyle's hard body against mine exploded in my head. I gasped as the familiar heat began to spread from my toes to the rest of my body. God, I was not over him. Not even close. I tried to smile but was sure I scowled instead. It still hurt a lot more than I was willing to admit to anyone. Even to myself.

"If you'll forgive me, I need to go straighten up in the back." I made my escape before I found myself confessing to feelings I was reluctant to admit to myself. On my way to the back room, I crashed against Cal. "Shit. Sorry, Cal."

His hands went around my shoulders to anchor and prevent me from stumbling backward, and I was suddenly crushed against a hard, sexy chest. I may have swooned a little.

"Are you okay, boss?" His wicked smile belied his meek words, and I could have sworn he pulled me harder against him. Had he no shame? What would his girlfriend say? "You look a little shaky."

I was shaky all right, but not from my near fall. Having that gorgeous body of his glued to mine was playing havoc with my senses, while my ridiculous conscience felt guilty for feeling that way so soon after reminiscing about Kyle.

"Well, I'm so sorry to interrupt such an intimate moment." It was Jenny, her arms crossed over her chest, tapping her foot. Her well-shaped eyebrows were arched high over her pretty blue eyes in a spot-on impression of an angry mother. "What are you two up to?"

I pulled away from Cal, who chuckled, obviously amused we had been caught with our hands in the biscuit tin, so to speak. "What makes you think we're up to something?"

"Well, for one the hands all over—" I grabbed her arm and pulled her forcefully away from Cal, who was still smiling from ear to ear, delighting in my discomposure. "What are you doing?"

"Preventing you from being fired for embarrassing your boss." She snorted. "Not funny, Jenny. He has a girlfriend, remember? This is the worst idea in the world right now." Not to mention I was still head over heels in love with my best friend. "Go attend to Mrs McGraig. She's waiting to pay."

* * *

Kyle

My armour reflected the sunlight as I tightened my knees against the horse's flanks to balance the long, heavy lance I held on my right arm. The glare from the reflecting metal was so intense I could only guess what lay ahead as I rode the snow-white horse. Even though fear weighed heavily on my shoulders, there was a stronger feeling carrying me, propelling me toward what I couldn't see but could easily guess was deadly danger.

When my vision cleared, I was startled to see a dragon, at least two-stories high with a wingspan that exceeded the width of a wheat field. It stood still, eyeing me with hunger, the only movement a slight flapping of the giant wings. Behind him, propped on a horse-pulled cart, Livie stared at me with a smile, a stream of sunrays making her shine like the angel she was.

To get to her, I had to defeat the dragon, slay it despite its size and strength. For a moment my courage wavered, but it was a fleeting hesitation. My friend was behind the monster facing me, and I could either flee or throw all caution to the wind and charge to kill. I braced the lance under my arm, kicked my heels against the horse, and took off running, hurtling toward the monster that held my heart hostage.

I woke up in a sweat, my heart pounding so hard in my chest I could hear it as clearly as my breath. I sat up, nauseous and out of breath, the meaning of the dream still hammering in my head and one question remaining: Had I been successful at slaying the dragon?

CHAPTER SIX
The Eagle Has Landed

Kyle

"I don't want you to go." Mia pouted like a five-year-old and crossed her arms over her generous breasts. "I want you here with me."

For what exactly? We hadn't slept together in a long time, and I often went for days without seeing her, choosing to stay at my old apartment instead. There was no love lost between the two of us, and yet Mia insisted on this ridiculous pretence. For the life of me I couldn't understand what she was getting out of this. Mia was gorgeous, with a body any man would kill for. And she was rich, filthy rich. The only child of the CEO of a big corporation, spoiled rotten her whole life, not a want gone unheeded, Mia would have no trouble finding a man to share her life—and fortune—with her. Why did she want me, especially if she didn't love me?

"I have to go, Mia." I folded two more shirts into the suitcase. She had shown up at my door unexpectedly. "It's my job on the line." I didn't like lying, but I couldn't tell her the truth.

She took a step closer to me and slid a hand across my chest. I cringed. "What do you need that silly job for? Now that we're married, you have all my money at your disposal."

I backed away from her, her touch making my skin suddenly crawl. "I don't need your money, Mia. That's not why I married you, and you know it." My hands, raised in front of me, shook. I needed this break like a drowning man needed a buoy. My soon-to-be ex-wife was physically painful and emotionally draining.

"You make it sound like I don't love you." Her voice had reached a whining pitch, and I fought the urge to cover my ears. "I do, you know? More than life." Her voice wavered, and I knew the tears would soon follow. Who was she trying to fool? She may have fooled me at first, but she hadn't bothered keeping up the deceit after we tied the knot.

I gasped for air, my chest tightening. I turned my back to her, taking slow breaths to keep myself under control as anxiety bubbled inside my chest. "Sorry. Mia, the papers have been drawn. We're getting a divorce." Her hands slipped over my shoulders to wrap themselves around me. I shivered as if someone had just walked over my grave. Mia rested her head against my shoulder blade, and I wanted to scream.

"But, sweetie. I forgive you. We don't have to go that far. We can save our marriage." I didn't answer and kept as still as I could manage. I was afraid that if I moved, I wouldn't be able to hide my repulsion. "Say you will give me another chance. I would do it."

With the excuse I needed to put more clothing items in my suitcase, I shook off her arms and walked away from her. "Mia, you know we are not for each other. I'm not sure why you pretended to care about me, but it's over. I can be stupid only for so long." Irritation was making me shake. Why was the same woman who'd told me I was a dumb fucker she was more than happy to see gone from her life before I had the divorce papers filed now trying to convince me she loved me? Nothing Mia did made any sense to me, and I was sick of it. This assignment had not been given to me. After much talking with my editor, I'd convinced him to let me go on assignment to Scotland.

"I'll pay for my own way and everything else, Samuel," I told him. "I know you don't need anyone doing this, but I'm offering it to you. Free of charge."

"Why would you want to do that when I can give you other assignments that actually pay well?" Samuel was understandably puzzled.

"I need to have a good excuse to go to Scotland and show up at my best friend's doorstep," I told him, beginning to doubt my own outlandish plan. "We didn't part on good terms, and if I don't have a good excuse to stick around for a while, she won't give me the time of day." She wouldn't. Livie was stubborn as a mule, and since she'd been right about Mia, she was also justified to keep me at bay.

After long discussions and begging, Samuel finally agreed to let me use his magazine as the excuse for my visit to Livie's bookstore in Scotland. "I will pull a few strings to have you stay at a nice place for a discounted price. I have some friends in Scotland," Samuel said. "And, Kyle, I'm sorry to hear about your divorce."

Everybody knew, and Mia was not happy about that. I hadn't told anyone, but the news had somehow leaked into social media and spread like wildfire.

"Thank you, Samuel. It's not final yet, but should be in another month or so." I paused. "We weren't right for each other, and I was the only idiot who didn't know."

Later that night, lying in bed, my arms cradling my head, I closed my eyes and conjured my best friend's pretty face. She danced inside my eyelids like a movie star in a classic film, her eyes twinkling in the dark and her hips swaying to the music in waves of pure loveliness. The weight that had lodged itself on my chest all day vanished suddenly, and I was soaring through the dark skies into Scotland where what was left of my heart now resided.

* * *

Livie

With a deceptively innocent expression, I stole a glance at the red-hot Cal standing beside one of the bookshelves, book open in his hands and lost in its words. Certain parts of my body were a bit too excited by the view. We had gone out to dinner the night before, and he had been nothing but a gentleman, pulling the chair out for me and taking me to the door and leaving me with a peck on the cheek. I couldn't lie—he had been the star in my dreams all night.

"Swoon much?" Jenny had the bad habit of sneaking up on me when I least expected it. I almost dropped the book I was holding. "Who can blame you? He's fine." She dragged out the first syllable and winked.

"You're a wicked Scot, and one day I'm sure I will rue the day my boss hired you." I carefully placed the book on the shelf where it belonged and started toward the counter. "But today is not the day. I need you to do me a huge favour."

Jenny followed me, her high heels clicking on the wooden floors. "Ooh, a favour. I like the idea of having something to hold over my boss's head."

I sighed dramatically. "Don't get any ideas, girl. It's not that big of a favour." Craving the comfort and warmth of a cup of coffee, I turned on the machine and made a mental note to buy a better one. It did not bode well that I much preferred the coffee from the Coffee Pot than that from my own store. "I need you to go to the Stables in Stonehaven and pick up the guy who's coming to write a feature on us. Well, on the store anyway." I had received word he had arrived the day before. "You can take my car."

"Like I'd want to." I had bought an old Land Rover that did not meet with my over-critical associate's approval. "I much prefer driving my Mini."

A chuckle left my lips as I poured the hot coffee into a mug. "The guy may not fit in your car."

"Stop teasing the lass, boss." Now even Cal was doing it—creeping silently up on me. "It's not very nice to tease your underlings."

Jenny perked up. "Right you are. I can always complain to the union."

Deciding to indulge a little, I pulled one of my chocolate spoons from a drawer and stirred my coffee with it. The scent of melted chocolate caressed my nose. I took a deep breath. "What union would this be exactly? The Bookstore Workers Union? Is that even a thing?"

"Don't see why it couldn't be," Cal added, taking a seat on a stool at the counter. Business was light this time of the day and allowed us to do what we loved best besides reading books and drinking coffee—tease each other mercilessly. We all seemed to enjoy the repartee and the jokes.

The coffee tasted as good as it smelled, and every muscle in my body relaxed in response. "Well, be that as it may, I still need you to go pick up this guy and bring him here. He's going to hang around for a while, so we might as well meet him."

Jenny came around the counter and took her purse from the small storage closet. "I guess I better do as you say, boss. What's this person's name?"

I froze. Shit. I had no idea. *Did I forget to ask?* "I don't know. Just ask for the Aussie that works for a magazine… I don't know. That hotel cannot have that many Australian guests."

"Never worry. Scots are amazing detectives. Why else do you think Scotland Yard got its name?" Jenny pulled her car keys from her bag and smiled that goofy kind of grin she always wore when telling a cheesy joke.

She left, throwing her purse over her shoulder and forgetting to wear her coat. She was going to freeze outside. "Didn't Scotland Yard get its name from one of the streets it was built on?"

Cal looked at me and burst out laughing. "You've done your research." I flushed, embarrassed to let my geeky side surface. I was a master of useless trivia, a fact only one person in this world knew about. The same person who was out of my life for good. "I didn't know that."

"I read something about it the other day when I was at the supermarket," I lied. When I was a kid, I was fascinated with everything British and spent hours of my life learning about the nation my father and his ancestors came from. I deflected. "Look, a customer."

Around lunch, Cal offered to go get us some eats from a neighbouring tea room. I watched him walk out the door, his step sure and relaxed, with a butt sexy enough to make a grown woman cry. Cal was offering a much-needed distraction from my Kyle-related woes, and I couldn't be more grateful. I knew he wasn't the solution to all my problems, but there was nothing wrong with a sweet and sexy Band-Aid.

Barely fifteen minutes later, Cal came back balancing a tray jam-packed with goodies. "I wasn't sure what you like, so I bought the whole menu." He was joking—or so I hoped. "We'll have to return the tray after we eat."

He deposited the contents of the tray on the closest table. He wasn't kidding; there were five or six different sandwiches and two different containers of soup. "Holy shit, Cal. I'm not that hungry." I laughed and began examining the sandwiches. "Which one do you want?"

"I'm kind of partial to the roast beef," he said, uncovering one of the soup containers. "Oh, my God. This Cullen skink smells amazing."

I threw him a glance, my eyebrow raised. "What in bloody hell is a Cullen skink?"

Cal burst out laughing. "You should see your face. Don't worry, we'll still make a Scot out of you." I glared at him, and he stopped laughing. "It's a thick soup made of smoked haddock, potatoes, and onions. Delicious."

It did sound good, so I opted for a cup of the soup and a toastie. We ate together while a couple of customers loitered around the store, scanning through books and keeping out of the cold air.

"Do you have a sweetheart in Australia?" The question was surprising because while Cal was constantly flirting with me, I knew he had a girlfriend, so it was a non-issue.

"No, there's no one." Was that bitterness I heard in my own voice? I hid my eyes and took a giant bite of the toasted sandwich.

"That is very hard to believe. A gorgeous woman like you?" I liked him more and more with each word. "Surely there must be someone."

Despite my best efforts to shrug the compliment off, I was sure I beamed. "Nope, not one single guy."

"A woman then?"

I choked on the bread, and a piece of it flew across the table and fell on his napkin. I was mortified.

"No woman either. I only swing one way." What had I just said? Could I have been any lamer? I wiped my mouth and pretend coughed into the napkin. "What about your girlfriend? Have you been together long?" *Deflecting. Nice.*

"What girlfriend?" His blue gaze had affixed itself to my eyes. "I don't have a girlfriend."

That was unexpected. "The girl you were with that night at the pub. I assumed she was your girlfriend."

Much to my surprise, he burst out laughing. "Maggie? You thought she was my girl?" His laughter made my cheeks burn. Was he making fun of me? "That was my sister-in-law, Maggie. The groom is her best friend, and my brother was working that night, so I offered to go with her to the party."

My face was on fire. "Shit. And here I was thinking you were taken."

Cal took my hand in his and heat sizzled between us. "Did it bother you? That I was unavailable?" His probing gaze had the double effect of melting my insides and causing my heart to flip-flop inside my chest. Not to mention what it did to my girl parts.

"A bit, I guess." Why lie? Might as well admit there was a strong attraction between us. "I thought we had a spark, but I don't do the 'other woman' bit."

He smiled—a wide, sexy smile that spread from his lips to his eyes like a rainbow after the rain. "I'm so glad it's not one-sided," he said, his voice a whisper. "Because I got it bad for you, boss."

Before I could reply, he had risen from his chair, stretched across the narrow table, and glued his lips to mine. The softness of his hot lips prying mine apart made me swoon.

Just a little. His tongue had just begun to tease its way into my mouth when we heard somebody cough loudly. I pulled myself away from Cal, my lips swollen and craving for more of his, and looked up.

Jenny was standing a few feet away from us, an amused smile on her face. "So sorry to interrupt that very important business meeting, boss, but your guest is here." She stepped aside, and I had to hold on to Cal in order not to fall. Standing right behind her, his lips set into a thin, rigid line and eyes as cold as menthol, was my childhood friend and true heart-desire.

"I would ask you how you're doing, but I can see you're doing just fine." His voice was even icier than his eyes.

"Kyle?" What in heaven's name was he doing here?

***

Kyle

I wasn't sure what I expected when I arrived at Livie's bookstore. Watching her stick her tongue down another guy's throat was not it.

A few months had passed—six, almost seven—and I knew she'd move on sooner or later. I couldn't expect she'd be single for the rest of her life when it had been me who broke her heart. But to actually witness it was another story. The urge to step forward and wrap my shaking hands around the other man's throat was so strong, I held on to a chair for lack of a better anchor. The irrational thought that I didn't want any man to ever touch her again took hold in my heart even as I told myself I had absolutely no right to ask for anything. Red-hot love mixed with anger flooded my lungs, and I gasped, struggling to inhale. What was this I was feeling? Love for the beautiful Aussie in the other man's arms, anger toward my soon-to-be ex-wife and the invisible emotional strings she pulled to work me like a puppet.

"What are you doing here, Kyle?" It was the second time she asked, but I was too choked up by contradictory feelings to answer. "Are you the reporter we've been waiting for?" She turned her gaze to the young woman who had picked me up from the hotel. "Jenny, is this him?"

Jenny had one finger in her mouth, chewing away at the nail as her gaze darted from me to my best friend. Livie looked like a painting by Vermeer as she stood in the middle of the store, a ray of winter light shining on her ivory skin and her dark hair. *I love you. God, I love you.* How had I not known this before? How could I have been so blind?

"Yes, he was the only Aussie in the hotel." The girl stumbled over her own words and then looked at me, a clear *help me* written in her eyes. "You are, aren't you?"

Still finding it hard to speak, I nodded and dropped my laptop carrier a bit too roughly beside me. I glanced at the man standing by Livie, and for a brief moment, I wished that looks could kill. My competition was tall and looked like one of those male models Livie often salivated over on Facebook. Perfect hair, perfect manly features, sparse, well-manicured stubble on his chin and cheeks—I hated him already, and I didn't even know his name.

I found my voice buried somewhere in the giant mangled mess of emotions in my chest. "I'm here to interview you and write an article on this new business venture." Without losing a breath, I added, "Who's your boyfriend?"

Livie prickled, her neck stretching like a fighting rooster's. "He's not my boyfriend."

You could have fooled me.

The man, who had remained silent while watching the exchange with curiosity, stepped forward, a hand stretched toward me. "Callum Miller, Livie's employee."

I hesitated but took his hand and shook it anyway. "Kyle Huang." The situation seemed so ludicrous—me, shaking hands with the same guy who had his tongue in Livie's mouth just a moment before—that I burst out laughing. "So, Callum, is this a common practice in Scotland? French kissing the boss?"

The young woman who'd brought me there, Jenny, let out a chuckle she quickly muffled with her hands. Livie's face was so red it looked as if she was ready to explode.

"I'm afraid you caught us at a rather… inconvenient moment."

I snorted. "Maybe next time you should get a room." I didn't mean it. The mere idea of the two together alone in a room made me break out in hives. "Like it or not, I'm here now. We need to go over a few things, if your boyfriend, employee, or whatever you choose to call him won't mind."

Callum raised his hands in mock surrender and walked away. Livie moved to stop him but thought better of it in the end. With a frown, she pointed to the nearest table and we sat together.

"I know this is uncomfortable, but my boss needed someone to come. So we might as well make the best of it." I had been planning this speech ever since my misguided heart had come up with this fake assignment. Now that I was actually saying it out loud, it sounded lame and stupid. "Where can we meet to talk?" Somewhere away from the eyes of the handsome Scot who even as we spoke was lurking around the corner, pretending to shelve books.

"I have a small office in the back," Livie said, biting her lower lip. God, I wanted to take those lips with mine and tease her until she swooned in my arms. I shifted uncomfortably on my seat.

"No, somewhere else." I overemphasized the words. Damn! I couldn't keep my cool around her. "Maybe at my hotel? It's quiet and they have great beer, I hear." She hesitated, her eyes darting briefly to the back of the store where the overly handsome Callum was still pretending to work. "We could meet tomorrow for dinner. It's a beautiful hotel. You'll love it."

Unconsciously, I covered her hand with mine. With a gasp, she jerked it away. "I'll meet with you, but it's all business. You married Mia, and we're done."

I sighed and cursed myself for the impulsive gesture. What was I doing? I had married Mia, convinced I was in love with her, and now there I was acting like a love-sick teenager toward my best friend. It was not fair to her. It was not fair to me. I needed to sort out all these unexpected feelings. I reminded myself of the reason I had crossed a couple continents: to come clean and apologize to Livie, not to win her over.

"All right, I'll meet you there tomorrow after I close the store." I was surprised she had given in so easily, prepared as I was for a fight. "In the restaurant area, not your room." As if I would even consider it—okay, maybe I'd *consider* it, but wouldn't dare asking.

"But for now, you should try our amazing house coffee from special arabica beans." Jenny had approached the table unnoticed and was holding a small tray with two cups of coffee. "You'll love it."

Livie giggled. "She's joking. We buy our coffee at the nearest Asda. You can get much better coffee at the Coffee Pot down the street." She took the two mugs from the tray and placed one in front of me. "But it's warm and doesn't taste bad."

I laughed as I wrapped my hand around the hot ceramic cup. "Well, there's a terrible endorsement if I ever heard one. I think I'd stick with Jenny's assessment if I were you." I winked at the young woman, and she clapped her hands in naked delight.

"Giving me business advice now, are you?" Her voice was stern, but I could guess a smile dancing in her eyes. "When did you get so smart about these matters?"

I decided to play along, a bit of our old friendship temporarily restored. "I could hook you up with a contact of mine who imports excellent fair trade coffee from Africa. I'm sure he'd give you a great deal." Her eyebrows arched, and the corner of her lip curled in doubt. "I'm not kidding you. I really know a guy."

"Ooh, wouldn't it be just lovely if we could have a great coffee to go with Mrs Riley's amazing rowies?" Jenny's enthusiasm was contagious, and even though I had started this conversation as a joke, I was now in earnest. I truly thought I could help Livie's dream business flourish—even if only in a tiny way. "We could be famous. Just imagine, Livie, people would come from Edinburgh and Glasgow just to taste your coffee." She had assumed a dreamy expression as if in her head she was actually seeing all of this taking place already. "The books we'd sell, Livie."

I looked back at my friend. She was so quiet, I was afraid she had tuned us both out. "Listen to the girl, Liv. I can really help you with that."

She blinked a couple times as if waking up from a long sleep. "I'll think about it." Both Jenny and I stared at her. "I will. I promise."

The Scottish version of a male model had inched his way closer to us. "Did I hear the words coffee and rowies?" I had no clue what a rowie was or why it would go along with coffee.

"I'll get you some," Jenny said, beginning to turn toward the counter. "Would you like one too, Mr—oh, shit, can't pronounce your name." She stared at me, a hand covering her mouth.

I was used to people's reaction to my hard-to-pronounce name. "Call me Kyle. And yes, I'd love one—whatever that may be."

Jenny giggled and skipped away. I had to admire her balance. With heels like that, how could she stand all day, much less walk so fast?

Callum sat down beside us, not waiting for an invitation. "So, I'm guessing you guys know each other." *Brilliant deduction, Sherlock.* "Friends? Ex-lovers?" *Didn't quite make it that far, mate.*

"Ex-friends." Livie saved me from having to address a question I was not sure could be answered. "Kyle is married to the biggest bitch on the face of this earth, who just so happens to be my childhood nemesis."

Even the Scot flinched at her words. Not that I disagreed with her summary of the situation, but it was still hard to hear. I wasn't sure why I didn't tell her then that I was getting a divorce, except that I was reluctant to have a conversation that pegged me as an idiot in front of her supermodel employee.

"What did she do to you, Livie?" *Good question, genius. I'd like to know that myself.* "I can't imagine anyone not liking you." *I think I may have vomited inside my mouth.* Was this guy for real?

"It's a long story, but she always tried to steal what I loved." *Ouch!* I could just guess what Livie was about to say next. "And she did it again. For the last time."

Jenny saved the awkwardness of the moment by arriving with another tray packed with goodies. She placed a small plate with an ugly-looking and almost flat roll on it. "Here's a hot rowie for the Aussie. Smother it with butter and then tell me what you think."

I was doubtful but did as I was told. The first bite took me completely by surprise. The stale-looking roll melted in my mouth in a buttery eruption, leaving my taste buds yearning for more. "This is like sex for your mouth," I exclaimed unwisely.

"Oh, love," Jenny said with a chuckle. "If you think so, then you haven't been doing it right."

CHAPTER SEVEN
Inverness Bound

Livie

One thing it was hard to get used to in Scotland was the fact that by three thirty in the afternoon, night had fallen. I had been told that during the summer the total opposite happened, with daylight by three thirty in the morning. As I drove along the coastal road, heading toward Stonehaven where Kyle's lodgings were located, the light of the full moon reflected off the ocean with a crystalline glitter. Kyle was staying at a renovated building that used to be the stables of a local laird, a few kilometres from the coastal town of Stonehaven and in the shadow of a castle.

As I drove up to the small parking area, I was struck dumb in awe. The castle was really a large manor house, complete with its own church at the end of the path. The owners had illuminated the paths with fairy lights, giving the whole scene a magical touch that made me quiver in pleasure. I was such a sucker for that kind of stuff. I stopped the car and got out, looking for the signs to the Stables.

"You're here." The melodic voice of my best friend reached my ears, and I immediately relaxed. Kyle had always had this calming effect on me. His voice, his eyes, everything about him could bring me from super stressed to totally zen in two seconds flat. I turned around and saw him walking toward me, a big smile on his face. *Jerk! Why do I have to love you so much?* "I was afraid you wouldn't find it in the dark."

The place was hidden from the main roads, rather rural and secluded. "Where's the restaurant?" I asked, suddenly wanting to end this meeting as soon as humanly possible.

"Come this way." Was that hesitation I heard in his voice? He was up to something. I knew him too well not to pick up on subtle changes in his voice or demeanour. I fell into step with him, following him away from the main building. "My lodgings are this way."

I stopped. Kyle continued to walk forward a few more feet before he noticed I wasn't with him anymore. "We're not going in your room."

"It's not a room. It's a flat. I have dinner for us." I gave him my what-are-you-up-to look, and he smiled sheepishly. "I didn't cook it. I bought it in town. The castle pub is closed today. The owner is on vacation somewhere in the Canary Islands."

All my red alarms were blaring. Being alone under the same roof with the man who could set me on fire with a look was not the wisest choice ever. But I was there, and I was hungry. I resumed walking, and he led me to the Stables, never uttering a word. I was intensely aware of his body, as if his heat had managed to cross the space between us, materialize, and caress me. A shiver ran through me.

We crossed the threshold into a dimly lit living room. I was expecting something grand, but the flat was simple. If I didn't know where I was, I'd have thought I'd wandered into a country cottage. Plain but comfortable furnishings gave the small space a feeling of home. I took off my coat and gloves and draped them over one of the armchairs by the fire.

"This is cute." It was. Quaint and cosy like a setting from an Agatha Christie novel. "How did you find this place?"

Kyle had also shrugged his coat into a chair and invited me to sit. "I didn't. My editor apparently spends quite a bit of time in Scotland every year. The owners are his friends." He sat on the opposite chair from me, gingerly hanging off the edge of the seat. "You should see the outside. It's beautiful."

An uncomfortable silence fell between us. It was strange to be with the one man I was the most familiar with in the whole wide world and yet feel so shy. I knew where all his scars were and the stories that went with them, where his secret tattoo was—upper thigh, almost at the bend of the leg—and why he kept it a secret—a tribute to his twin sister who died shortly after birth. I was there when he broke down in tears the day his parents got a divorce, and he held me while I cried over my first broken heart. His scent was as familiar to me as the air I breathed, and yet I felt awkward and uneasy sitting in that small living room across from him.

"Do you want to go over the interview process first or after dinner?" The soft light of the two floor lamps reflected off his almond-shaped eyes, and my insides liquefied. Why did he have such an effect on me even after all that happened? I wanted to hate him, to name him number one in my blacklist, but I seemed incapable of doing so.

"How long are you staying?" I ignored his question and went straight to what was important. I wanted him out of my life. No, that was not it; I *needed* him out of my life.

"Not sure. A few weeks." I straightened my back and gasped. *What?* "It's not just the interview," he added, obviously aware of my surprise. "I have to observe the daily business, interview your local customers, write the draft… and my boss wants me to visit the branch that's opening on the west coast too."

I scratched my jaw, confused. "A west coast branch? No, that's not possible." My boss would have said something.

"Competition. A French company had a similar idea." I was floored. It was true that great minds thought alike, but I had been so sure we were in the vanguard of this type of franchise. "You may want to have a look too. Check out what the others are doing. A mild version of corporate espionage." He laughed at his own joke. "Without legal penalties."

It wasn't a terrible idea. The smart thing would be to check them out, see what they were doing differently from us, adjust and adapt. Flexibility and acquaintance with customers were the magic dust that made or broke a business. "Right, good thinking."

He lifted his chin and stared at me, a question in his eyes. "Really? You're coming with me?"

"What? I didn't say that." *Did I?* "I can go there another time."

He scooted even closer to the edge of the seat. "It makes sense. I don't have a car; you do. We might as well go together."

It made all kinds of sense, but it was a terrible idea no matter how you looked at it. The two of us stuck in a car for hours? I shivered in apprehension.

"I'll think about it." *What? Am I losing my mind? Retract it right now!* "I'll see if I can get away for a few days." All was lost. I had finally gone totally bonkers.

We talked business for a while and then had a simple but delicious dinner in the small nook by the kitchen. Despite all the bad blood between us for the past few months, I couldn't help but feel safe and happy around Kyle. Our souls had been connected since we were children, and there was no one in the world I'd feel more at ease with. Kyle was home to me.

"Shall we walk a bit? I'm stuffed."

The offer would seem ludicrous to anyone who did not know my friend, but I was used to his unusual whims. Yes, it was cold outside, but there was magic in the winter nights. True magic. The kind that made the hairs on your neck stand up and your skin break out in goosebumps. We grabbed our coats on our way out and skipped like little kids into the chill of darkness.

"Let's walk to the creek. It's pretty there." Kyle's breath

came out in puffs of white clouds. I wrapped the scarf tightly around my neck and clapped my gloved hands in an attempt to warm them up.

As we turned the corner around the Stables, a vision appeared before our eyes. Fairy lights, white and flickering, lined the path we followed up to the small bridge across the creek. It looked enchanted, something out of a fairy tale. I might have sighed because Kyle stopped suddenly to look at me.

"I knew you'd love it," he whispered, his voice a gentle caress. I shivered and not from the cold. "It looks like a magical kingdom. Like fairies could be hidden behind the trees and trolls could be charging tolls under the bridge."

We used to imagine such things when we were young and met by the river. We'd spend hours making up stories about the magical beings we thought inhabited the land, unseen and unheard. A flutter in my chest caught my breath for a moment, making it hard to breathe.

His gloved hand had somehow found mine. The warmth of his palm crossed the fabric barrier between our hands and made my heart sputter as if about to stop beating altogether. *No, no. This can't be.* I pulled my hand free from his a bit too abruptly, and the look on his face made me cringe with guilt. He held his hand as though he was still holding mine and stared into my eyes. His pain was so acutely obvious I had to fight the urge to hold him in my arms and comfort him.

"I better go." It was the only thing I could say or do. The magical atmosphere around us was having some unexpected and unwanted effects on both of us. I hated Mia, but I was not going to be "the other woman." No way in hell. "I guess I'll see you tomorrow at A Cup of Fiction?"

Kyle didn't say anything, and after a moment's hesitation, I turned around and began retracing my steps up to the Stables to retrieve my purse. I needed to get away. Quickly.

"I love the name of the bookstore, Liv, but I don't want it to be our tag line." I stopped and turned to him, not sure what he was getting at. "I don't want our friendship to turn into something fictional, something that never happened, do you?"

Out of nowhere, tears flooded my eyes and threatened to roll down my cheeks and betray what I was feeling inside. I turned back to the building and ran as fast as I could. Away from my love. Away from more heartbreak.

* * *

I hadn't felt this excited since I was a kid, a lifetime ago. It was probably an ill-advised situation, but I couldn't care less at this junction. I was over the moon thinking of a long drive alone with Livie as my captive audience. The opportunity to tell her the truth about my relationship with Mia. The fact that in the end Livie might still be angry and unwilling to forgive me didn't dampen my enthusiasm. And hope. A stupid, relentless hope that maybe Livie still loved me.

That she may have forgiven me and that somehow she'd be willing to give us a chance. Maybe—just maybe—we could still recover our friendship and take it to the next level.

"I can't believe you managed to convince her to go on this trip." Jenny had quickly become a friend to me. Her easy-going, bubbly personality was hard to resist. "A whole drive stuck in the car with you. And she went for it?"

"Surprising, I know, but yes." I was flabbergasted myself—flummoxed, discombobulated, and all those fun expressions that so accurately described what I felt when Livie had called to tell me she was coming with me to the northeast coast. "How far is Inverness?" I had absolutely no clue, but I was hoping it was far away.

"I don't know—three, four hours' drive tops. Possibly less." Disappointing. I was hoping for a much longer drive. "You can make it longer by going the scenic route. Lots of things to see on the way." Could I be that devious? Or crafty? "I can help you come up with some ideas for delays."

A sudden click-clack on the wooden floor made us turn around. "What are the two of you plotting?" Livie's raised eyebrow gave her a comical look. "I'm not sure I trust either of you."

Jenny was hanging from Livie's neck in a few quick steps. "You know I love you," she squealed. I wondered whether I'd get away with doing the same thing, but decided against it.

Livie laughed. "Crazy woman, we have customers to attend to." We all glanced toward the counter and saw a couple of people waiting for service. "Would you please do your job?"

Jenny sauntered in their direction, and Livie turned to me, a question twinkling in her eyes. I shrugged and smiled coyly. "We were just discussing literature." She hmphed and sat down at a table, setting down the bundle of papers she'd been carrying. I sat across from her. "Jenny was telling me about the wonderful things along the way to Inverness. We should make time to visit a few of them."

Livie blinked. "It's a business trip, not a tour." She began shuffling the papers in front of her with no apparent focus.

"But, Liv, it would be the perfect way to get to see a lot of Scotland." I could be persuasive when I wanted, especially when I batted my lashes—or so Livie had once told me. "You've been here for just a little while, and you love castles—and sheep."

She giggled. "Sheep? Really?" I was winning her over, I was sure of it. "I don't know what makes you think I like sheep."

"What's this about sheep?" Callum, the Scottish male model, had once again managed to sneak up on us unnoticed. He was not only handsome but also stealthy like a snake. I hated him. He stood behind Livie and placed a possessive hand on her shoulder. She twisted to look up at him and smiled. I really hated him.

"When we were about ten, you badgered your parents for a pet sheep, remember?" Damned Callum could not beat me when it came to personal memories. I almost snorted in victory. "You wouldn't stop."

Livie burst out laughing. "Oh, my God. I had forgotten."

Take that, Scot. "My mom gave me a toy goat instead, and I threw a huge fit."

Callum brushed his hand across the width of my girl's shoulders, and I had to hold on to a chair so I wouldn't jump forward and punch him.

"Are you ready, Livie?" Callum asked. Was he smirking at me? And ready for what? "Can't wait to show you that new restaurant in Forfar."

With a smile that rivalled the shining stars, my friend stood up and held on to the Scot's arm. The familiarity in that simple gesture crushed me, the memory of them kissing as I first arrived driving the proverbial nails in my coffin. I turned around abruptly and walked away and out of the store, unable to stand the sight. I knew I had no right to feel that way. I was the one who had ruined any possibility of a romantic relationship between us, to marry Livie's archenemy. I had absolutely no right to be jealous or expect any different from her. Yet, I did.

Get a grip, idiot. You don't deserve her.

I walked aimlessly down Montrose's High Street, barely aware of humanity around me or the cutting chill of the winter breeze. My eyes blurred with tears of anger and frustration. I felt helpless and hopeless, and I hated it. I had always been the kind to have a solution for every problem, but I was lost this time. This time I couldn't find the light at the end of the tunnel. Livie looked so happy with Callum, who was I to deny her that? The phone vibrated in my jeans' pocket. I pulled it out without stopping and pushed the talk button. "What?"

"Well, hello to you too." A chill ran up my spine. That was the last voice I wanted to hear. Mia. *Fuck! What does she want now?* "I have a huge surprise for you, Kyle."

My fingers had gone cold, almost frozen, holding the edges of the phone.

"You're going to love this. Can you guess?" Unless she was about to tell me the divorce was final, there was nothing she could say that would please me. "I'm coming to Scotland."

My feet stopped even before my brain digested her words. "What?" *Please, God, tell me I heard wrong.*

"I'm coming to join you in Scotland." *Fuck, fuck, fuck.* "Isn't it great?"

Great was not the word I would use to describe what she had just told me. My hands began to tremble, and I had to lean against a building's wall.

"Think about it, Kyle." I couldn't think of anything else. "Me and you together in Scotland. What could be more romantic and conducive to our reconciliation?" What could be better? A bullet in my head for starters. What in heaven's name made her think I wanted us to get back together?

* * *

Stunned, I dropped to my bed, a rock into a soft patch of sand. No, it couldn't be true. Mia had encouraged me to file divorce papers. *"You bore me, Kyle. I've had enough of this marriage, so go ahead and file the papers. I will be more than glad to sign them."* And a few days after that conversation, she had called me to ask me to speed up the process. *"I want to be free from your dead weight. You're cute but not the right calibre for my husband."*

After all of that, why would she be refusing to sign the final papers? I had just finished a call with my lawyer, and I needed a stiff drink. The bigger the better.

"If she continues to refuse to sign the divorce papers, you only have one way out," my lawyer had told me a few minutes before. "You can always go into litigation. Unfortunately, that will be very expensive, especially considering she's rich and has access to the best lawyers in town. She can drag the process out forever and put you in the poor house. You want to avoid that at any cost."

I choked on my own breath. I was not poor, but I was also far from wealthy, and lawyers were not cheap. Besides, I didn't want to stretch out my marriage with the poisonous snake Mia turned out to be. "I'll find a way, Ted. I can't stay married to her. I just can't."

"Did you say that she's planning on joining you in Scotland?" My stomach churned. "Maybe you can convince her to sign the papers. I will email them to you, just in case."

I sighed and ran an open palm over my face. "Is there anything else I can do?"

Ted coughed on the other end of the line. "Only if you have something to hang over her head, mate, and knowing you, I'm sure you wouldn't use it against her even if you did indeed have it."

Mia was pushing all my buttons, so I just might do

something totally out of character and dig up some dirt on her. Except I wouldn't know where to start. Her friends and acquaintances were loyal to her as long as she paid for their silence, and Mia had no problem with that. It hadn't been enough that she betrayed me by making me fall for a fictional side of her, but then she didn't even bother to continue with the act as soon as she had me.

"Thanks, Ted. Keep me informed, okay?" Not that he would have much to say, especially if Mia was indeed coming to Scotland to attempt a reconciliation. What in heaven's name had happened for her to change her mind so radically? As soon as I'd announced I was going to Scotland, it was as if she had suddenly fallen in love with me again. Too late, of course. I had seen the real Mia, and I didn't plan to stay married to her. But she could still make my life pretty complicated with her decision to go against the divorce.

I wasn't sure how long I sat on that bed, staring at the walls and breathing heavily and unevenly. This was the last thing I wanted to hear now that I had finally realized how an old crush for my best friend had turned into something much deeper, something I wanted to explore to its full extent.

Fuck, Mia. Why are you doing this now?

CHAPTER EIGHT
Stranded

Livie

"I don't know why I ever agreed to do this." My breath came out in smoke-like puffs as I stuffed my suitcase in the trunk of my old Land Rover. Jenny handed me a small toiletry bag. "He's already driving me crazy, and we haven't even left."

Kyle had insisted on leaving later in the day, claiming he had some important calls to make that morning. I had a strong suspicion he was up to something. Kyle had always been mischievous, and I had learned to expect the unexpected with him.

"Cal is not happy with this either." Not that I really cared. We had been out twice and exchanged a couple kisses. Yes, the lip action had been toe-curling, but it didn't mean I owed him anything. We were not an item, and I was not looking for a romantic attachment. "I must be out of my mind."

"What are you talking about, lass? You're heading to beautiful Inverness with a hot Aussie who obviously worships the ground you walk on." Jenny had an irritating habit of telling it as she saw it. Except she also tended to ignore the nuances. "What's there not to like?"

"You forgot he married the woman whose life mission is to make me as miserable as possible." Kyle's suitcase was already in the boot, standing next to mine in the kind of intimate contact we couldn't have anymore. "It's going to be a long trip." I closed the boot with a heavy sigh.

Kyle came out of the coffee shop, bundled in a black peacoat and carrying a small box in his hands. "Mrs Bailey insisted we take these pastries with us." He waved a large thermos in the other hand. "And some hot coffee."

With a grunt, I opened the driver door and slid on the seat. "Take good care of my store, Jenny. And tell Cal I'll call him from Inverness." Kyle mumbled something under his breath. "What was that?"

He sat next to me on the passenger seat and smiled—a boyish, up-to-no-good smile that spoke volumes. "I didn't say anything." I was certain I had heard the words "Cal" and "idiot" emerge from his otherwise undecipherable mumbling.

Jenny waved until we were out of sight, driving down High Street and heading toward Aberdeen. Kyle had somehow convinced me—what was this power he had?—to go A96 instead of a more straightforward way. "We might as well see the sights," he had said. I was convinced there was a much more devious plan behind it.

The old Rover sputtered and roared down the road in a poor imitation of a lion as Kyle fiddled with the radio.

"Does this thing even work?" Screeching and beeping sounds made me cringe. "Why did you buy such an old car?"

"It was the only thing I could afford that was all-terrain. And it's not that bad." It was worse. "But the radio doesn't work."

Kyle gave up and leaned back in the seat. "Not sure why you needed an all-terrain, but I'm so happy you agreed to come with me."

I was already regretting my decision. It was tougher than I had thought to sit next to him, pretending nothing bad had happened and that everything was just as it always had been between us.

Since I didn't answer him, he stopped talking and pulled out a book from his backpack. So much the better. I couldn't handle much more "normal" conversation and banter. I focused on the road ahead and pretended I was all alone in that old, forest green car. Maybe this would end up being a good thing—a last hurrah of sorts, a closure.

We drove for almost two hours before my travel companion lifted his eyes from the book he was reading and scanned the land around us. He stretched, opened his bag, and removed a map.

"They still make those?" I chuckled as he unfolded and studied the paper map with the intensity of an old scholar pouring over a treasure map. "What are you looking for?"

"A castle I read about." His voice was muffled by the big map in front of his face. "I know it's between Aberdeen and Inverness, and I really want to see it. It's supposed to be haunted."

"Sounds like fun." Not! I was not too excited about ghosts. I reserved a healthy respect for all things supernatural. "It's getting late, and it will be dark soon. I don't think we should make any stops."

With a loud crackling of paper, Kyle dropped the map to his lap and stared at me with an expression of disbelief. "Really? Who are you and what did you do with my best friend? The one who loves to explore old ruins?"

Yes, I had always enjoyed historical architecture. The idea that people who lived centuries before me had walked the same floors and touched the same walls was a magical feeling, almost time traveling, in a way. But it was different now between my old exploring companion and me. The last thing I wanted to do was be caught somewhere alone with him. Dark would be falling soon, even though it was barely the middle of the afternoon.

"She grew up." The bitterness in my voice surprised even me.

"Well, I insist. It's just a little detour." God, he never gave up. I used to admire that trait in him, but now it was plain irritating. "In about a mile, we need to turn left. Why don't you have a GPS in this car?"

"Because I didn't need one." Until he decided to take me on this trek across country. "Do we really have to do this?"

"Come on. Where is your spirit of adventure?" *Gone, along with my faith in you.* "Shit. We're in Scotland. We made a hundred plans to come here someday, remember?"

Yes, I remembered it well. How could I forget? We had

spent many hours sitting side by side, our legs draped over each other's in that way that came only with years of familiarity, dreaming about that trip. We'd visit and explore every castle in Scotland—an almost impossible feat considering there were castles in every corner—and then cross to the Isle of Skye and make friends with the puffins. My stomach twisted into a knot.

"That was a lifetime ago, Kyle. Let it go."

Silence enveloped us for a while, and I thought he had given up on the idea, until he told me the exit was coming soon. We veered off the motorway, and a few moments later we were driving on a narrow country road. The population became sparser and sparser until the houses came at large intervals and eventually became virtually non-existent. The early winter night had descended upon the land. Driving along roads that twisted and turned, weaving between the growing mountains of the Highlands, I had a sudden surge of panic and almost reached out for Kyle's hand.

"I wish it was lighter. This must be beautiful." Kyle had his nose glued to the window, straining against the darkness.

"Where is the fucking castle?" Was that a squeak in my voice?

Kyle turned to me, his eyes widening. "Wow, you must be pretty nervous." He knew I barely ever cussed unless my nerves got the best of me. "There is nothing to be anxious about. We're almost there. Just another couple of kilometres ahead."

"Shit, Kyle. There is nothing here but empty country." My knuckles were sore from my tight hold on the steering wheel.

"I don't like this."

I felt it before I saw it—his hand on my leg. Not intrusive but comforting. "We'll be all right, Livie. We'll be all right." Why did it sound like he was talking about more than our situation there?

We drove in silence for the next mile or so. The Rover's purring became more of a roar and then a sputter. I cussed again, tightening my hold on the wheel even more. The car engine went silent, and the car rolled quietly on momentum for a few more feet before coming to a total stop on the side of the road.

"Are we out of gas?" Kyle stretched to check the gauge.

"No, we're out of a working engine." I dropped my head to the wheel, willing the nightmare to fade away. "Holy shit. We're stranded in the middle of nowhere."

"Calm down. The castle should be just a few minutes' walk down the road. We can take shelter there." He was talking as if he was suggesting a night at a comfortable, safe hotel instead of a ruined medieval fortress. I snorted. "It's our best chance. Better than staying in this car in the dark."

"It's a freaking ruin. It probably doesn't even have a wall standing, and it's freezing cold out there." Much to my mortification, I felt tears of frustration burning behind my eyes.

He ignored me and opened his door. A second later, he opened mine and held my hand to help me out of the car. It was dark, with the only light coming from the cloud-covered moon. The frigid air slapped me with the sharpness of an open-palm hand, and I shivered, shrinking inside my heavy winter coat. I scanned the limited horizon and rubbed my hands on my arms, trying to dispel the sense of foreboding and apprehension the eerie contours of dark trees and mountains were settling in my chest.

I pulled the phone off my pocket, punched in the emergency number, and listened. Nothing. Not a tiny buzz. The signal was non-existent. "We're in a freaking dead zone," I whined.

Kyle had gone around and was digging through the trunk and our luggage. "We need blankets, food, and water." Without moving, I studied my friend as he proceeded with the search, efficient and sure of himself. I loved that about him and hated Mia even more because of it. Around her, Kyle seemed to totally lose his sense of self-worth, his confidence. He stopped for a moment and frowned at me. "Are you going to help me?"

Snapping out of my mind freeze, I joined him in his mission to find what we needed to survive the night in relative comfort. We found a couple blankets—thanks to Jenny's constant badgering about the hit-or-miss heat of the Rover—the box of goodies Mrs Riley had sent along with us, an old scented candle I must have forgotten, and a couple bottles of water Kyle had insisted on bringing. It was not much, but it was better than nothing.

We followed the road on foot, Kyle frequently checking his map with the small flashlight I always carried in the glove compartment, until the impressive dark silhouette of a castle materialized ahead of us. "There it is. We have to find the footpath. Keep your eyes peeled." Not that it made much difference. It was so dark, I could barely make out my own hands, much less a small dirt path branching out from the main road. "Found it."

"You must have the eyes of an owl." I swung between being annoyed and grateful for his sharp vision. I followed him off the road, making sure I kept close to him. "Why did you say this castle is supposedly haunted?"

He stopped for a moment so I could catch up. The terrain was rough and hard to navigate without light. "Most Scottish castles are rumoured to be haunted. But this one is known as the Dark Castle because its laird was infamous for his unsavoury appetites."

I turned my face in his direction. He was nothing but a shadow next to me. "What do you mean by 'unsavoury appetites'?"

Kyle chuckled. "He had a taste for blood, especially for the blood of young women." I heard the crunch of his boots against the rocky surface. "The locals had cleansing ceremonies in the castle for decades after he died. They were afraid his evil still lingered even though he had long left this earth."

I kicked a rock as hard as I could without hurting myself. "Just peachy. I'm about to spend the darkest night of the year in a castle haunted by an evil vampire. Lovely."

Kyle's laughter seemed to echo through the valley. "You've got me with you. You know, I'm a great vampire slayer."

"Oh yeah? Who taught you?" In spite of the situation, I was amused by the resurfacing of the old Kyle, all huff and puff but no bite.

"Buffy, of course." I burst out laughing. We used to spend our Saturdays watching *Buffy, the Vampire Slayer* and taking bets on what apocalyptic evil was about to befall the world that night. "Only the best masters for me, my friend. Only the best."

We arrived at the castle—or what was left of it—and aided by the flashlight, we began searching for a space where we would be sheltered from the elements, which wasn't easy in a castle that was little more than a ruin. Eventually we found a small space, maybe what used to be a niche in the staircase, that still boasted walls and only a narrow doorway. We'd be better protected from the chill of the night.

We sat side by side, as close to each other as I could bear, and draped one of the blankets over our legs. Kyle dug up some matches from his coat pocket and lit the rosemary lavender candle we had found in the trunk. It was nice to be able to see Kyle's face again, even though the flame threw weirdly shaped shadows on the walls around us, giving the whole space a ghostly appearance. I was still cold, and my body craved the heat Kyle's could offer. *I can't. I just can't.*

Kyle opened the box my neighbour had given us. "Good old Mrs Riley," he exclaimed, his hand inside the box. "Rowies and cheese sandwiches. We won't go hungry tonight." He pulled a sandwich from the box and handed it to me. "She even packed some chocolate. Remind me to ask her to marry me."

I went cold all over, and not from the weather. "How

many wives do you think you can get away with?" My voice reflected the ice in the air. Kyle flinched. "Apparently marriage means very little to you."

"That's not at all what I meant, and you know it." Hurt coloured his voice, reminding me of times when we were young and had fought about stupid stuff. It had been so easy to hurt him back then because he wore his heart on his sleeve, open and exposed. "I asked Mia for a divorce."

Maybe the castle was indeed haunted because I couldn't possibly have heard what I thought I had. "What did you say?"

Kyle's eyes seemed to flicker along with the candlelight. "I'm getting a divorce. Mia and I are separated."

We were silent for a moment. My mind was reeling from the unexpected news. What did this mean for us? *Are you crazy, woman? Nothing. This means nothing at all.* Nothing had changed. He had still betrayed me by marrying Mia, my sworn enemy and the biggest, certified bitch in all of Australia and beyond. Nothing changed. I was still hurt and mad at him, and knowing that he had finally come to his senses didn't make it any better.

"Good for you, Kyle," I said, bitterness freezing my words. "But too late for us."

She slept like an angel resting on a cloud, beautiful and peaceful. I wanted to brush the hair that had come loose from her bun and flown over her cheek. Instead, I sat on my own hand, afraid to touch her. The silence around us was broken only by the melodic sound of her breathing caressing my senses. I leaned against the wall, cherishing the icy stone's bite crossing the layers of clothes to my skin underneath and keeping me grounded. My whole body was alive with yearning for my best friend, and there was nothing I could do about it. I took a deep breath and closed my eyes, willing the need to draw her into my arms and hold her there forever to go away.

Livie moved and scooted closer to me, her hands searching my body, taking hold and pulling me against her. I stiffened at the contact, conscious of the dangerous ground we were treading. Her cold hands—when had she removed her gloves?—sneaked under my shirt and inched their way around my waist and back. I gasped and held my breath for a moment, her touch electrifying me. Slowly, I exhaled and allowed my muscles to relax against her, guilt-ridden for taking advantage and enjoying her moment of vulnerability. As much as I'd have loved nothing more than to ignore the cold, rip her clothes off, and make love to her until the sun came up, I was happy with the simplicity of that moment— us caught in an embrace, nothing more, nothing less.

I must have dozed off, lulled into serenity by the heat of Livie's body against mine, but I woke up suddenly when the sound of voices echoed in the cavernous halls of the castle. Reluctantly, I let go of Livie, who was also beginning to wake, and strained my ears, trying to identify the sounds. Definitely voices—whispering or maybe chanting in a language I didn't understand. Gaelic, perhaps. Livie, eyes still glazed by slumber, looked at me in a silent question, and I quickly snuffed the candle. As darkness fell around our little shelter, my heart pumped fast, blood throbbing in my ears and neck. This place was a bit too remote to be the target of criminals, but it was never a bad idea to be cautious. Who in heaven's name would be visiting a ruined castle in the middle of the night, after all?

* * *

Livie

"*Sireadh thall... sireadh thall.*" I recognized those words. Growing up with a Scottish father had me researching everything I could find on my ancestry. I had delved into ancient Gaelic poetry and *fuinns*, ancient chants that led into a meditative state. Seek beyond, it said. Over and over again. There was more than one voice, singing in quiet tones that grew in volume as they echoed between the remaining walls of the castle. Who was singing?

A flare of sudden light illuminated the dark, quickly fading into wavering ribbons of pale light licking the stony surfaces around us. A fire had been lit. I looked at Kyle, whose eyes searched for the source of the mysterious chanting and light before settling on mine.

"What's that?" I barely spoke, moving my lips to form the words without actually uttering them. Kyle shrugged, his forehead creased in worry. "Do you think we're in danger?"

We moved together as if reading each other's minds, on our tiptoes, being careful not to kick or step on anything as we made our silent way to the entrance. Hoping not to reveal our presence there, we got to the corner and reached out at the same time, his hand accidentally stacking on top of mine. I was scared, and the rock beneath my palm was frigid, but the warmth from Kyle's hand found its way to my heart. I repressed the sigh of relief that bubbled up my throat and peered around the wall. We gasped at the same time.

The room just beyond the tiny space we'd been sharing seemed to be alive with the flames from the fire in the centre, dancing shadows on every surface. Around the roaring fire, several people, their locked hands forming a human circular chain, swayed. "*Sireadh thall… sireadh thall.*" Seek beyond… seek beyond. Their presence there in the middle of a bitter cold night in a castle so remotely located was troubling at best. But even stranger was the fact that both men and women, all ten or eleven of them, were dressed in anachronistic clothing—seventeenth century, if I had to guess, with long heavy skirts and tight corsets for the women and voluminous short pants for the men.

I threw a panicky glance at Kyle. His mouth had fallen open and his narrow eyes had widened into circles. *Holy shit. This is really happening.* Instinctively, I leaned back against his body, seeking the comfort of his touch, and he wrapped his arms around me, pulling me away from the doorway and into the connecting wall, where we could not be seen by the odd dancers in the Great Hall. We slid together all the way to the floor, me settling between his outstretched legs and Kyle still holding me tight against him. I covered his hands, flat on my stomach, with mine and leaned back further. I held on to him for dear life, afraid that the universe was about to pull an *Outlander* on me and that I'd wake up in the morning in another time, another lover's arms. I didn't want another lover. I wanted Kyle.

His breath caressed the side of my face. "What do you think they're doing?" Hell, I didn't care what they were doing. The bigger question was *when* were they doing it? Had we somehow fallen through some time hole? "What are they saying?"

"It's a chant, kind of a meditation to call on spiritual and physical enlightenment or healing. Very ancient." My voice shook as I spoke those two last words.

"Like a druid thing?" Kyle liked his urban fantasy novels a bit too much sometimes. But he was not too far from the truth. I nodded. "What do we do? Do we go join their singing and dancing?"

Had he lost his mind?

"No, we just sit here and hope they leave soon." And that the time gate shut tightly behind them. "We're not moving an inch."

A blast of warm air hit the side of my face in small bursts. Kyle was laughing. "I'm not complaining. I like it where I'm at right now." The hardness pressing against the small of my back was plenty proof he was telling the truth. Heat ran through me and gathered on my face and other less well-behaved parts of my body. "I won't move if you don't."

We remained in that spot as if glued to it, our bodies so close together I could almost imagine we were one. It was unsettling and heavenly all at once. We hadn't been that close in a long time, and all the feels came back to me in a tidal wave. I hated that I loved Kyle that much. I hated myself for not being able to get him out of my system. But I couldn't help loving the way he made me feel.

I wasn't sure how long we waited, painfully aware of each other's breathing, Kyle's chest rising and lowering against my back, his hands burning under mine. The voices kept chanting, an oddly soothing sound that settled both of us into a semi-hypnotic state, only half aware of our surroundings. My senses, lulled by the drone of the murmuring voices, were jarred by the sudden silence. For the first time in the last hour or so I straightened my back, breaking the connection with my friend's body. Did he groan?

"I think they're gone." I risked a whisper and crawled a couple feet to the doorway to peek around it. The fire in the centre of the Great Hall was dying out, reduced to glowing embers, and there was not a single human in sight. "They're gone. Do you think they were ghosts?"

A strange rumble grew in the silence, and I realized Kyle was laughing again. "Ghosts? You're a riot, girl."

I guess I won't tell him my Outlander *theory.* "What else am I supposed to think?" He could be so annoying.

"Reenactors? Modern druids?"

Hell, I hated when he made sense. Why had I not thought of that?

I scowled at him, crossing my arms in front of me. "Make all the fun you want. I don't care."

Still laughing, he bent forward and pulled me toward him. It was such a sudden and unexpected move, I fell on his lap, enfolded by his long arms. "You're so funny, Livie. That's why I love you."

Time froze. Our faces were mere inches apart, our breath and his words hanging in white clouds between us. Like magnets, our faces slowly inched together until our lips met. It was a hesitant, barely there kiss at first, but it quickly developed into a roaring fire, a hunger of such girth I thought for a moment it would swallow me whole. God, I loved those lips. Warm, soft and perfect around mine, nibbling and prying mine open. Lips parted, my tongue darted to meet his, unwilling to wait any longer. He tasted of sunshine and bitter chocolate—my favourite. I moaned against his mouth, my hands sliding inside his coat and under his shirt. Strange how my fingers seemed to recognize every ridge of his muscles and every valley in between. We had never been together that way, and yet it was as if we had.

What am I doing? He picked Mia instead of me. For all I know, he may go back to her. My mind knew this, but my heart and body weren't listening. For once my irrational side had taken over and I wanted to find out how it felt to have him inside of me. I frantically struggled with his clothes, the thick winter coat becoming my most hated enemy. Kyle wriggled his hands under and in between the two layers of shirts I was wearing and got stuck short of reaching my breast. Damned tight clothes!

"Maybe we should resume this once we get to the hotel." Kyle chuckled, still wiggling his fingers, trying to stretch the unyielding fabric of my shirts.

He was probably right, but by then I was hyperventilating, so far lost in wanting him that I was beyond reason. I jumped to my feet, almost taking his hand along with me, and began stripping. Kyle's eyes grew round in the dim light. With the fire dying down, the light was quickly turning into shadows, and I knew that soon we'd be drowned in darkness again. My body, burning with desire, seemed impervious to the bitter cold as I removed one layer after another.

"Are you just going to sit there and stare?" Kyle's mouth had gone slack and he looked paralyzed, sitting with his back to the wall. "If you don't get naked with me, there's not much point in this, is there?"

Intoxicated by my own desire and the look of yearning in his eyes, I must have broken the record for the speediest striptease ever. Kyle was not so quick, hesitant and sluggish. I stepped forward until my naked body touched him. He moaned, his shirt still half covering his head. I slid my hands over his bare chest and smiled when he shivered. Closing my fingers around the edges of his shirt, I pulled it out once and for all. A quiet curse crossed my lips—I could barely see him now. I wanted to drink him in, devour him with my eyes, and I couldn't. All I could see were contours and shadows.

With my fingers, I felt my way to the waist of his pants

to unzip them and pull them down. He was ready for me. I moaned in anticipation and pushed him against the wall, crushing the middle of my body against his hardness. *Who is this wild woman?* I didn't recognize myself. This was my best friend, the cute, mischievous boy who had dropped creepy crawlies down my shirt in school. He had graduated to something much better.

Kyle captured my mouth with his again, suckling on my lower lip until I writhed against him in desperate need for more. I knotted my fingers behind his neck and pressed harder against him, feeling him swell in desire. "Take me, Kyle. Please."

My beautiful friend pushed away from the wall, slid his hands under my arms and scooped me up in his arms. I wrapped my legs around his hips as he brought his hands under my bottom, supporting me. He backed into the wall again and slid down gently until I was sitting on his lap, his hardness against my softness. I was finally going to know how it felt to have Kyle fill me, love me completely.

"Do you have a condom?" With the blood pumping hard in my ears, I didn't hear it at first. "A condom, Livie. Do you have one?"

Why would I have a freaking condom? I hadn't dated in a while, and my few in between dates had always been prepared. Didn't guys carry those in their pockets like candy? "You don't have one?"

"Fuck! I left them in the car inside my toiletry bag."

I was so close to him, his heat mixing with mine, my girly bits all afire—and no protection? I might have been drunk with desire, but I was not about to risk getting pregnant. Not here. Not now. Or was I? "I don't care, Kyle. Make love to me."

Kyle lifted me up and gently sat me down beside him. I felt bereft, now that my body was not touching his anymore. "No, we can't. I'm not going to ruin your life by getting you pregnant. God knows, I've ruined enough lives already."

I groaned, frustrated. All I could think about was how I felt now that we were separated—I loved Kyle and I didn't want to lose him. The sudden realization brought me down from the high I had been riding and crushed me. I knew then I was going to forgive and fight for him. At any cost.

* * *

Kyle

Her creamy white skin glowed in the darkness, a faint beam of moonlight falling on her like stage light. Livie was so beautiful, her pixie hairstyle crowning a small face spattered with freckles and big, blue eyes. I longed to touch her again, but it wouldn't be right, especially not without protection. I couldn't risk getting her pregnant. I had come to Scotland to tell her about my impending divorce from Mia, to let her know I had no love left for her nemesis. Most of all, I'd come to Scotland to ask for her forgiveness and try to restore our friendship. Damn! What kind of an asshole would risk getting his best friend pregnant, right after betraying her with another woman? "What did you mean by ruining enough lives?" Livie's big eyes landed on mine, a frown creasing the skin of her forehead.

I handed her a coat. The cold of the night, which in our frenzy we had managed to ignore, was back in force. Livie slipped into it, never once moving her eyes away. She put on her discarded underwear and shrank inside the jacket.

"Never mind, Livie. It's nothing you should worry about." I lowered my eyes, unable to face her.

She grabbed my arm and made me look at her. "No, you're going to tell me. You've been my best friend forever, and I know there is something strange going on with you. Tell me now."

I swallowed hard and bought some time by picking up my jeans and putting them on. "It's hard to talk about this with you, Liv." Dressed and warmer, I covered myself with my jacket and leaned back on the wall. "It's embarrassing."

"I think we are beyond embarrassment." She shrugged off her coat and put on the rest of her clothes. I watched transfixed as the soft mounds of her breasts bounced with her every move before she covered them with the woollen sweater. "We've seen each other naked, for God's sake. Just tell me already."

The knot in my throat had grown into a ball I couldn't swallow. How did you tell the woman you loved that you'd been suckered by another woman's pretty face and sexy body? That you'd been fooled by what you wanted her to be, rather than seeing who she really was? That the woman you thought you loved humiliated you after sex and ignored you the rest of the time? How could I tell her I'd been blind to the fact the woman I truly loved had always been there for me?

"Fuck, Kyle. Will you just tell me the truth? You owe me that much." She was right, of course.

It came out in a tidal wave—all the secrets, the humiliation, the fear and shame of the past months. The shock of finding out Mia had a flawed personality that thrived on humiliating and hurting others. The sense of responsibility and shame that led me to hope things would get better given some time. The feeling of doom that had filled my heart, knowing I had tied myself to someone I couldn't love and feeling guilty about it. And now the fear that despite my resolve, Mia would drag me down the litigation path and into financial ruin.

Livie listened to my barrage of words, her round eyes open wide and mouth agape. I wished I knew what she was thinking. Probably how stupid I was, how ridiculous it was for a grown man to get himself into such a situation. She wouldn't be wrong. I felt stupid, like a half-witted moron who didn't deserve a second chance. When Mia had walked out on me at the wedding, I was crushed, thinking the love of my life had walked out on me, when in fact love had been beside me all along. How could I have been so freaking blind?

"I'm sorry, Liv. I'm so sorry." I hung my head, despondent and broken.

She wrapped her arms around my shoulders and surprised me into near paralysis. "Shit, Kyle. Why didn't you tell me?

I thought you were still going for that whole bitchy-sexy-and-rich package of hers. That you were so enamoured by her curves and pouty lips you were more than willing to believe the witch loved you." In spite of the bile gathering in my stomach, a chuckle escaped my lips. Livie had a flair for spinning comedy into everything she said. "But I still don't understand why you didn't see it when she left you at the altar."

Her words shook me. It was nothing I hadn't told myself before. I had come close to grabbing the phone to call and break up with Mia then. But when her shaky voice had reached my ears with the familiar complaint, the teary woe-is-me words that filled me with what I thought was love, I felt crushed under its weight. Love was forgiveness, wasn't it? Now, all I felt was shame and guilt for a failed marriage and a love that never was.

"You realize you don't owe her anything, right?" Livie had her face smashed against my shoulder. She knew me all too well. Inside of me, and despite all that had happened, I carried a hefty sense of guilt. Maybe Mia didn't love me because deep inside she knew I didn't love her either. "You made a mistake, nothing more, nothing less. Shit happens all the time. Staying married to someone you don't like and ruining your life because you feel responsible for what happened does not serve anyone. You'd be miserable, and so would she in the long run."

I knew she was right. Her words triggered something in me though; my resolve wavered, not sure anymore that I couldn't live with the guilt. Maybe I could be happy again.

When I lifted my friend's face to me, I feasted my eyes on the depth of her ocean-blue eyes and kissed her, long and hard. "You're right. There is nothing to feel guilty about. It's over."

"And us?" The moonbeams played in her eyes like on two sapphires. "What about us?"

Her scent, a mixture of lavender and lemon, tickled my nose. I smiled. "We have some unfinished business, I think."

Her smile was all the assurance I needed. Maybe I could do this—leave guilt behind and follow my heart down the path it had been begging me to take. Was it really possible I could be happy again?

CHAPTER NINE
On The Banks Of Loch Ness

It had been a relief to wake up to find myself still firmly rooted to the twenty-first century. In spite of Kyle's assurances and all that happened—or not—afterward, that little scene of medieval-looking people chanting in Gaelic around the fire had truly spooked me. Kyle and I slept in each other's arms, hanging on to each other with all we had, the blanket swaddling us like a cocoon. I woke up first and had a few moments to admire my best friend's handsome features. Last night's revelations still reeled in my mind. I couldn't wrap my head around the idea that such a strong-willed man like Kyle could be so gullible when it came to Mia. I didn't think anyone had believed Mia was really in love with Kyle—Mia loved no one but herself, her parents a distant second. Except him, of course. What I couldn't understand was why Mia had wanted to marry him. Could she be so shallow and evil that she'd use Kyle as a trophy against me?

When Kyle's eyes fluttered open, I couldn't resist cupping his cheek with my hand. The roughness of his day-old stubble scratched the palm of my hand and made me smile. *I love you so much.* "Good morning, sleeping beauty."

Even before his eyes were completely open, his lips stretched into a smile. "Hey, beautiful. So I wasn't dreaming."

My face burned at the memory of our almost lovemaking session. "All real, Kyle."

He lingered against my shoulder for a few more moments before sitting up. "I guess we need to figure out how to get out of here. We probably should have reached out to the Gaelic chanting troupe last night."

I scowled. "Are you nuts? What if they took us with them to another time? No way."

Kyle laughed and kissed me lightly on the forehead. "You're too funny, Liv."

We collected our things, straightened our crumpled clothes, and began the trek back to where we had left the car. Walking side by side, our hands brushed against each other until Kyle slipped his fingers between mine and held them. There was no need for words, so we continued in silence along the lonely back road until we came across my old Rover. If we couldn't get it started, we may be in for a long wait. I checked my phone but still had no signal. *Damn mountains!*

Kyle opened the bonnet and looked inside, his stance one of someone who knew what he was doing. I laughed out loud.

"What are you laughing about?" Kyle looked up suddenly and almost hit his head.

I loved his expression of utter confusion. "You. Pretending you know anything about cars." We were both totally hopeless when it came to mechanics. I could fix just about anything around the house, but cars were not within my range of expertise.

"I know a thing or two." His protest was as weak as my phone signal. He shrugged. "Okay, so I have no idea what anything is under here. Sue me."

Still laughing, I slid onto the driver seat. I inserted the key in the ignition and turned it. The engine, dead as a doornail the night before, revved up into life within seconds. I whooped and kissed the steering wheel. "You sweetheart of a car. I love you."

Kyle opened the passenger door and sat down beside me. "I'm a bit jealous of the car right now."

When Kyle smiled, his whole face opened. His eyes, pulled into narrow slits, beamed along with his lips. I couldn't resist; I bent toward him and kissed him. It was a brief, fluttery kiss, but it set all my senses on red alert. I didn't give him time to say anything, putting the car into gear and speeding away.

I wished my radio worked so I could fill the silence. As it was, I could hear the pumping of my heart against my ears and was overly aware of Kyle's presence next to me.

He broke the silence first. "What's the deal with the pretty boy?" The question surprised me enough that I swerved a little.

"You mean Cal?" Of course, he meant Cal. Who else could he have been talking about? "What about him?"

"When did you start dating him?"

Loaded question. I could just have told him the truth: we weren't really dating. We had gone out a couple of times, kissed a little, nothing else. Nothing serious. Instead, I said, "We started dating the day you got to Scotland."

Kyle winced, and I felt guilty for a fraction of a second. But after what he had put me through, I had the right to make him cringe.

"Is it serious?"

Idiot. If it was serious, would I have got naked with you last night?

"Not sure yet." I was sure. Yes, Cal was a great kisser and as handsome as they came, but I wasn't thinking of him as a relationship past a date or two. I didn't want Kyle to know that.

Silence filled the cab again, and I held on to the steering wheel as if to a buoy, drowning in my feelings. What did all of this mean? Was he going to pull the same stunt he did before, give in to his guilt and go back to his soon-to-be ex-wife? Or was he capitulating and considering staying by my side? My decision stood either way; I wanted to avoid all the what-ifs of the future. I wanted to make love to him, know how it felt to have him inside of me even if for one time only.

"Why did you come to Scotland?" I bit my lip, avoiding his eyes, and focused on the winding road ahead. Had he come because I was better than nothing, now that his sex-bomb wife didn't please him anymore? Was I a second choice, a consolation prize?

Kyle coughed, clearing his throat of whatever had lodged there.

"I'm not sure. I wanted to see you and apologize. I wanted our friendship back on track." He coughed again and brushed a hand over his mouth. "But when I walked in your store and saw you kissing the Scot, something cracked inside of me. I realized that I'd had the one I loved right there with me all along and I was too blind to see it."

"Are you sure it wasn't a case of 'she's mine and you can't have her' rather than you actually loving me?" It was out before I could stop myself. I bit my tongue, but it was too late.

"No, of course not." With a sigh, Kyle dropped his hands on the top of his thighs with a loud clap. "I can see how you'd think that. Hell, I would think that if the same happened to me. But that's not what happened; I was just too dumb to see through all the Mia-glitter."

At the risk of making him mad, I asked, "What made you realize she didn't love you?"

Kyle turned his eyes to me, blinking too rapidly.

"It wasn't one thing but a combination of things. The way she treated me, the things she said, the things she did. I kept making excuses for her behaviour, sure that she had a good reason to do it." Kyle's faith in people didn't always serve him well. "And when I couldn't justify it any other way, I reminded myself of my responsibility as a husband to love her no matter what."

"Didn't any of your friends point out she was using you? For what I'm not sure but still…."

"Liam did all the time, but I wouldn't listen to him. I couldn't bring myself to admit to failure." He blinked again and shook his head. "I was embarrassed and hurt…. I feel so stupid, Liv. So fucking stupid." Kyle rubbed his temples.

"Are you okay?" My hand landed on his arm as I held on to the steering wheel with the other. "You look pale."

"Just a headache." So much more than that, I was sure. "Can we not talk about Mia anymore? Please."

I squeezed his arm gently and then returned my hand to the wheel. "Of course, Kyle. She's not my favourite topic of conversation anyway." I giggled, and then he burst out laughing. We laughed together for a while until my foot hit the brakes suddenly. I couldn't believe what I was looking at. "Shit. Traffic jam."

Kyle looked at the road ahead of us, probably wondering how there could be a traffic jam when there were no cars on the road at all. A whole flock of sheep spilled over the road from one side to the other, being prodded by a shepherd who didn't seem in any hurry to move them off to the side. Kyle and I stared at each other and burst out laughing again. Some of the unconcerned sheep bleated as if annoyed. We were going nowhere for a while. At least we were in good company—sheep and all.

* * *

If I hadn't been in such good company, this would have been the ride from hell. It was official: sheep had way too much freedom and there were way too many of them in Scotland. We arrived at our destination, a cute inn on the banks of Loch Ness, after dark already. A trip that should have only taken four hours tops ended up taking us two whole days. I carried most of the luggage up the few front steps and then up the narrow stairway to the rooms while Livie was taking care of the registration paperwork. Our rooms were next to each other and tiny, but they both had an extraordinary view of the loch. I was standing by the window in her room when she came in.

"Looking for Nessie, are you?" She giggled and stood beside me.

I threw her a glance and smiled. "Well, do you blame me? I am truly hopeful I can take a snapshot of the famous monster before we leave."

Livie threw her head back and laughed. "You know they do boat tours on the loch."

That would be amazing. "Really? In the lake, the same one Nessie calls home?" I had long been fascinated by the Loch Ness monster.

"Sure. We can do a tour tomorrow after we visit the bookstore."

My best friend looked gorgeous with her hair totally dishevelled and her clothes just slightly askew from sitting in the car for so long. I had the urge to hug and kiss her until her lips were swollen. I didn't. Now that we were here, I was suddenly hesitant, not sure of what to do next. Was the tryst in the castle a product of a strange and eerie night? Or was she still willing to give me the chance I didn't deserve?

We stood side by side, hands barely missing each other, as much in awe of the glittering waters of the loch under the moonlight as from each other's proximity. It was like a magnetic field had been created, and I could almost hear the crackling of electricity between us. I sighed deeply and loudly, but she didn't move, keeping her eyes in the distance where Castle Urquhart's dark contours carved a space out of the night.

"Are you coming to dinner?" We both turned at the same time and almost bumped into each other. Our hostess was standing in the doorway, looking curiously at us. "It's served downstairs if you'd like a bite to eat."

We followed Mrs Grant down the stairs and into the cosy dining room where several small, square tables had been set with white linen tablecloths, old-fashioned floral china, and a small vase with fresh greenery. Shortly after we sat down, Mr Grant came in carrying a crockery pot filled with something steaming and deliciously scented.

"Stovies for the guests," the older man announced with a big smile. "A special Rose of the Loch recipe."

Livie's face opened into a smile. "My favourite. Kyle, you're in for a treat."

I loved her smile, the way the corners of her lips curled up and forced the fleshy part of her cheeks to dimple. *God, I want to kiss you.* I could still taste her on my tongue, sweet and tantalizing…. I covered my lap with the cloth napkin in an attempt to disguise my reaction to the woman before me.

Oblivious to my state of discomfort, Mr Grant spooned large portions of the hot concoction into Livie's plate and then came around to do the same with mine. It did smell heavenly, but then again, I was starved. We had barely eaten the night before—Mrs. Bailey's rowies notwithstanding—and even less all day as we navigated the rather lonely back roads of the highlands.

The delicious dinner was followed by cranachan, a fabulous boozy trifle-like dessert made with raspberries and fromage frais. I didn't eat it. I must have inhaled it, because it was gone before I even had a chance to fully appreciate its flavour.

"This is so good." Livie was still working on hers, a bit of the white cream stuck to her upper lip. For a brief, crazy moment, I saw myself stretching over the table and licking it off her lips. I choked. "Did it go the wrong way?" God, no. That was the problem, it was going the right way—right to my heart and certain misbehaving parts of my body.

We finished the meal and sat by the fireplace for a while, talking softly about everything and nothing at all. I wasn't even sure I could recall the theme of our conversation. It felt so good to sit side by side, the warmth of the flames kissing our cheeks while I listened to the soft voice of my love. It was intimate and felt so right.

Soon we retired to our separate rooms. I changed into some thin joggers and slid a loose T-shirt over my head before stretching on the soft double bed. As exhausted as I was, I couldn't sleep. My body was still alive from the night before, every nerve, every fibre of my being awakened by desire. But I didn't dare act on it. I had left Livie right after she declared her love for me. And then there was the not-so-little issue of my marriage. I had lost the right to expect or ask anything from her. So I lay there, staring at the faint light playing tag with the shadows on the ceiling and wishing things were different.

A rasping sound at the door snapped me from my daydreams. I lifted my head, not sure I had heard it correctly, but there it was again—a single knock, weak and hesitant. I jumped to my feet and opened the door, my heart not daring to hope. Livie was standing there, shivering in a sleep shirt that covered her legs down to her knees, no shoes on her feet.

"Livie?" I held on to the door, afraid that if I let it go, I'd draw my friend into my arms.

She didn't move at first, her hands rubbing her crossed arms and her chin quivering. It was as if time had frozen and we were stuck in some weird vacuum where neither of us could move.

"Can I come in?" I had never known her to speak so softly, so timidly—not around me anyway.

I trembled and nodded, the words caught in my throat. She stepped in the room, and I closed the door behind her, studying her as she kept her back to me, slowly moving toward the window, her arms still tightly knotted across her chest.

"What happened in the castle...." Livie paused as if

looking for words.

"We don't have to talk about it if you don't want to." I wanted to assure her she didn't owe me a thing. I, on the other hand, owed her everything and hated myself for not being able to give it to her.

Silence followed my words, and I thought I saw her shoulders move as if she was crying. I stepped forward and wrapped my arms around her, tucking my chin in the crook of her neck. "Please, don't cry, Liv. I can't stand that I've hurt you."

Livie turned around within my arms until she was facing me. I wiped the tears rolling down her freckled cheeks with a finger and tasted the salty wetness on her nose in a gentle kiss. She gasped.

We were so close, our bodies touching, our chests rising and dropping together in unison. My heart had taken off in a race, and my whole body was lit on fire. I fought the need to slip my hand behind her neck and pull her face to mine until our lips met in a kiss. "I'm so sorry, Liv. I never meant to hurt you, and I definitely never meant to bring this all up again."

Never ceasing to amaze me, Livie rose on her tiptoes and glued her lips to mine in a hungry kiss. For the next few moments, I forgot where I was. I may even have forgotten who I was, lost in her embrace. I wanted to stay there, hanging on the threads of the fictional bliss holding us in each other's arms. Reality be damned. Forget Mia, forget my stupid mistakes, forget the life that was waiting for me back in Australia. All I wanted—all I needed—was right there, yielding against me.

"I may be making the biggest mistake of my life, Kyle," she whispered over my lips, breathless. "But I need to know how it feels to be with you. One time, Kyle, I need this one time before you go back to Australia."

Selfishly, I wanted that too. I knew one time wouldn't be enough. I wanted more, or the memory of that moment would haunt me for the rest of my miserable life, but I had no right to ask or demand anything from her. "Are you sure?"

I wasn't sure what I'd have done if she had changed her mind, but she didn't. She nodded emphatically and took my lips with hers again.

***

Livie

The room was stuffy and claustrophobic. The music coming through the crackling speakers by the fireplace was repetitive, and even though soft and wordless, it grated on my nerves like nails on a blackboard. My stomach was all in knots, and I couldn't relax long enough to take a deep breath. I had walked in my sleeping T-shirt down the stairs to the guest living room, hoping the change of setting would calm my nerves. It wasn't working.

"Stop that music," I whispered to no one in particular. The slow, smooth, and characterless tune ignored me, and I threw a murderous glare at the speakers. "You're not cool. Just shut up!"

I dashed out of the room and almost barrelled into a couple of people coming in. I mumbled my apologies and continued to walk toward my destination.

I may throw up. Maybe not. Oh God, what am I getting myself into? What am I doing? Why can't my heart and my brain agree on anything?

I climbed the steps one at a time, my legs heavy with anxiety, and ambled to Kyle's room. The door stood in front of me, ominous in its faceless personality. My heart's calisthenics made me feel lightheaded, and I had to shut my eyes for a moment to collect myself.

Are you going to do it or not?

Making a decision, I lifted my hand and knocked. Twice. It was more like a hesitant rap, the knocking of someone who didn't want to be heard. Not really.

Yes, you want him to hear it. Knock harder.

I had just lifted my hand again when the door opened, and the handsome body of my friend filled the gap. My heart went crazy but this time in a pleasant way. Kyle always had that effect on me. It was a mystery to me how a single person could make me feel like this—nervous and happy at the same time. My tight muscles relaxed, and all the anxiety of a moment ago dissolved into a smile. He was the reason I was there. And what an amazing reason it was.

"Livie?" His soft voice caressed me, and the butterflies inside my chest took flight. I loved him so much it hurt sometimes. The thought of losing him forever to the arms of another woman made all my muscles cramp again.

"Can I come in?" I spoke so softly I wondered whether he'd heard it, but he nodded and stepped aside.

I entered the room, avoiding his eyes and staring out the window where the beauty of the moonlight reflected on the great loch provided me with some soothing assurance that all was not lost. Not yet.

"Have faith," my otherwise unwise mother had always told me. *Have faith.* Didn't humans hold faith in what they couldn't see or totally comprehend? Didn't we hope that something extraordinary lived in the dark, cold waters of that loch? Then why couldn't I have faith that something—however small, however simple—may happen to change things around and give Kyle and me the second chance we both wanted and needed?

Tears welled up in my eyes, and in spite of my resolve, nerves got the best of me and quiet sobs climbed in my throat. Like gentle waves in the ocean, my shoulders shook and rolled until I felt the body of my best friend glued to my back. He wrapped his arms around me and tucked his chin in the crook of my neck.

"Please, don't cry, Liv. I can't stand that I've hurt you."

I knew that. Kyle had always had a kind soul. So kind and empathic that sometimes he forgot who he was, his own needs, to attend to others around him. Even as the mischievous boy who stuck creepy crawlies down my shirt, he had struck me with his ability to notice every change in my moods, every hint of trouble, and be ready with a sympathetic word or a shoulder to cry on. I sometimes worried, afraid that one day he would lose himself looking after someone else's needs.

I wasn't quite sure what happened next—what I did or what I said. By the time I was aware of my actions, I was in Kyle's arms, lips melded into his. Did I kiss him, or did he kiss me? Not that it mattered. I wanted to have him inside me; I wanted us to be one.

At some point, he asked me if I was sure, and I replied with another kiss. My body burned with desire, and my heart had taken over my senses. Mistake or not, I was going to make love to my best friend.

We stumbled to the side of the bed, entangled in each other's arms, my lips refusing to leave his even for a few seconds. I drank him in, intoxicated by his flavour on my tongue and the urgent pressure of his against it. Blindly, I sought the edges of his T-shirt and began pulling it up until it slid between the two of us, over his head, and across the room in an elegant arch. I moaned at the sight of Kyle's well-defined biceps and chest muscles. Before I could touch him, he pulled my sleep shirt all the way over my head. I heard his sharp intake of breath as he realized I was wearing nothing underneath.

"Shit, Liv." His throaty voice filled me with goosebumps as he ran a hand from my neck to my breast, lingering there. "Have we lost it? Are we really going to do this?"

I pressed myself against his hand, pinning it between us. "You do have the condoms, right?" I giggled at the words, remembering the night at the castle.

Kyle laughed and slid his hand downward to my belly

and then around to cup my butt. "Yes, millions of them." I pulled away just enough to look him in the eye. He shrugged. "I carry them around in case of the apocalypse or a zombie attack."

Leave it to Kyle to make me laugh even when I had very little else in my mind than sex at that moment. I undid the ties of his joggers and pulled them down. He wasn't wearing anything under them either. It was my turn to brush my hand along his slim, hard body. There was no disguising how much he wanted me, and when I wrapped my hand around his arousal and pressed myself against him, he groaned.

We fell onto the bed, Kyle under me, his legs dangling awkwardly off the edge. I pulled away then, leaving his naked body open to full view. He was the most beautiful man I had ever seen. They say that love is blind, and those words had never made more sense than at that moment. Love colours the object of your affection in such rare and beautiful hues, you can't help but being blinded to any flaws. Kyle lifted his head and looked at me, a question in his eyes. "What are you doing?" He pulled himself farther onto the bed so his legs weren't dangling anymore.

"I'm admiring you, idiot."

He rose on his forearms. "Why admire the painting from afar, when you can have it for yourself?"

I snorted, and he laughed.

I climbed onto the bed beside him and kissed his chest, one pec at a time, teasing him with my tongue. "I'm hoping for no interruptions this time." Kyle turned to the side and took me halfway underneath him. "And as much as I want to see Nessie, I hope to God she doesn't pick tonight to make an appearance." He captured my breast with his mouth, and I closed my eyes, whimpering in pleasure. "Tonight is all about you, Liv."

As he transferred his attention to the other breast, I wove my fingers into his silky hair. "I love you. I've always loved you."

Kyle moved down and settled between my legs. "I love you too, Liv," he said before kissing me, his tongue caressing my folds and driving me near the edge. I laid a hand on his head and pushed him closer to me, riding the waves of pleasure his touch unleashed in me.

"Get a condom." I surprised myself with the urgency in my voice. Deep inside I was afraid that something would happen and we couldn't finish what we'd started. More than the pleasure he so expertly and generously was giving me, I wanted to be one with him—two bodies joined in a way only two people who loved each other could. Mind, body, and heart.

He pulled away from me to retrieve the necessary item from his suitcase, and I felt forlorn, like something vital was missing. I willed him to hurry and watched him as he fumbled to the corner of the room where his luggage was. He had an amazing body—wide shoulders that sloped into well-defined biceps and tapered down to his waist and the sexiest butt the world had ever produced.

"Come on, hot arse, are you ever coming back to me?"

He turned around, a little flustered, and waved a small blue square wrapper in the air with a smile. "Got it." My heart nearly stopped at the sight of my beautiful naked friend. The V of his hip bones hugged his abs and narrow hips and made all my bones turn into mush. He rushed to join me on the bed and handed me the condom. "You do the honours."

I lost it. Not in a sexual way. This was my best friend, the same young boy who had first tormented me and later become my fiercest defender. My whole body was overcome by a wave of love so strong I sobbed and sat up, wrapping my arms around his neck and pulling him against me with all my might.

"Whoa, girl." Kyle sounded choked, and I loosened my hold just a little. "What do I owe this sudden and weirdly timed show of affection?"

I cried against his neck. "I love you. I love you so much. I can't believe I'm here with you right now." I was blabbering, I knew, mirroring the confusion of feelings in which I was drowning. "It all just feels so unreal, like a storybook thing."

Kyle nuzzled behind my ear and nibbled my earlobe. "It's not fiction, Liv. We're real. What we have is real." The heat of his body against mine was causing magic. "We've just been… derailed for a while. But we're back on track."

I pulled away and looked him in the eye, tears still rolling down my cheeks. "Are we really real? You're not going back to your wife?"

He winced, as if the mention of Mia had physically hurt him. "No, I'm not going back to her," he said after a moment of hesitation. "You're my future, not Mia. This is very real." He pointed at the two of us, emphasizing the word "this" before leaning closer and covering my mouth with his. "We're real."

***

I meant every word. At that moment, the doubts that had been swimming around in my head had coalesced, and I was now determined to call my lawyer and get my divorce to Mia moving faster, even if that meant running the risk of drowning in debt—not that my head was too clear right then, as I lay skin to skin with the love of my life. Livie quickly ripped the wrapper off the condom and rolled it on me, the touch of her fingers nearly driving me to the brink.

Before I could do anything—my reactions had slowed down to a crawl—Livie slid over me, straddling my hips. "I want you to stay with me, Kyle, but I won't make you do it. I won't pressure you into it."

I shook my head and opened my mouth, but the words got stuck in my throat. Despite the confusion in my mind, in my heart, my feelings for Livie were as clear as crystal.

"I didn't come to your room expecting anything in return," Livie said, her hands splayed across my abs. "I just want a night with you so I don't spend the rest of my life wondering how it would feel. No regrets."

The breath I had been holding in escaped through my open lips. "No regrets." It was a whisper, almost a prayer.

Livie smiled, the corners of her big, blue eyes crinkling. She moved over my hips and slid higher, her softness meeting my hardness. My groan collided with her moan as she rocked on top of me, her hands braced on my chest, her eyes semi-closed. I arched against her, wanting to be even closer. She lifted and lowered herself on me, sheathing me in her heat. I lost all control. My mind went blank, my only thought the need to drive myself deeper into her, not wanting to leave any space between us—our bodies fused as one, our souls blended. We danced the lover's waltz, bodies moving in sync, our rugged breathing setting the rhythm to the beat of our hearts.

We came together, climaxing so high I thought I'd never come down. I soared, lifted by the pleasure and my love for that tiny wisp of a woman. Livie shuddered in my arms, whimpering against my skin and pressing herself harder against me. There was so much I wanted to say, but I couldn't find the words. Instead, we lay together, enveloped in each other's arms, still connected and silent. Earth had come to a full stop, but the world hadn't ended. In fact, in the skies above, a new star shone brightly. Whatever happened, that star would forever reflect our first night together.

* * *

Livie

Waking up within the cocoon of my best friend's arms was

better than what I imagined it would feel like waking up among the angels. I remained still, afraid that if I moved even an inch, I would break the spell we were both under. Because this couldn't be true, could it? This sense of infinite well-being was totally new to me. None of my previous relationships had ever provided me with this peace, this deep-rooted joy. I wanted it to be real, but I was terrified to wake up and find out I had dreamed all of it.

"Are you awake?" Kyle whispered, as if afraid to wake me up. Or maybe he was also afraid he was dreaming.

Reluctantly, I wiggled in his arms. "Yes, you?"

He turned to me, sliding the arm supporting my head until his face was almost above mine, his head supported on his hand. His luscious lips were stretched into a blissful smile. "Hello, gorgeous."

I stretched like a cat, bumping my legs against his. I shivered. "Hi. So nice to wake up to your smile." I barely recognized my own voice, languid and soft, the voice of someone fully satisfied with life. So not me.

He bent down and kissed me, a tender, barely there kiss that sent all my senses into overdrive. "All right then, I'm not dreaming." He smiled even wider. "You really are here with me. We made love, right?"

I nodded, giggling quietly. "We sure did."

Kyle licked his lips, his smile becoming crooked as his eyes closed to almost a slit. "And it was epic."

A loud chuckle escaped my lips. "Well, don't get too cocky. I had better."

A sudden warmth covered my breast, and I gasped.

"Right! You are totally immune to my superpowers." He bent down again and ran his tongue over my lips teasingly while his hand, cupping my breast, continued to cause havoc to my girly bits. "You love me."

The breathy whisper caressed my lips just as effectively as his fingers on my oversensitive skin. I sighed, incapable of fighting the overwhelming feelings washing over me. "I do love you, Kyle. I do."

His face was still mere inches away, his onyx eyes trained on mine with such intensity I thought he could see inside me. "I love you too. My best friend, my love."

We didn't leave the room until much later, irresponsibly late to Kyle's appointment with the bookstore owner. That morning, recklessness seemed the way to go, the feeling of optimism and happiness making me feel invincible. Kyle had given the owner of the store a courtesy call to let him know we were coming, but it was not a business visit. "More like corporate voyeurism," Jenny had said with her usual aplomb and a wink.

The bookstore was bigger than mine and employed five people. It was a busy place with customers wandering around by the shelves or lingering by the coffee counter with Z-shaped chrome bar stools lining its whole length. It was modern and clean with lots of interesting and colourful graphic art on the walls and bright wall-to-wall carpet.

"I like yours better," Kyle whispered in my ear while he was setting his tablet on one of the few tables. "A Cup of Fiction has a lot more personality and a more welcoming atmosphere."

I wanted to pull him into my arms and kiss him, but it seemed like an unprofessional thing to do. So I just beamed at him and was rewarded by the sunniest smile this side of the Milky Way.

While he interviewed the owner, a short man in his late fifties with a full mop of red hair, I wandered the aisles, checking out their stock and studying the artwork on the walls. Kyle was right; as beautiful and well put-together as the store was, mine was so much more. A Cup of Fiction had a real soul, the kind that attracted bookish people like me or Kyle, a mixed feeling of home and fantasy. Fictional-ish was the word I was looking for. This one was too grounded, too real for the taste of fiction lovers. Inverness was a much larger city than Montrose, and business seemed to be thriving. *No matter.* I had my faithful patrons who would sooner starve than go without books from my store. A growing sense of pride swelled in my chest.

After sampling their coffee—better than mine—and their pastries—nowhere near Mrs. Riley's rowies—we left. Kyle was determined to look for Nessie, so we got in the car and headed for the loch. We bought two tickets on a small boat with a rather rudimentary sonar machine, and soon we were in the middle of the loch lulled by the sound of the beeping contraption.

"This is absolutely amazing." Kyle had been chatting with our pilot, who was more than a little amused with our Aussie accents. "Can you swim in the loch?"

The old sailor chortled. "Only if you have a death wish, lad." The man pointed at the expanse of the dark waters.

"This water is never above six degrees Celsius, winter or summer. You jump in and you have a very short time before your body goes into shock."

"Hypothermia? Not a fun way to die, is it?" Kyle said. "So how can Nessie survive in this water?"

"There are animals that can easily survive in even colder waters, so who's to say Nessie is not one of them?"

"Have you ever seen her?"

I smiled, amused by Kyle's child-like question.

The sailor shook his head. "I may have a long time ago, but whatever it was emerging from the waters was too far for me to see clearly."

I sat in the back of the boat where a toddler was busy trying to climb on the small bench that ran along the stern. His mother was doing her best to keep an eye on him while watching the breathtaking scenery. The loch was incredibly wide and dark, its mucky waters not allowing us to see anything beneath the surface. I understood now how such a legend had started and been kept alive for so long. At that moment, looking at the almost black waters, I could easily believe that a never-before-seen creature lived in that loch. The weak sun warmed my cold cheeks, and I closed my eyes, images of fantastic beasts becoming solid in my mind.

"Are you dreaming of me?" Kyle had sneaked beside me, his hand sliding along my shoulders.

I giggled. "Only if you are twenty feet long and can spit fire." I dropped my head on his shoulder, grateful for the small intimacy. "This is so beautiful, Kyle. Did you ever think you'd see it with your own eyes?"

"I'd hoped." His head leaned against mine, and I closed my eyes, enjoying the moment. "Just like I hoped one day you'd love me as much as I love you." I felt the warmth of his lips on mine, and I was instantly on fire.

"Ewww." The sound of the childish voice broke us apart. The little boy's face was screwed into a funny grimace as he stared at us. "Kiss, Mum, he kiss."

The mum laughed nervously and shrugged an apology. "Come here, Stevie. Stop bothering the nice couple."

Kyle looked at me, eyes twinkling with amusement. "Do you think we'll have one or two of those?" He pointed at the toddler who, tired of watching us, had turned his attention to the gunwale. I must have looked positively horrified because Kyle quickly added, "Okay, a conversation for another time then."

A scream of sheer terror made us jump to our feet. There was a big commotion happening on the opposite side from us, centred around the young mother who was hysterically screaming. The captain left the helm and ran toward her. "What happened?"

"My baby, my baby," she cried, waving her hands in the direction of the lake. "He fell off the boat."

Kyle moved so fast I didn't have time to stop him. While the captain returned to the helm to turn the boat around, Kyle took off his shoes and jumped overboard into the freezing waters of the loch. I wanted to scream after him but choked with fear. Hadn't the captain just said that the cold water could kill quickly?

I managed to walk closer to the gunwale he had gone

over and joined the frantic woman. As much as I wished I could comfort her, my eyes couldn't move away from Kyle swimming away from the boat toward the bobbing orange figure of the toddler. The boat had gone some ways from where the child had fallen in, and Kyle was going to make it there before we were. Even though the boy was wearing a life jacket, he had somehow flipped and had his face submerged in water.

"Can you move this boat faster?" I yelled at the captain, my chest so tight I thought it would crush my heart.

The sailor mumbled something I couldn't hear, and I turned my attention back to my best friend. He had reached the boy and managed to turn him around so he could breathe. From that distance, I couldn't tell if the child was moving or not. If an adult could reach hypothermia in ten minutes, with a child that tiny it would happen a lot faster. Kyle was holding the toddler against him but making no effort to swim back, which could only mean one thing: his body was going numb.

As soon as the boat reached them, the boy was pulled in by his mother, and I reached out for Kyle. "Give me your hand." He wasn't moving, and his skin had a sickly bluish tint. I yelled, "Kyle, give me your hand."

He raised his eyes to me then and sluggishly lifted his hand to mine. I was teetering on the gunwale, stretched as far as I could be without falling in the water to grab hold of his hand. His skin was a piece of ice, cold and slippery, as I pulled him closer to the safety of the boat. The captain appeared at my side and helped me pull him up and inside.

"I'll get him a blanket," the man said before running into the small cabin.

Kyle lay motionless on the floor of the vessel, the out-of-control shaking the only sign he was still alive. I began stripping him of the soaked clothes, down to his underwear, and wrapped him with the blanket the captain brought back. I propped him up against me and rubbed his arms, trying to bring some circulation back to them.

"Kyle, speak to me. Are you all right?" His wet head was tucked in the crook of my neck, and I heard him utter a sound. "Kyle, say something."

After a few seconds, I felt his icy hand come to rest on my arm. "I'm just a little cold, that's all," he said, lifting his face to mine. "How's the boy?"

The sobs that I had somehow managed to restrain were now running free, making me hiccup with every word I said. "He's going to be fine. You idiot. You could have died." I was not sure whether I was angry or happy. Maybe both. "We would have turned the boat around soon enough." But even as I said it, I knew that was not true. If he hadn't turned the boy around when he did, the child would have probably drowned in the murky waters.

Kyle made a weird sound with his throat, and I realized he was laughing. "I'm actually really disappointed," he said, stuttering as the shivers shook his body. "I'd hoped that Nessie would rescue the boy and me."

Nessie may have not made an appearance, staying well-hidden in the mysterious waters of Loch Ness, but I was delighted my man was alive and well—even if very cold.

Nothing a good cup of hot cocoa wouldn't fix, the doctors at the ER had told us. By the time we arrived back at our inn, he had forgotten about Nessie and was focused on us and the heat we could conjure together. I selfishly loved the fact he couldn't stop touching me or whispering sweet nothings in my ear. For years, my dreams had been filled with these moments, and now they were finally a reality.

That night we didn't even pretend to sleep in separate rooms. It was our last night in Inverness, and I couldn't care less what people thought. Kyle was my hero, my friend, and my love. I would have my time in his arms. God knew I had waited long enough.

CHAPTER TEN
Back To Reality

Kyle

I may have floated instead of walked. Every time I glanced at the beautiful woman sitting next to me in the car, I had to pinch myself to make sure I wasn't dreaming. I couldn't say for sure when I realized I was in love with my best friend, but I knew it went back a long time. I may have been in love with her when she had two pigtails and I chased her around at recess. All I knew was that I had loved her for what seemed like forever and having her in my arms was a dream come true.

Following my near-drowning the day before and much discussion, we had decided to take the same out-of-the-way route back. Livie wanted to have a second and better look at the castle where we had spent the night and look for the strange people who had haunted it. "But you can't chase ghosts during the day." The teasing was just for show. I wanted to see it again too.

"What are we going to do when we get back?" Hands gripping the wheel, Livie stole a quick look at me before turning her attention to the road again.

Even though she had not been specific, I knew what she meant. "You're going to break up with the Scot, right? I want everybody to know we're together now."

Livie's freckles moved as her cheeks rose in one of her lovely smiles. "He's not my boyfriend."

"What?" I was confused. "But you told me…."

Her laughter was like bubbles of joy bursting inside my ears. "I was mad at you still. I lied. We went out on a couple dates. He's a good guy, but we never committed to anything at all."

I didn't know whether to kill her or kiss her. I chose the latter. "You're a mean one when you want to be," I whispered over her lips. "I was so jealous."

"Good, that's just the way it should be."

Deep inside I totally agreed with her. I had been cruel without meaning it and oh so dumb letting Mia hoodwink me thoroughly. I kissed her again before Livie steered the car out of the side of the road, ready to head home.

I looked out the window at the beautiful green hills and lochs. Peaceful and simple. Something my life hadn't been in a long time. After my brush with death, I was even more determined to make my relationship to Mia a thing of the past. Quickly. "As soon as my divorce is finalized, hopefully in the next couple months or so, I will be totally free of Mia and her poison."

"Not a minute too soon." She smiled, but I could see the slight twitch in the corner of her lips. Damn! She was still not sure I wouldn't go back to my wife. Then again, could

I blame her?

After a couple of encounters with the inevitable herds of sheep, we came across our castle. Funny how I thought about it that way. We stopped the car and walked along the beaten path to the ruins of the old stone building. It was a small castle, like most in Scotland, but even in its state of disrepair, the buttressed home was an impressive sight.

"How did I not notice how beautiful it is?" Livie sped up, her eyes glistening in excitement. "Hurry."

I laughed. "It's not like it is going to vanish or anything."

She grabbed my hand and pulled me behind her toward the old building. "You never know. After all, we saw those people from another time."

"Liv, they were reenactors or modern druids, not people from the past." There was no point in arguing. Livie was truly enchanted by the place and the events of two nights ago. Who was I to ruin her fun?

She dragged me all the way to the castle until we were standing in the same spot where we had spent the night together. As soon as we crossed the broken threshold, she swung around and cornered me between her and the wall. "If we ever get married, I want the wedding to be set right here."

"Whoa, girl." I chuckled, the sound bouncing off the tall walls. "We just had a night together and you're already making plans for the future?"

She pressed her body against mine, and I melted. The icy wall behind me disappeared, and I was leaning on a feathery down cloud. Her touch held magic.

"A girl can dream. And it wasn't one night; it was two. I thought I was going to lose you yesterday. Again." She stood on her tiptoes and kissed me, prying my lips open with her tongue and inviting mine to dance. With a sigh, she slumped against me, her face against my chest. "I can hear your heart singing. I know you feel it too."

I did feel it. Everything and then some. If I could, I would probably marry her right then and never let go again. Had I ever felt like that with Mia?

Shit. Mia is coming to Scotland!

I had conveniently erased that fact from my mind. There was still time. As soon as we arrived back in Montrose, I'd get on Skype and make sure she wouldn't get on that plane.

"We really should be going." I was suddenly in a hurry to get back and make that call. A giant weight had settled in the pit of my stomach, an uncontrollable fear of being too late.

Livie cuddled even closer. "What's the hurry, Kyle?"

She nuzzled the dip at the bottom of my neck, and I wondered whether what I felt was what women referred to as swooning—wobbly legs and a fast-beating heart that robbed me of normal breathing.

"I want to call Mia as soon as possible." She flinched, and if I already resented my soon-to-be ex-wife, I now resented her so much more. Even from afar she was able to cloud my happiness. "She told me she was coming to Scotland soon." It was a whisper, and I couldn't be sure Livie had heard it.

For a moment there was silence. Livie, still glued to me, didn't move, and I thought she hadn't heard it.

Probably better this way.

"Did you just say that the bitch to end all bitches is coming to *my* Scotland?" Okay, so the deep growling tone in her voice negated my previous assessment. She had heard every word.

"Well, it's not really your country, per se...." Livie pulled away from me and glared. *Uh-oh, I must tread carefully.* The killer look she gave me could melt iron. "What I mean is, I can't stop her from visiting, can I?"

"You certainly could try." The ice in her voice made me shudder. Literally. Livie could let you know exactly how she felt with a simple sound and look.

I needed an escape. "That's why I want to call her as soon as I can. If I tell her we're together, she won't want to come." I looked at her, hoping for a smile, but I got a scowl instead. "Liv, I forgot she had told me that. I don't want her here any more than you do."

Holy shit, the look!

"Why? Because you'll feel guilty for still having the hots for her? Because when you look at her all you can think about is having sex? With her?" Livie separated the words and spat them out, each one a bee sting in my heart. Not because it was true any longer, but because it had been at some point, and the shame and regret that came with it still burned a hole in my soul.

She tried to step away from me, but I held her still, desperately wanting her to know she was the only one in my heart. She had held that place since our schooldays and nothing much had changed even through all my stupid mistakes and lapses of judgment.

"Don't be mad, Liv. Please. I love you." The frown on Livie's face was like a slap, and I wanted to wipe it away and make it disappear. "Mia is my past and not a good one. You're my future… I don't know why I ever thought I was in love with her."

"Because she's good in bed." *Ouch! A bit too close to the truth for comfort.* "Don't you think I've heard all the guys she dated broadcasting her expertise in the bedroom? I mean, she has made sure she's dated all of my male friends at one time or another. They were happy to share that bit of unwanted information with me."

What could I say? "I'm not saying that didn't weigh in my decision to date her. I'm an idiot, Liv, and sometimes I do think with my dick." Might as well go with the truth. "But the real reason why I started dating her was because I thought I didn't have a chance with you. If I had known that we could have a chance, I'd never, ever have even considered asking her out." She blinked, and I took that as a sign her anger was wavering. "I love every inch, every quirk, every detail of you, Liv. Please, don't be mad."

She raised her round, blue eyes to me and smiled. "I'm not mad at you." I exhaled in relief. "I'm mad at Mia. That manipulative, spiteful bitch—"

I covered her mouth with mine and squeezed her against me. I wanted to inhale her, make her part of who I was, part of my body and soul. Hungrily, I searched for her tongue with mine, intoxicated by her heady flavour. I slid against the cold wall, all the way to the stone floor, Livie settling on my lap as I swelled at the contact. I could have stayed there for the rest of my life and been perfectly happy, but life never stopped, and we had to get back home. So, after a while we jumped to our feet, shook ourselves off, and walked hand in hand to the car to resume our drive back.

The rest of the drive was a quiet one as I focused on the beautiful scenery around us, in awe of what had happened and wondering what other surprises and joys were in our future.

* * *

Livie

Still swooning from our two nights together, I parked the car in front of the store and slid off my seat into the street. Kyle was already opening the boot of the Rover and retrieving our bags. I was walking around to join him when I noticed Jenny tottering toward us on her usual high heels, a frown on her face.

"Hey, Jenny." I waved at her, worried she would fall in her rush to meet us. "Slow down. You're going to trip."

Jenny waved her hands as if in distress and finally stopped by us. "Oh my God, I tried to call you a million times. Why didn't you pick up the phone?"

I was beginning to worry. Jenny was not the type to panic over nothing. "The signal was non-existent for most of the way. What happened? Are you okay?"

Jenny threw a glance at Kyle before continuing, "She's here." It was a weird screamed whisper, as she held the sibilant sound of the first word for longer than necessary. Kyle and I looked at each other, confused. "The snake has landed." Again, she held that *s* sound for too long.

"Snakes don't fly, Jenny." Was she high on something? I had never seen her do any drugs, but she was acting so strangely. I touched her arm, trying to calm her down. "You're not making any sense."

Kyle had gone pale. His tanned complexion had turned into a sickly beige as his eyes turned to the store. "Mia."

I knitted my eyebrows and stared at him, a bit miffed he was uttering that name. "Her name is Jenny, not Mia."

"Well, look who's here. If it's not Little Miss Muffet and my husband."

I was pretty sure I'd be able to identify that voice in a crowd of thousands. It was a sound that clawed at my eardrums and made my blood boil. I turned to the always gorgeous shape of my nemesis. Jenny was right; the snake had indeed landed.

"What are you doing here?" My voice was so cold my tongue went numb. After such a happy couple of days, this was not what I had been hoping to find at the end of our journey. How dare she come to my store?

She squinted in the winter sun. "Don't get your knickers all in a bunch, girl. I'm here to see my husband." She took a few steps and, to my total mortification, pulled Kyle into an embrace and kissed him full on the lips. Bile rose to my mouth, burning everything in its way, and I thought I was going to vomit right there. "When he didn't show up at the hotel, I thought he might be here interviewing you." She licked her lips and smiled.

I was too scared to look at Kyle, afraid he was also smiling, his lips swollen by her hungry kiss and cheeks tinted with excitement. I stared at Jenny instead. "Can you help me with my bags, Jenny?" Then I turned to Mia, still avoiding Kyle's eyes. "I wish I could say I'm glad to see you, Mia, but we both know it would be a lie. Run and go back to whatever hole you crawled from, because you are not welcome in my store."

"Liv." Kyle grabbed my arm as I passed him on the way to the store. "Please, don't go."

I did look at him then. His cheeks were not flushed, and he was not smiling. Instead, there was a shadow over his beautiful dark eyes, a quiver to his lips. I hesitated for a moment before covering his hand with mine and smiling at him. I wanted to stay with him, but he had to do this alone. We would never be happy together if I ever thought I had somehow pressured him into it. I dropped my hand and walked inside, leaving him standing on the sidewalk with my frenemy, his back slumped and suitcase beside him.

"You're back." Cal was behind the counter of the coffee bar, a kitchen towel in one hand and a cup in the other. "How did it go?"

It was heaven. But now hell had reclaimed me. I hoped Kyle would have the strength to stand up to Mia, but part of me was being eaten by doubt and fear. He'd looked so despondent, so unlike him. My usually strong friend was reduced to a fraction of who he was at the mere sight of his wife.

Jenny was close behind me, my bag in her hands. "Shit, Livie. I tried to warn you she was here."

"I know. It's all right." It wasn't, but it was a hurdle both Kyle and I had to conquer. "How long was she here?"

Following me to the back room, Jenny's heels set the rhythm of her voice. "She's been here since yesterday. I just couldn't get rid of her." I took the suitcase from her hands and placed it in the corner of my office. "What a horrible person. She spent hours making fun of every person who walked through that door. When she wasn't mocking our customers, she was shamelessly flirting with Cal."

Not Cal too! Why did she feel like she had to seduce every male in my life? "Miss Perky has been a royal pain in my arse for most of my life. I think she has perfected it into an art form." Jenny laughed. "But she *is* Kyle's wife, at least for now. Let's just hope she won't show her perky self around here anymore."

Jenny looked up at me, her lower lip caught between her teeth. "For now? Did something happen while you were away?"

I avoided her eyes and turned around to leave the room. "Nothing serious."

"No, you're not getting away with that answer." She held my arm and gave me the laser-eye. "What happened? Something happened."

Shit. There was no escaping Jenny's probing eyes. "Well, we may have…."

She squealed, and I placed a finger in front of my lips. "You had sex."

I shushed her, afraid Cal would hear it.

"You did the nasty," she added, ignoring me.

"Can you please quiet down?" I took a peek through the door and glanced toward the counter where Cal was still happily towel-drying the cups. "And it was not even remotely nasty." We giggled like two silly schoolgirls. "It was like I've always thought it would be and so much more."

"What about the wicked witch of the west? What is he going to do about her?" My friend had no trouble asking the hard questions.

I sighed. "He's divorcing her, but I saw the look of panic in his eyes when he saw her outside the store. She has broken a part of him, I think. As much as I hate to say this, Kyle really thought she loved him." The question was, would he cave in to her wiles?

It was not planned, but the events of the last few days had made me overly emotional—our lovemaking, Kyle's near-drowning, and now Mia's appearance. So it happened anyway, I spilled my guts to Jenny, crying my eyes out as I told her the whole insidious tale of my friendship-turned-love, his betrayal, and my fear he'd go back to his wife. My Scottish friend was trustworthy, and I needed someone to talk to about the one thing that kept me awake at night. She listened attentively to my sob story, patting my arm gently once in a while, a strange motherly gesture coming from someone just a couple years younger than me.

"What makes you think he may go back to her? She's obviously a bitch."

I had asked myself that same question. Kyle was sometimes too trusting, and I wouldn't put it past Mia to take advantage of that and lie to him again to win him over. "I don't know. If she makes him believe she really wants to work on their marriage, he just might. He's always been true to his word, so I'm afraid he'll feel obligated." I blew my nose loudly. "Shit, Jenny, I'm just a mess of conflicted feelings and insecurities. I don't know what to think anymore."

"Are you two lovely lasses coming out of hiding anytime soon?" Cal stood in the doorway, looking every bit the romance-novel hunk that he was—minus the kilt—with a towel over his shoulder and a swoon-worthy smile on his lips. Why couldn't I just fall for him instead? He seemed like a simple guy with no major emotional baggage. Because he wasn't my best friend, that's why.

Both Jenny and I stood from our perches on the arms of the office chairs and followed him into the store. There were a couple of customers browsing by the shelves, but Kyle and his witch were gone.

Cal noticed my brief searching glance outside. "They left," he said, placing a hand on my shoulder. "Is the woman a friend of yours? She said she's known you since childhood."

I snorted. "More like she has made my life miserable since we were kids." Cal raised an eyebrow. "Long story, Cal. Did she tell you anything else?"

"She was very… friendly." He chuckled at his own choice of words. "Why is she here? For such a small town, our Montrose has been attracting a lot of Australians."

Focusing on making myself a hot cup of coffee, I rushed to the coffee counter. Both of my employees followed me, and a picture of a mama duck and her ducklings popped into my mind. I laughed.

"She's Kyle's wife." Those simple words left a terrible, sour taste in my mouth.

Cal's jaw dropped. "*That's* the wife? Are you sure? She spent the whole time trying to get me to ask her out on a date." That caught my attention. "I almost did. I mean, she's not very nice, but she has the body to make a grown man cry."

Men! They can't keep it in their pants.

"Wait a minute, big boy." Jenny had both hands on her hips and was tapping her foot. "I thought you were interested in our boss."

Damn it, Jenny!

Cal smiled at me, his intense eyes softening. "I was—I am, but it's obvious her heart belongs to the Aussie lad. Who am I to stand in the way of true love?" His melodic Scottish accent made that last sentence sound like a line from a movie.

My cheeks were burning, and I couldn't make myself look at Cal. "That's very sweet of you, Cal, but this true love's fate is riding on what happens with the sex goddess."

Jenny tiptoed her way to my side behind the counter and leaned against me, a certain covert attitude to her demeanour. "We need to find out what she's up to. Why is she here after the divorce papers have been filed?" Her whisper made all kinds of sense. Mia was up to another one of her tricks, and knowing her, nothing good could come of it.

***

Kyle

The taxi drive to my hotel was painful. Mia wouldn't stop talking about everything and anything, mostly negative stuff as per her usual, but after a while, I blocked her out. My head was throbbing with thoughts of Livie—how she had looked right before we left the store. It broke my heart to have seen that fear and pain in her eyes. Maybe they reflected my own panic at finding out Mia was not a phone call away anymore—she was right there in flesh and bone.

I paid the driver, grabbed my bag, and walked the gravel path to the main building, Mia by my side. I couldn't bring myself to look at her, terrified my resolve would melt away as soon as our eyes met.

"Fucking rocks! Can't these barbarians pave this road?" The barbarians in question were the Scots—not any of them in particular, just a general idea of them as a whole. She had already accused them of several acts of backwardness while we were inside a car driven by one of the aforementioned barbarians. I had whispered an apology to the driver at the end of the ride and hoped the poor man had not taken it too hard.

"You shouldn't be wearing high heels," I muttered under

my breath, angry that I didn't have the balls to say it loud and clear. I opened the door to the reception while saying a little silent prayer that her room was on the opposite end of the building from mine. "What room are you in? I'll take you there."

Mia let out a loud laugh. "You silly man, I'm in your room, of course."

I dropped my bag, and its contents splashed across the reception's carpeted hallway. Shaking in anger, I dropped to my knees to pick up my personal items. Thankfully, Mia didn't offer to help me and stood next to me prattling on about how small the rooms were, considering the hotel used to be a grand manor some years ago. I remained on my knees far longer than I needed. I didn't want her to see me as anger and frustration rose in the shape of heat to my face.

"You can't stay in my room." I finally rose to my feet and looked her straight in the eye. My father's words from long ago reached my ears as clearly as if he had been standing there, *"Don't be a coward. If the going gets tough, you must face it and keep going. Only cowards run away."*

Mia stopped talking and pouted. Once I would have thought her puckering lips were irresistible, but now they were quickly becoming revolting. "What do you mean, I can't stay with you?"

"Fuck!" *All right, Dad. I'll do the right thing.* "Mia, you're not staying with me. We're legally separated, and our divorce will be final very soon. We need to talk."

Her pout turned into a frown, and the frown soon became an angry scowl. "About what?" Her voice carried poison arrows, ready to strike me down. I knew it wouldn't be long before she began working me, bringing all the guilt to the surface and trying to make me rethink my decision to divorce her.

"I'm tired, Mia. It was a long trip from Inverness." I brushed my hair back with my hand. "We'll talk later. I'll send your stuff to your new room."

She was about to protest when I stepped to the registration counter and asked the receptionist for another room. For once it looked as if I had surprised her into silence. Her usual comebacks were absent, but I knew they'd be back, and I wanted to be away from her when that happened.

Once in my room, I placed her bags outside the door for the porter to take away. I locked the door and closed the heavy curtains, not wanting to give Mia any chance to peek in. I needed to gather my courage and build up my defences to withstand the guilt attack I knew was coming. It was Mia's trademark. I threw myself on top of the bed, shoes and all, and stretched over the blankets. Closing my eyes, I thought of Livie, of her taste and her scent, how her breasts had felt underneath my hands, how her little moans of pleasure had melted my heart and electrified my senses. I had said it before; she was my better half, and I couldn't allow anyone or anything to stand between us.

I must have fallen asleep because when I opened my eyes again the room was dark and the phone was ringing. *Mia?* I switched on the bedside lamp, jumped off the bed, and picked up the phone.

"Mr. Huang, this is the reception. Ms. Stück asked me to

tell you she's waiting for you in the dining room." How had she managed to get the dining room opened for her? The owner was still on vacation and the restaurant was closed until she came back.

Making no effort to rush, I took a shower, got dressed, and sat for a few minutes on the armchair, staring at nothing. This was it. Ready or not, I had to face the woman who knew how to play me like an instrument. My confidence and happiness of a few hours ago were gone, replaced by a heavy weight in my stomach and chest. Would I be able to convince her to sign the damned papers?

Mia looked regal, sitting at a table by the window, her beautiful features glowing by the light of a candle. The red dress clung to every sexy curve of her perfect body and left her legs bare from thighs to ankles, her skin a flawless imitation of silk stockings. Any other man would be turned on at first sight, but her sexual overload had worn off on me a long time ago. She used that body of hers as a weapon, and I had grown impervious to it. I just wished I was as immune to her emotional guns.

"You're here. Good." She smiled and waved at the chair across from her. "I can't believe they closed the restaurant just because the owner is on vacation. That's the most ridiculous thing I've ever heard. I made them open it and serve us dinner." God only knew how she had accomplished that, but I had more pressing matters to think about.

I sat, the hard wood of the chair reminding me of how I wanted my guard to be. "Why did you come?" I had to ask even though I knew the answer.

A dazzling smile spread across her full lips, and I cautioned myself against it—snakes could be as beautiful as they were dangerous. "To be with my husband, of course. We're going through a rough patch, and we need to fix it. Husband and wife shouldn't be apart ever."

My throat was dry, so I took the glass of water to my lips and gulped it down. "Mia, we're not that kind of couple. Never been and now even less. I'm not going back to you. Our marriage is over."

"I don't know what you mean by that." Her lips puckered into a tiny circle. "We had a little bump in the road, nothing that can't be patched." She interlaced her fingers and rested her chin on them.

"What's your problem, Mia? You know our marriage is beyond repair. You've never loved me, and whatever I felt for you it's gone." I couldn't hide the frustration and anger that coloured my words. "You're not being fair to me or you. We need to go our separate ways."

Mia could summon tears at will. As soon as those words left my lips, her eyes were brimming with them, but this time, instead of the usual guilt they ignited in me, they hardened my heart. "You can't be serious. After everything we went through together? We were so good as a couple."

We weren't. Outside the bed, we were like oil and water. "Don't make this any harder than it is. We were never good together. Never."

The waterworks had started, tears rolling down her perfectly made-up cheeks and gathering around her equally exquisite quivering lips.

"How can you say that? We're fire together." *Fire destroys, Mia.* "You promised to love me forever, through good and bad times. How can you stop loving me just like that?"

I had to admire her guile. Even though she'd been the one who had done everything in her power to push me away, she was now blaming me for our failed marriage. The worst part was that she could make me feel two inches tall even then. I rubbed my eyes, a dull headache gathering force behind them.

"We're making a terrible mistake, Kyle. We can still make it work."

That did it. I stood up so abruptly, my chair skittered backward on the wooden floor. "I'm the one who made the mistake of believing you loved me, Mia. You know you never did." A wave of sobs escaped her wet lips, and even with a scrunched-up face, she managed to look beautiful and well put-together. For a moment, I wondered why she didn't hide her face in her hands like most would in similar circumstances, and then it hit me; it would prevent me from seeing the distress in her eyes, the pain in her expression. Anger lit a fire in my gut. How dare she? How dare she guilt me after I'd offered to stand by her and love her, even while she treated me like an annoyance rather than someone she loved? When I had given her the benefit of the doubt while she kicked me down over and over again? I felt my remorse begin to dwindle, escaping like sand between my fingers and being replaced by white-hot resentment. I bit my tongue to prevent myself from uttering the words I knew I'd regret later.

"Why are you so intent on hurting me? Have I not forgiven you for leaving me?" Relentless in her emotional finger-pointing, Mia turned down the corners of her lips just enough to make any man falter. "I have no intentions of signing the divorce papers, and I'm sure you don't want to go into litigation. Have I not convinced my dad to come up with the funds to help your father's failing business? What would happen to him if my dad insisted on full payment now? He hasn't been keeping up with the payments, you know. Do you want your father to lose his business?"

Straight to the heart. My whole body froze in shock. Mia did not want to let me go, and she was willing to use any ammunition she had available to stop me. With that last question, she had me, one perfectly shaped hand fisted around my heart. She knew it too, for her lips curved into a barely there smile. She knew she'd won this battle.

But she was yet to win the war.

***

Livie

The picture on my screen made me sigh, melancholy taking hold of me. The Dark Castle stared back at me with its ruined walls and well-hidden secrets. I could almost feel Kyle's big hands on my naked skin, his lips against mine. I shook my head and closed the laptop.

"Looking at pictures of *Magic Mike* again?" Cal was leaning against the door frame, his handsome face opened into a smile.

I smiled back and stood up. "I wish. Researching castles." I walked out of the office with him. The store was full of customers, unusual for a weekday, but I wasn't complaining. Business was hopping. "What's the deal with the crowds today?"

"Writers conference in town." That explained it. *How did I miss that bit of news?* Because I was too busy thinking of Kyle.

I hadn't seen him in a couple days. He hadn't called either. As worried sick as I was, I was even more scared of what he might tell me. What if he had decided to get back with Mia? She had somehow made Kyle believe he was in love with her once, she could do it again. *No, no.* Kyle wouldn't let himself be manipulated like that again. Would he?

"How come your friend Kyle hasn't been around much?" Cal waved at one of the local girls who crowded into the store every day to gawk at him and smiled. The girl almost fell off her chair. I laughed. "Is he with his wife?" My smile died on my lips.

"Ex-wife," I hurried to correct him. "Or soon to be. They're separated. He's probably busy with his writing." I knew that wasn't true. Kyle had told me about his ruse. He was under no obligation to write an article, since he had come of his own accord. But hearing those words uttered out loud gave me a measure of comfort. "He'll come back when he's ready." I hoped.

"We should go to the pub after work today." Jenny was walking by, a pile of books in her arms. "You need a night out, boss."

I opened my mouth to refute her assessment, but Cal raised a finger in front of my lips. "I concur. You haven't been out of this store in a while." He grabbed me by the shoulders and looked at me, squinting. "You will have fun if I have any say in the matter."

There was no escaping those two crazy people. Sometimes I wondered who worked for whom. I nodded, and they hooted in unison. Apparently, we were going to the pub that evening. A couple of beers wouldn't hurt and might help me forget the whole Kyle/Mia debacle.

By the time we closed the store, we were exhausted. A constant stream of customers had flowed through my store all day, buying books, drinking coffee, and swooning over Cal. My energy was depleted, and all I wanted to do was take a nap, but my friends wouldn't hear of it. After I slipped into my coat and gloves, they practically dragged me to the local pub.

"Let's find a cosy spot and enjoy the local fauna." Jenny enjoyed what she called hunk-watching a little too much. According to her, in spite of its small-town feel, Montrose had one of the best collections of hot guys in a hundred-kilometre radius.

Navigating through the throng of people, Jenny and I headed to the far side of the pub in search of a seat while Cal collected a pint from the bar. Even though the place was pulsating with life, there were quite a few seats available. Strange how most of the pub guests preferred to stand or circulate through the crowd in a flowing stream of humanity. We found good seats by one of the darkened windows and waited for our drinks to arrive. We couldn't see the bar clearly from where we sat, our vision obstructed by all the other patrons in the pub, and after a while we began wondering what had happened to Cal and our most sought-after beers.

"Sorry, lasses." He finally arrived, balancing a pitcher and a few glasses. "I got caught up at the bar by your friend's wife—I mean, ex-wife."

My stomach immediately filled with rocks. "Kyle's here?" As much as I wanted to see him, I was afraid he would greet me with the kind of news I did not want to hear. And I certainly didn't want to see those two together.

"No, just the lass." Cal settled on one of the stools and poured everybody a drink, tilting each glass. "She has had more than her share of beer, it seems, and became very handsy."

I opened my eyes so wide, the skin in the corners actually hurt. "What do you mean?"

Cal laughed and took a swig of the lager and then wiped the foam from his upper lip with the back of his hand. "I like to think I'm a gentleman who doesn't kiss and tell."

I slapped him not so gently across his shoulder. "Oh, come off it, Cal. Just spill the beans, will you?"

Rubbing his shoulder in mock pain, Cal gave me that dazzling smile of his. "Let's just say I now know how she tastes, and she might have some of my DNA under her fingernails." He licked his lips to punctuate his words, a visual I didn't need or want.

I frowned. "Eww, Cal. You kissed her?"

He lifted his hands in a big show of outrage. "Ach, no. She's the one who stuck her tongue down my throat and her hands down my pants."

Both Jenny and I scrunched our faces in disgust. "How could you, Cal? She's my nemesis and a bitch too." I was totally aware of the hypocrisy of my words. Cal was single and totally free to date whoever he wanted, but it stung that he might be considering Mia of all people.

"Get a hold of yourselves, lasses." Cal could put on a show as well as any actor on the big screen. "I had nothing to do with it. I ordered the pint, and the next thing I know she's all over me, drunk as a sailor, and not particularly worried we're in a public place." Cal pointed in the general direction of the bar. "I had to put some muscle in to push her away and escape with our drinks."

At that moment, Mia, carrying a large glass of lager, emerged from the thick crowd and approached us. Cal actually flinched, and if it weren't for my revulsion toward her, I'd have laughed.

"Miss Muffet and her crew." Her voice slurred, and she wobbled her way to an empty stool next to Cal. "Mind you, I have to give it to you, Livie." She always pronounced my name as if she was tasting something sour. "You picked a good one here." She set the drink down and brushed a hand over Cal's shoulder. "He's so yummy."

I had never seen Cal in such distress. He normally thrived on being the target of female attention, but this time his lips were curved into a frown that shouted disgust as clearly as words. "What are you doing here, Mia? I thought you came to be with Kyle." My tone dripped with bitterness. Inside, however, I was dancing for joy. Kyle was not *with* her.

Mia burst out laughing. "My sweet and hot-as-lava hubby is having a little sulk in his room." The alcohol in her system was loosening her tongue. "So I came to check out the locals." She cackled like the witch she was.

I couldn't hold it in. "What the hell made you think he'd want to be with you? After the way you treated him since you got married? Are you surprised Kyle finally saw through that beautiful veneer and into the darkness of your soul?"

She didn't like that. She bent and stretched across the small table, her hands shooting out to grab me. Cal was quicker and caught her hands before she could hit me. "You bitch. You'll never have him. Ever." She shook Cal's hands off and took a gulp from her glass. "I have him wrapped around my little finger, and I hold all the strings. I've broken him, and he will never be whole again. Make no mistake, he's not going anywhere."

"Even if he was considering reconciling, which he's not, how will he feel when I tell him what you just did to Cal by the bar?"

Cal threw me a worried look.

She cackled even louder. "Tell him whatever you want. It won't work against me. He's mine." What was she holding against Kyle? She turned to my Scottish friend and gave him a drunken but still gorgeous smile. "What do you say we go to my hotel room and get to know each other, sugar?"

Cal's grimace was almost comical. "Listen, lass. You're drunk, and I don't take advantage of women like that." Lovely Cal. "So, I'm going to call you a cab and send you home, okay? You need to sleep it off."

He didn't wait for her to answer. In one smooth move, he had swept her up into his arms without much resistance and walked out. I was left speechless, my brain trying to process what she had said. How could that be possible? What could Mia have on Kyle that made her so sure he'd reconsider the divorce? Mia obviously had no intention of staying faithful to him and was not afraid he would find out.

I stared at Jenny, who for the first time since I met her was silent, her mouth slightly agape and a rather wild glint in her eyes. She looked like I felt: bewildered and clueless. "What does she mean, she's holding all the strings? What strings?"

* * *

Kyle

After a couple hours of tossing and turning, my mind reeling with scattered thoughts that mixed and mingled into nightmarish pictures of what my life would be if I stayed married to Mia, I gave up on sleep. It had been a few days since I'd seen or talked to Livie. Mia had upped the cruel games she'd been playing on me since the day we got married. First it was only noticing me when she wanted to have sex or putting me down every chance she had, then it had progressed to belittling me in front of her friends and relations, and now she had brought my father into the ring. The clarity and peace I had achieved in the past few weeks was now obscured by Mia's veiled threat against my dad. I wanted to clear my head before talking to Livie. But I needed to talk to someone.

I checked the time and calculated the time difference—it was early morning in Australia. Liam should be up, getting ready to go to work. After a moment's hesitation, I punched his phone number and waited for the click on the other end. I didn't have to wait long; my friend's sleep-slurred voice rang in my ear.

"Liam, it's me." Maybe things would make more sense if I talked through my doubts. "I didn't wake you up, did I?"

"Kyle?" A loud yawn interrupted him. "Dude, are you back in Australia?"

"No, I'm still in Scotland." I didn't know where to start. "I—shit, mate, I don't even know why I'm calling you."

"Whoa, what's going on? Did something happen to Livie?" Concern coloured his voice. "I hadn't heard from you, so I figured things were going well."

I sighed. "They were, until Mia showed up at my door."

Silence filled the airwaves between us. Then he cleared his throat. "Wait? I may still be asleep. Did I just hear you say Mia is in Scotland?"

Forgetting I was on the phone, I nodded. "She followed me here, mate, and she wants to get back together."

I heard his sharp intake of air, and before I even realized it, I was telling him the whole sordid story. Just like when I had opened up to Livie about my failed marriage, I felt as if a weight was being removed from my shoulders. With each word I uttered, the stronger my conviction became; I still didn't know how, but I couldn't let Mia win. I couldn't allow her to use my own family and sense of duty against me. I may be a people pleaser, but I was not a pushover—or wasn't until she began her war against my conscience.

"Mate, she's using my dad's situation to make me stay with her." I brushed my hand over my face and groaned. "I don't know what to do. I can't let her ruin my father's life, but I can't go back to her either. Not now, not after Livie and me—"

"Are you telling me that you guys got it on?" Despite the way I felt, his choice of words made me laugh. "What?"

"You sounded like a bad version of Marvin Gaye," I said. "And yes, I suppose we 'got it on.' It's quite a lot more than just physical, mate. I love her. I want her to be my wife, not that psycho."

"That's a tough spot you're in, my friend," Liam admitted with a whistle. "But you've always had a good head on your shoulders. You'll figure it out. Don't give in. When you showed her you were not the puppet she thought you were, she got desperate. She's probably just pulling on strings."

He could be right. Then again, Mia had proven to be

crazy and relentless when she set her sights on something she wanted. And for some bizarre reason I couldn't fathom, she wanted me.

"Not to change the subject or anything, but I read about your heroic dunk in Loch Ness. You're lucky Nessie didn't get you." Liam's laughter was interrupted by a loud yawn.

"How did you find out about that?" I doubted very much that such local, unimportant news had made it to Australia.

"Livie emailed me a local article from some small publication in Inverness," Liam said, with another yawn and the sound of day-old stubble being scratched. "Mate, you're a hero, a bona fide fucking hero."

I had to laugh. Bitterly. What kind of a hero was I, a man riddled by guilt who seemed incapable of standing up to his own wife? "I'm no hero, Liam. The child was drowning. I did what anyone else would've done in my position."

"Don't be so modest. I don't think I'd jump in those frigid waters even to save the kid." A loud noise exploded in my ear. "Fuck. Dropped my phone. You're a real hero, like it or not. Like your father would say, you're made of good fibre." He laughed at his own words. "I'm proud of you, mate. That's all I'm saying."

After mumbling a thank-you, I coughed to cover up my embarrassment at being called a hero for simply doing what I should do.

"Sorry, I have to go to work, mate," Liam said. "Whatever you decide to do about the psycho wife, make sure you tell Livie though. She doesn't deserve this emotional push and pull you've put her through. You're better than that, Kyle."

His words stung, but I knew he spoke the truth. Livie deserved so much better. "You're right. Thanks, Liam."

"Call me later," he said, huffing. I heard him turn on the water in the shower. "I want to know what you decided. Bye now."

Even though Liam had hung up, I held the phone to my ear for a while afterward. I shook my head, as if trying to shed confusion off my brain, and then collapsed onto the bed, an arm over my eyes. Sleep was not on the books for me that night. I had to come up with a plan to refuse to give in to the woman who had singlehandedly shattered my confidence, while keeping my father out of the mess I had gotten myself into.

CHAPTER ELEVEN
Revealing Secrets

Kyle

I hadn't eaten since the day before, except for a granola bar I'd had inside my laptop bag. It had been a beautiful sunny winter day, but I refused to leave my hotel flat. Mia was out there, and I didn't want to talk to her. I was mad at myself and so angry at her I was afraid I'd do something stupid. I tapped away at my keyboard, organizing words into sentences that I'd have to rewrite later because my mind was not in the right place. But I needed to do something, anything, to keep busy and my head away from thoughts of my wife and her emotional bullets.

A soft knock snapped me out of my reverie, and for a moment I thought I had dreamed it, but then I heard the knock again, a little louder this time. I hesitated. What if it was Mia? The knock was too soft for her though. Mia would want to make sure I heard it. This was a hesitant knock, almost as if whoever was behind that door was not sure of himself… or herself.

I got on my feet and, setting my anxieties aside for a moment, opened the door. "Livie."

My heart jumped inside my chest at the sight of my best friend. She stood on the gravel driveway in a pair of white sneakers, skinny jeans, and an oversized sweater that seemed too flimsy for the cold weather outside. She hugged herself, her fingers fidgeting. I wanted to draw her into my arms and never let go.

"I need to talk to you." Her voice was barely audible, and her chin quivered. Was she crying? I searched her face for tears but couldn't find any. "Can I come in?"

Can you come in? Can you stay forever? I moved aside and made room for her to cross the threshold into the small living room. Before closing the door, I scanned the area outside, searching for Mia, but thankfully there was not a soul in sight.

"Are you okay?" I hadn't seen her since we came back from Inverness a few days ago, and I was like a starving man staring at a royal feast. I wanted her with every fibre of my body but knew I shouldn't. Not until I had figured out what to do about Mia.

"Why haven't you called me?" Her voice trembled. "What power does Mia have over you? Tell me, Kyle. I need to understand."

I wrapped my arms around her and pulled her to me. "I'm sorry, Livie. I'm so sorry." How do you tell the love of your life that your wife has your life in her hands? That she's holding it with an iron fist and won't let go?

"Why won't you trust me with whatever it is she's got

on you?" Her face was against my chest, her voice muffled by my shirt. "I know that you thought you loved her and that, knowing you, you probably feel guilty you couldn't make it work. But no matter how guilty you feel, it's not fair to me—or even you—to keep the truth from me. What is it, Kyle? What is she holding over your head?"

The thought of telling her the whole truth made me cringe. I didn't want Livie to think of me as a weakling who couldn't stand up to a manipulating, sick woman with no morals. I wanted to be the hero in Livie's eyes, the man she always thought I was, and not the disappointment I had turned out to be.

"I'm sorry."

My feeble words triggered something in her. Raising her head from my chest, Livie closed her hands around a bunched-up layer of shirt and pushed me backward. I was so surprised by her actions, I almost fell. She didn't stop; she kept pushing me backward, using her tiny body as leverage. My back hit the wall hard enough to steal a breath or two.

"Livie," I managed to whisper, trying to get hold of her fisted hands. She wouldn't let me.

"Why can't you just tell her to get her arse in a plane and leave us alone?" Her usually sweet voice was soured with frustration and anger.

She let go of my shirt and began pounding her fists on my chest, harder than I ever thought she could. It smarted—physically and emotionally. My love was angry at me enough to do what I had never seen her do. I ceased trying to stop her. After putting her through emotional hell,

I deserved every pounding of her hard knuckles against my chest. I deserved so much more.

Livie stopped for a moment and looked at me with suspiciously shining eyes. "I love you, Kyle. Doesn't that count for something?"

Of course, it did. It counted for everything—the only thing that still made me get out of bed in the morning these days.

I bent down to kiss her, but she beat me to it. With unfamiliar roughness, Livie crushed her lips against mine and assaulted me with her tongue, thrusting it so hard and deeply into my mouth, I gasped. Her hands bookended my face, pressing it closer to hers until there was no space left between us.

"Livie," I uttered again when she pulled away from me for an instant. I was lost for words. I had never seen her like this: angry, almost violent.

"Shut up. Unless it's to tell me why you let Mia rule our lives, just don't say anything." She slid her hands down my chest and pulled on my shirt, untucking it from my jeans and unbuttoning it by sheer force.

"You're scaring me, Livie." She was. Not because I was afraid she was going to hurt me, but because this was my gentle-hearted friend who had never lifted a hand in anger to anyone. This enraged creature stripping me of my clothes was foreign to me—and I was certain also foreign to Livie herself.

She had ripped my shirt away and was working on my pants when I finally managed to hold on to her hands, capturing them between mine and the waist of my jeans.

"Stop, Livie. This is not you."

She freed her hands from mine, stood on her tiptoes, and covered my lips with hers again. I wanted to stop her, to be the voice of wisdom, but I couldn't. My traitorous body responded to her touch in an almost visceral way. My hands moved on their own accord to wrap around her and press her closer to me. Her taste was pure ambrosia even when tainted by bitterness.

Our lips were still connected when she resumed unzipping my pants, her fingers brushing against my bare skin, making me hard, driving me insane with desire. With my pants and underwear out of the way, she surprised me again—pulling away, backing a couple steps, and leaving me breathless and strangely exposed.

"I don't know what she told you or made you believe about yourself, Kyle." There was no question about who *she* was as my beautiful friend stood before me, completely dressed and yet vulnerable. "But I want you to know you are the most amazing man in my life. You're kind, smart, passionate, handsome, and deserving of everything good."

I shivered at the tenderness in her words. She took a couple steps toward me, her anger magically dissolving into a crooked smile, and brushed her hands down the sides of my body, dropping to her knees in front of me, her eyes never leaving mine. Every cell in my body electrified in anticipation. After a quick smile, she latched her lips around my arousal and tasted me, her mouth working in an ebb and flow motion that turned me into liquid. I moaned and placed one hand on the back of her head to press her against me. In the height of pleasure, I wondered whether I was hurting her and I loosened my hold, but she flattened her hands against my bottom and pressed us even closer. I may have screamed or maybe I just thought I did. I was lost in heaven and didn't want to come down from it.

"Livie, please stop." The words didn't come easy, but they begged to be said. This was my better half, the woman I loved, and I wanted her to feel the same bliss I felt—the two of us together.

Livie pulled away from me, and I almost lost control as her warm tongue and lips glided over my oversensitive skin.

"Don't you like it?" She looked so young then, like the girl I used to torment with creepy crawlies. I smiled and pulled her up to her feet. "I want you to feel good, Kyle. To know you deserve better than Mia. To know that I love you, no matter what."

Oh my God. I so didn't deserve this angel.

* * *

Livie

I hated what Mia was doing to my Kyle. The confident, almost cocky man he had been just a few days ago was gone. The beautiful man who stood naked before me had a sadness in his eyes and a hesitance in his stance that I didn't recognize—vulnerable and broken, the muscles on his arms and chest quivering in surrender.

"Kyle, what is she doing to you?" I had to know. I searched his face for a hint, a sign that he would tell me the whole truth. "Please, Kyle."

Instead of answering, he took a step forward and lowered his mouth on mine, running his tongue along the inside rim of my lips and driving me crazy with desire. I wanted to be in control, ask all the right questions, but he was making this difficult. My body came alive, and I gave in to his kiss, matching each stroke of his tongue with mine and softening into mush in his arms.

I must keep my wits. I wanted to find out what exactly was going on, but I was quickly losing hold of rational thinking. That man could do amazing things with his lips, conjure feelings I didn't even know existed. I moaned into his mouth as his hands crawled under the edge of my sweater.

"Oh, hell!" All bets were off.

I pushed him away from me and began stripping as fast as I could, my clothes flying over my head and scattering around the floor. As soon as I threw the last item of clothing across the room, Kyle picked me up and carried me romance-book style to the bed. After our exchange earlier, I half expected him to drop me roughly on the flowery bedspread, but instead, he laid me down gently, as if I was a fragile piece of art.

Kyle slid slowly over me, our bare skin rubbing against each other, making me shiver in delight. He stopped about halfway and suckled on my breast, mimicking the rhythm of what I had done to him earlier. I screamed and locked my legs behind his back, pressing myself against his hardness, wanting more. When he moved, I felt his heat touching mine, and I thrust my hips against it. I wanted him inside me, to feel that he was mine—that Mia had no claim over him and would never have him. To trick myself into believing everything was all right.

Obligingly, he eased his full length inside me with a groan, his eyes closed and his head tilted toward my chest. I moved my hips, frantically trying to take him to the highest height with me. I knew he wouldn't last long, not after our earlier make-out session, but I wanted to make it count. If he was going to leave me again, I wanted to give him something to remember me by, a memory of what could have been.

We climaxed only a few seconds apart, our bodies clashing and collapsing, breathless and sated. Kyle tried to move, but I held him in place. "Don't. Stay a little longer." *Be mine for a few more minutes.*

We must have fallen asleep, still joined, our hearts beating in unison. When I woke up, Kyle had slid off me, lying beside me with his head nestled in the crook of my neck. I could feel his seed still warm between my legs, and a sense of total sadness came over me. Was I going to lose Kyle again? Our bad timing was epic.

Kyle stirred, his hand brushing against my breast. My body vibrated, goosebumps erupting all over my arms and legs. It was cold in the room now that evening had fallen. Trying not to wake him, I stretched and grabbed the edge of the bedspread to pull it over us. I tucked it gently around Kyle's shoulders and watched him sleep. Serendipity. The worry lines wrinkling the skin of his face when I first arrived at the hotel had been erased by the peace of slumber. His eyes were dark, thin crescents on his face, the perfect structure of his cheeks and nose giving him the look of a classic statue by Michelangelo.

He stirred again, his narrow eyes opening slowly. "Livie?" The warmth of his hand made me tremble in pleasure. "You're still here." It was as if he was surprised. Did he really expect me to make love to him and run?

"Of course, I'm still here, dummy." I bit my lower lip, trying to hold the question on the tip of my tongue. "I'll always be here if you let me."

For a moment he was quiet, blinking as if trying to clear his vision. Then he lifted his head, supported it with his arm, and looked deeply into my eyes. "I want you to, Livie, more than anything, but I'm not sure I can."

Here we go again. "Why, Kyle? Why can't we be together? What is going on between you and that witch?"

Kyle dropped onto his back again and sighed. "I owe her. I owe her big time, Liv, and she won't let me forget it."

I sat up suddenly, the spread slipping off my chest and exposing my breasts. Kyle's eyes opened wider and his breath caught. "Mia has always been good at making people feel like crap. It's her superpower, I guess. Whatever she's telling you is most likely not true. She's a manipulator, Kyle."

He covered his face with an arm and growled. Causing him

pain was the last thing I wanted to do, but he needed a good shake-up. Why couldn't he see Mia was playing him?

"It's not that simple, Liv." His voice was muffled by his arm, and I almost didn't hear him. "You don't understand."

That's it! I've had it. Leaning over him, I pulled his arm away from his face so I could see his eyes. "Kyle Huang, you look at me right now." I hadn't used my I'm-dead-serious voice in a long time and didn't hold much hope he would actually listen to me, but I was desperate. "Yes, I do not understand and that's because you're holding something back. Make me understand. Tell me!"

Kyle blinked and swallowed a few times. If it weren't for his Adam's apple bobbing up and down, I would have believed he was a small boy again, remorseful and not sure of himself. Suddenly I wanted to stop talking and envelop him in a hug, whisper sweet nothings in his ear, and make him forget there were people like Mia in this world.

"Please, tell me," I whispered, tears burning in my eyes and a knot in my throat.

He swallowed again and licked his lips. "I want a divorce, Livie, I do."

It was not what I was expecting to hear. "What?" Then why were we having this conversation? I didn't dare get excited yet.

"After we got to the hotel, I met with Mia for dinner and told her she needed to go back home because we were not getting back together." Where there should have been a smile, there was a frown, his lips turned down at the corners. "But she wouldn't hear of it, told me she wouldn't sign the papers, and then dug up a blackmail card I didn't expect and am not sure how to deal with." My back went stiff and my stomach clenched in apprehension. "My dad owes her father a lot of money."

I wanted to say, "So what? A lot of people owe him money. He's a rich guy." But I shivered in anticipation of what he was about to say. This was Mia we were talking about—she never did anything without a conniving motivation behind it.

"A few years ago, my dad needed money to save his business, but couldn't get any bank to give him a loan." Kyle propped himself up against a pillow, and I sat back on the bed, still stunned by what he said. "Mia and I had just started dating, and I happened to tell her about it. She offered to talk to her father and ask him for the loan."

I wasn't sure what to say. "So what? It was a loan. It's not like your father stole it or anything."

"It was a lot of money, and my dad's business has not been doing well." He sighed. "Mia has threatened to make her father demand a full payment."

I took a deep breath, having trouble breathing. I could guess where this was going. "And if he can't make it?"

"The loan was a verbal one. Even though some papers were drawn, the agreement was mostly reached in front of witnesses, one of which was Mia. At the time, Mia made me believe it was because they didn't want my father to feel like he owed them anything, that it was an agreement made between friends."

Typical Mia. Nothing she ever did was for free. "But what

she really wanted was to have leverage over you."

Kyle nodded. "One of the terms of the contract is that if my father can't make a couple of payments, Mia's dad reserves the right to collect the full balance or collect my father's business as payment. He's sacrificed a lot for his business, and he's not a young man anymore." A groan of frustration left his lips. "I can't let her do that to my father."

I bit my lower lip, deep in thought. I had known Mia's father since I was a kid. He had been a workaholic who never seemed to think he had enough money, but he had never struck me as mercenary or cruel. "Her father is a nice enough guy. He used to take all the kids in the neighbourhood on trips to the zoo when we were little. He would rent out a bus, buy everybody tickets, and then volunteer as a chaperone. Everybody loved him."

With another sigh, Kyle sat up, his face now level with mine. "Well, I guess his business persona is a bit different from the fatherly figure." Possible, I guessed, but something told me there was another side to that story.

"Can I ask you a question, Kyle?"

His eyes wandered to my exposed breasts, momentarily distracted. He looked up.

"How can you be sure that Mia is telling you the truth about this? She lies about everything else. Did you ask your father if he has skipped payments on the loan?"

His narrow eyes widened. "No, she told me herself. I...." Kyle lowered his eyes to his lap and was quiet for a moment. "You think she's lying?"

"I think you should have a candid conversation with her

father about the loan before you decide to destroy your life because of what she's telling you." I brushed my hand on his cheek and smiled. "I think you should question anything that comes from Mia's mouth. She's never been too fond of the truth."

For the first time that evening, there was a glint of hope in his eyes, and it made my heart sing. I leaned forward and caught his lips with mine, losing myself in his taste again. It wasn't until I had gone back home that I realized we hadn't used a condom.

CHAPTER TWELVE
Green-Eyed Monster

Kyle

I had been staring at the phone for the past thirty minutes. Mia had called me earlier, and when I didn't answer, she came knocking at my door. I ignored it, paralyzed by doubt. Was Mia lying to me? If so, I felt like a dunce. I wasn't a child or even that young anymore. How could I have let her confuse me to the point of not being able to tell when I was being played? Confusion had scrambled my thoughts to the point I couldn't tell them apart. Everything in my head was jumbled up together—the good and the bad, the sad and the joyful…. Oh, hell, what was wrong with me?

I had heard of people using emotional blackmail so well their victims were only half aware of it. But me? I had always thought of myself as someone impervious to the machinations of others. I had never been bullied in school because I wouldn't allow it, plain and simple. Was it possible that I had allowed my adult self to be bullied into submission?

I shook my aching head. There was no point in torturing myself like this. Livie was right; I needed to have a conversation with Mia's father. I picked up the phone and dialled his number with shaky fingers. I hardly recognized myself as I fumbled with the keys, punching the wrong ones, deleting them, and punching them again. It shouldn't have taken that long to dial a number I knew by heart.

The female voice on the other end of the line was vaguely familiar. It was Ms Bellamy, the secretary. I had met her on occasion when Mia had insisted on visiting her father's offices and showing me around the massive building. I could never be sure she wasn't just showing me off, like some kind of trophy she had won in a competition. Stupidly, I had been flattered at the time, but now I was interpreting everything differently—every conversation, every action, every situation.

"Is Mr Stück available?" I managed to say, my voice sounding unfamiliar to my ears.

"Who's asking?"

As soon as she found out who I was, she told me to wait a moment while she transferred the call. I shuddered and counted each and every beep in between.

"Young man, what's going on?" Mia's father sounded worried. "Did something happen to Mia? I told her not to go, but you know how stubborn she can be."

I rushed to assure him everything was okay. At least where Mia's health was concerned. "I was calling to ask you a very difficult question." How did I ask the father of the woman I was divorcing whether she'd been lying to me? "It's about my father's loan." My voice skipped like a needle on a scratched record, and I had to cough to recover.

"What about the loan? Is there a problem?" Mr Stück sounded concerned. "Is your father all right?"

He sounded so sincere, I almost gave up on asking him. "No, he's fine, thank you. It's something Mia told me."

The sound from a sudden blast of air exploded from the other end. "What has my princess done now?" That simple question made me wonder why, after all the time I had been dating Mia, I never knew her father that well. In fact, other than on rare special occasions, I had not been around him much, and even then, it seemed like Mia always kept me away from her dad. "What did she tell you?"

I took a deep breath and exhaled before answering. "Are you considering asking my father to make a full payment of the loan's balance?"

"What?" The man broke into laughter. "Of course not. If I thought your father had that kind of money, I'd never have considered loaning it to him."

My lungs hurt from withholding air. "Even if he falls behind on the payments?"

I heard a sigh from the other end. "Listen, Kyle. I know how difficult business is in today's economy. It's hard to make a profit. I don't expect your father to be an overnight success, and I fully expect that there will be times when he can't pay the loan."

I hadn't asked the hardest question yet, and I braced myself for a bad reaction. "But if—say, Mia and I get a divorce…."

There was silence for a moment. "Son, I love my daughter and I'll do anything in my power to make her happy." *Uh-oh, this doesn't bode well.* "That said, I would never do something that would hurt someone else just because I'm angry." I let out the breath I was holding. "Even if my Mia asked me to."

I couldn't say anything. Livie was right about Mr Stück. He was indeed a good man, a man of principles despite what his daughter said.

"Is everything okay between the two of you?" he asked in a quiet voice.

"Not really, sir." Apparently, Mia had not told her parents about the divorce, but there was no point in lying. "Things are not well, but if you don't mind, I'd like to talk to your daughter first."

Surprisingly enough, he didn't insist on details and said his farewells before hanging up. I had been so busy trying to stay afloat on Mia's mire of subtle threats and blame game, I hadn't noticed her father was a decent man.

The sense of hopelessness I had been feeling was thinning out, and I could breathe easier finally.

I punched in Livie's number, wanting to hear her voice. It rang a few times before I heard the telling click. "Livie, you're not going to believe this—"

"Who's this?" Either Livie had a terrible cold or this was not her. The male voice took me by surprise, and I flinched. "Hello?"

It took me a few moments to recover. Why was this guy answering my girl's phone? "This is Kyle. Who are you and why do you have Livie's phone?"

"The Aussie reporter? This is Cal."

I literally saw red, like a thick curtain of fire falling over my eyes. Cal was everything I wasn't—handsome, debonair, Scottish, and free, as far as I could tell. I had noticed the way he looked at Livie, as if he wanted to devour her in one bite. The fire in his eyes every time Livie walked by was unmistakable.

"Where's Livie?" I almost choked on the words, my throat was so tight. For a moment I wished I could reach through the airwaves and wrap my hands around his neck.

"She stepped out for a minute." Still didn't explain why he had her phone. Livie rarely forgot her phone. She had been known to hide her phone in her bra so that she wouldn't leave it behind. "Do you want to leave a message?" *No, I want to chop you like an onion and dump you down the drain.* "She should be back soon. Was she expecting you today? I can check her schedule and see if she has any free time."

You fucking Scottish turd! I don't need to be fitted into Livie's schedule. She would always have time for me. We loved each other—had loved each other for years. I would have a place in her life no matter what. Right? Except I was still technically married to another woman, a woman I had picked over her. I could not blame Livie if she wanted to move on. A picture of my sweetheart locking lips with Cal popped into my head and made me gasp. *No, no. She wouldn't do that.* Or would she?

"I'll tell her you called."

Since I couldn't free any words through my jealousy-constricted throat, Cal gave up and hung up on me. I must have sat there with the phone to my ear for a while because the light that seeped through the cracks in the curtains shifted. What was wrong with me? I had obviously lost my ability to make decisions and had acquired an annoying and frustrating knack of doubting myself at every step. What the hell was happening?

Shaking myself off, I freshened up in the bathroom, called a taxi, and left for town. It was almost closing time at A Cup of Fiction and usually a good time to talk to Livie without having to vie for her undivided attention. The taxi driver dropped me off in front of the bookstore, and I rushed to get out of the cold evening air.

I pushed the front door open and was struck by paralysis. A few feet away from me, Cal had his hand around Livie's waist and was pulling her toward him. Another wave of red-hot jealousy hit me, and without stopping to consider the consequences, I crossed the space with a couple wide strides and punched Cal right in the face.

* * *

Livie

"What the hell, Kyle!"

I stood in disbelief of what I had just witnessed. Kyle was holding his hand as if in pain—*serves him right*—and poor Cal had a hand over his face, trying to stop the flow of blood erupting from his nose. Jenny had rushed to us and pulled a chair for Cal to sit, returning to the kitchen to fetch ice and a towel.

"I'm okay, lass, really." Cal was being too optimistic. His nose was bleeding profusely, and his skin was turning a rabid shade of purple. "It's just a nosebleed."

I turned around to face Kyle, who was still rubbing his knuckles and frowning in pain. "What do you have to say for yourself, mate?" I barely recognized my angry voice.

"Fuck, that's a hard nose he has," Kyle exclaimed. Really? Was that all he had to say about this whole mess? "I may have broken my hand."

"You deserved it." Still, I reached out to check his fingers. They were swollen, but nothing seemed broken. Jenny had returned with the ice and was applying the small bag to Cal's nose. "Jenny, get another bag for this idiot."

Thankfully the store was empty of customers. Montrose was a small town, and this would be on the front page of the local newspaper if anyone happened to have witnessed the commotion. Jenny brought me a bag of ice that I unceremoniously slammed on Kyle's sore knuckles.

"Care to explain what possessed you to do such a stupid thing?" Kyle looked at me and frowned. "Well?"

"He was all over you." Still hugging his hand, Kyle pulled out a chair and sat down.

I shook my head, confused. "All over me how?" Then it dawned on me. "You stupid man. I slipped on the rug and Cal caught me before I fell. That's all."

Kyle blinked a few times, his expression that of a child caught with his hand in the biscuit tin. "But it looked like he was going to kiss you."

I rolled my eyes with the same ferocity I used to as a teenager. "Oh for goodness' sake, Kyle. Are you ten again?" I was reminded of a time when Kyle had decked another boy in my class because he thought the child had groped me. To be fair, he had, in fact, grabbed a handful of my butt, but I was perfectly capable of defending my honour back then and still was—not that I needed to defend myself from Cal.

"Come on, Livie. You guys had a thing going when I first got in town. How can I be sure that's over?"

I felt a hot wave erupting from my core to my head and could have sworn I had steam coming out of my ears. "How dare you? You, of all people, have no right to doubt my word. I told you there was nothing between me and Cal, and I meant it." I tasted bile and thought I might puke. "Unlike you, I've always known who I truly loved."

Kyle's eyes were open wide, and his chin had slacked into an expression of disbelief or pain—I was not sure which. As much as I loved him, he was being a total dick and I wanted to strangle him. Instead, I turned my back on him and walked away to cool down in my office. I sat at my desk and lowered my forehead to the cool table. *I am calm. I am at peace.* My yoga mantra and some deep breathing soon soothed my nerves, and I was able to go back to the main room where Jenny was fussing over Cal's bloodied shirt. Kyle was nowhere to be seen.

"Where's Kyle?" I scanned the whole room, hoping he was maybe behind one of the shelves.

Cal looked up at me, his lovely nose swollen to double its size, and chuckled. "I have a broken nose and you're asking about the bloke that did it? I'm deeply hurt, boss."

I pulled up a chair and sat by him, examining his nose a bit closer. "It's not broke, just a little… mangled." It looked worse than it probably was. He would surely have two black eyes and a snout to rival that of a long-nose monkey, but nothing serious.

"Did he really think I was about to kiss you?" Cal gingerly touched the area around his nose. I nodded. "Not that the idea didn't cross my mind, but it's been very clear who the object of your affection is, boss. A little insecure, isn't he?"

That was the understatement of the year. I had never known Kyle to be so unsure of himself. Mia was seriously messing with his head. I was suddenly scared he may do something stupid. "Where did Kyle go, Cal?"

He cocked his head and blinked. "Are you kidding me? Did you really expect me to keep track of the crazed Neanderthal who attacked me? Out. He went out."

I stole a guilty look at Jenny who shrugged and nodded toward the door. "He just left in a big hurry without saying anything. He looked awful."

Before Jenny could say anything else, I grabbed my jacket and rushed through the doors into the already dark evening. I looked both ways, scanning the street for my friend. No luck. There were still quite a few people walking up and down the sidewalks, wrapped in heavy coats, but none was Kyle. *Where could he have gone?* I decided to turn to the right and strode along the shopfronts, checking side streets and doorways. Kyle was nowhere to be seen.

"Shit, Kyle. Where in heaven's name have you gone?" I had stopped by a fishmonger shop and yelled out, so worried I didn't even care if people thought I was a madwoman.

"You're going to be known as the crazy Aussie if you keep talking to yourself like that in public." Kyle was leaning against a poorly illuminated niche, his right foot flat against the wall.

I flew at him. "Fuck, Kyle. You scared the shit out of me."

Startled, he barely had time to open his arms. "Whoa, I thought you were pissed at me." With my face buried among the folds of his shirt, I felt his arms come around and pull me against him. "I'm sorry I punched the Scot, but I was so jealous."

"I *am* pissed at you. You have no right to doubt my love for you." My voice was muffled by the fabric, but I refused to let him go. I inhaled his scent and absorbed his warmth as a drowning woman craving fresh air.

"I'm an idiot, Livie," he whispered in my ear. "I need to do better, to recover to my former self—strong and sure. Someone who you—and I—can be proud of."

Pulling my face from the warmth of his chest, I looked up at him, surprised by his statement. "You think I'm not proud of you? Why would you think that?"

"I've been weak, letting Mia control my life," he said,

brushing his hand over my head and tugging at a loose lock of hair. "I allowed her to muddle my thoughts to the point I didn't know what was true or false." He sighed. "To the point of almost losing myself—and you."

I rose on tiptoe and kissed him. "You're human, Kyle, and humans are all susceptible to being manipulated." I cupped a hand over his icy cheek. "I'm so proud of you, Kyle. Even as Mia threw everything she could think of into the rink, you managed not to fall. Hell, you jumped into a freezing loch to save a child from drowning. You're my hero."

Kyle chuckled softly and kissed my forehead. "Hardly. I guess I should thank Mia for being such a bitch. We wouldn't have split up, and I might have never realized how much I love you."

The thought made me shudder. "You knew. Deep down inside, you knew," I said, surprising myself. I'd hoped he would come to his senses, but at some point I'd lost faith. "I knew you would realize it eventually."

Without a word, Kyle captured my lips with his and relaxed into a long, passionate kiss that left me weak in the knees and burning for more. "I'm not so sure, Livie, but I love that you think so. Your love makes me stronger."

I touched my lips to his again, a butterfly touch that lit another fire in me. "And yours makes me stronger too. Isn't that how a good relationship should work?"

The cold of the night was numbing my fingers. I thought of going back to the store and checking on Cal again, but I knew Jenny would take good care of him and close the store for me. So, I walked home, hand in hand with Kyle, happy for those few moments of togetherness and avoiding thoughts of what might have happened if he hadn't been able to shake this strange power Mia had over him.

* * *

Our hiding place by the river had been by far my favourite place in the world. We had met there when we were kids and later as teenagers to plot and sometimes carry out our mischievous plans. It was always my favourite place. Until now.

This was my new haven—Livie's bed in her small flat above the ironmonger. For the first time in my life, I needed a safe place, a hole in the wall where my psychotic wife couldn't find me. This was even better because it held Livie within its walls. She was lying beside me, her beautiful pixie face half buried in the pillow, her worries washed away by the peace of slumber. I turned on my side and brushed a few fingers softly over her face, not wanting to wake her up. I sighed, the weight on my chest releasing as I exhaled, in awe of my good fortune—how many guys could boast to have an angel as their lover? I wanted to stay here forever.

"A penny for your thoughts."

Livie stared at me with sleepy eyes, a bit of mascara smudged on the skin below her eyes. On her, even messed-up make-up looked sexy. I bent down from my perch on my arm and kissed her tiny nose. She giggled. I dipped lower and brushed my lips over hers, teasing her mouth open. Her breath caressed my sensitive skin and invited me in. Intoxicating, her flavour and scent took over all my senses. I swelled against her as she draped a leg over mine and pulled herself closer to me.

"I want to wake up like this every morning," she whispered against my cheek, sliding her hand along my back to cup my buttocks. "Tell me we will. Tell me this hot bod of yours will be mine forever." She giggled. "Along with your soul."

I meant to laugh, but it came out as something between a groan and a chuckle. Livie could make me lose control without even trying, and she was doing a good job at trying, wiggling her delicious body against my arousal. I wanted to promise her we would; that whatever happened she had me, one body, one soul. But I couldn't. Not yet. Not until I freed myself completely from the dark shadow of my marriage to Mia.

Livie's lips were performing some kind of magic on my earlobe and neck. I closed my eyes and arched toward her, willing the little space between us to disappear completely. She had always been so easy to love. Funny, bright, and full of life, my friend had captured my heart the first time she removed a worm I had placed inside her shirt, her face scrunched up in disgust but no shrieking, no running in panic like the other girls.

"Love you, Livie."

Smoothly, she lifted her body from the bed and straddled my hips, surprising me into near ecstasy as her warmth enveloped me. I moaned, and she gyrated on top of me, rhythmically bringing me higher and higher into climax.

"No condom, Livie," I managed to utter, the rational part of me getting lost in the sensual pleasure of our connection.

I thought I heard her whimper, maybe say something, but couldn't make it out. Too far gone into each other, we rode the waves of pleasure together before she collapsed on me, sated and breathless.

"Tell me, Kyle. Tell me you'll be here for me always." It was a mere whisper, muffled by my skin.

I brought my hands around her and flipped her gently to the side so I could see her face. "I will for as long as you want me. I love you, Liv."

We lingered in bed, entwined and reluctant to acknowledge we had to get out of bed eventually. Livie had to go to work, and I needed to begin writing the article I had promised my editor. My time in Scotland would come to an end sooner rather than later, whether I liked it or not. I got up first and cooked breakfast while she got ready. By the time she came down the few steps to the kitchen, I had a decent meal ready for her.

"Wow, I could really get used to this," she said, sitting across from me at the small table and spreading a napkin over her lap. "When did you learn to make crumpets?" She took a dainty bite of an apple slice.

I chuckled, almost spilling the coffee I was pouring in her cup. "I didn't. Those were in your fridge. I only warmed them up and scrambled some eggs for the topping. My skills in the kitchen haven't improved much over the years."

Livie giggled and dug into the small but filling breakfast I had put together for us. A sigh escaped my lips before I could stop it. I looked up at Livie to see if she had noticed it, but she was concentrating on slicing the eggy crumpet in small bites. This was amazing—this intimate moment over something as simple as breakfast. It felt so right, but it was also painful because part of me knew it wouldn't last. Life was out there, beyond those protective doors, and I was still tied to Mia. She had wrapped herself around my ankles and was weighing me down to the bottom. I had to let go of the weight before it was too late.

"What are you going to do with yourself while I'm at the store?" Livie lifted her eyebrows.

"I guess I'll go back to the hotel and write." Even as I said it, I knew I didn't want to. My whole body cringed in revulsion, not wanting to see Mia, talk to her, or feel that deep sense of betrayal I always felt every time I laid eyes on her.

In tune with my feelings, Livie held my hand across the table. "You have your laptop here. Why don't you stay? And maybe come and spend some time with us at the store."

I half laughed. "I'm not sure Cal will be too happy to see me." I had seen him briefly a couple days after our "incident," and I couldn't believe how purple his eyes and nose were.

She waved a hand in the air and shook her head. "Are you kidding me? Ever since you gave him the black eyes, he has been even more popular among the ladies. Women of every age and marital status have been coming to the store and pampering him silly. And Jenny keeps asking me about you."

A smile stretched across my face. I liked Jenny. In fact, I liked Montrose. I had never expected to feel so much at home in a foreign place. I had been there for just a few weeks, but it felt as if I had lived there my whole life.

"Sure, I'll come." I bent over the table and kissed her. "But don't get any ideas. I'm only coming because I love Mrs Bailey's rowies."

After she left, I took a shower and then sat by the large bay window, laptop in front of me but no wish to write at all. I stared at my lawyer's email, the one that had my divorce papers attached, and sighed. If only I could come up with a way to convince Mia to sign them. If I never left this room, maybe I would be successful in avoiding any chance encounters with the woman who had made an art form out of making me miserable.

CHAPTER THIRTEEN
The Witch's Heid

"Boss, can you please come and help me out?" Cal sounded desperate, not the tone of voice I had gotten used to. Something must be seriously wrong.

I could hear voices in the background. He was at the Witch's Heid pub where he often went at lunch for a bite to eat. "What happened?"

"This Aussie friend of yours is a fucking handful, Livie." Kyle? Was he talking about Kyle? "Your guy's ex-wife, I mean."

"Mia? She's no friend of mine, Cal. You know that." But curiosity gnawed at me. "What happened?"

There were more voices in the back and some commotion. I heard Cal yell out, "Grab a hold of the lass, Graham, will ya?" Then back into the phone. "She's drunk as a sailor and wanting to get in my pants." That did sound like her.

"What do you want me to do, Cal? Just tell her no—unless you do want her to." He was a guy and very unattached at the moment. Mia did know how to make the men lust over her.

"Ach no, boss. As much as I'd love to taste that lovely body of hers, I would never take advantage of a drunk." My respect for him just climbed a few points. "And I'd never betray you that way either, Livie. I know how much you hate her."

I sighed, happy that he was the good man he was, but a bit confused as to why he had called me. "What exactly do you need from me?"

"I have to take her home, and to be honest, I need a female with me. She's not the nicest woman I've ever met, and I'm afraid she may accuse me of raping her or something if I take her to her room alone." He laughed humourlessly. "And, friend or frenemy, she knows you. Come on."

Jenny was away visiting her mom in Edinburgh, but this was Montrose. I shrugged. "All right. I'll close the store for a bit and come to you."

"Thanks, boss." Cal sounded decidedly more cheerful. "And quick. She's actually trying to strip in the middle of the pub."

I hung up and without delay grabbed my jacket and purse and left after locking the front door. I was not sure what I was going to do when I got there, but I was tempted to encourage her lewd behaviour. God knew she deserved it for making my life miserable when we were young and now messing up Kyle's. *Who am I kidding? I don't have the heart to do it.*

There was a huge commotion outside the pub, and as I

approached, I realized Cal had somehow managed to bring my BEF outdoors. He was patiently trying to keep her away from the curb and place a coat on her back. She was wearing a skimpy shirt draped loosely over her tight jeans, and I was once again reminded of the reason why I called her Ms. Perky. Mia was as slippery as a worm, and the Scot was obviously having a seriously hard time keeping her under control. I chuckled under my breath and moved forward to rescue him from the witch.

"Thank heavens you're here, boss." Cal dropped his hands along his body. "I don't know what else to do."

Mia turned around at his words and met my gaze, her eyes scanning me from head to toe as she wobbled on her high heels. "Look what the cat dragged in—Ms. Perfect." I had never heard her call me that before. "Well, you're not so perfect after all. I stole your sweet little friend, didn't I? And if you don't watch it, I'll steal this delicious piece of Scottish arse from you too."

Cal threw me a look and shrugged apologetically. "I called a taxi, boss. Should be here anytime."

There was a small crowd outside the pub watching the show. I recognized a few of them, and the heat of blood rushing to my cheeks tempted me to turn around and leave the bitch to her own devices. Maybe she would strip right there on the sidewalk and get herself arrested for indecent exposure.

"Here's the taxi," Cal yelled, waving a hand over his head. "I'll grab her and stuff her in. You give the taxi driver directions to the hotel." Efficient as usual, Cal shared his plan of attack with me just as he made a move for the drunken Mia. She yelped in surprise and then groaned, pissed off at the way Cal was pushing and shoving her into the back seat of the car. He slid beside her and closed the door while I got into the front seat and told the driver where to go.

"Come on, sweet Scot." Mia was sprawled over Cal's lap, trying to unbutton his shirt. "We could have so much fun."

"Yer aff yer heid, lass!" Cal was so flustered he had fallen into his strongest brogue. He tried in vain to hold her hands away from his shirt, but even in her intoxicated state, Mia's bedroom expertise was coming through. Within a few moments, Cal's shirt was unbuttoned all the way to his waist and being pulled from his pants. "I should skelp yer wee behind, lass. Stop it already."

Amused, I draped my arm along the back of my seat and looked at the two struggling for supremacy in the back. "For God's sake, Mia. Stop being a freaking slut for a second, will ya?" She stopped in her tracks and lifted murderous eyes to me. "Did you act like this while you were married to Kyle? Is this how you hoped to win back your husband?" I choked on the last word.

"Don't even think you can win this one, Livie." Mia's voice poured out of her lips like viscous black acid— malicious and cruel. "You never stood a chance. Your pathetic friend couldn't keep his hands off these." She cupped her hands on her large breasts for emphasis. "I can do things with my tongue you cannot even dream of. It's like catnip for sex-starved guys like Kyle. It doesn't matter what I do, stupid, he's mine. All mine."

I fought the urge to jump over the back of the seat and punch her in her ridiculously well made-up face by sitting on my hands. "We'll see about that, Mia. Kyle is not a thing to be owned, and there are things stronger than your…." At a loss for what to say next, I added, "Thighs." Crap, I was not the best at barbed comebacks.

She didn't notice. Her face contorted into what she probably thought was a sarcastic expression but ended up more like a grimace. "I wouldn't bet on it, bitch. My thighs hold the honey guys kill for."

I stole a glance at Cal, who was buttoning up his shirt and looking perplexed. "I may *boke*." When I looked at him with a question in my eyes, he translated, "Puke, I may puke. Honey between your thighs? Lass, you sound like an actress in a bad porn movie."

We had arrived at the hotel. I paid the taxi driver while Cal dragged Mia out. Her state of intoxication was getting worse, her step more unsure and her speech slurred. After a few steps, Cal gave up trying to hold her up as she slipped to the ground for the third time and swept her up in his arms to carry her to the room. I walked behind them, admiring his nice butt despite the situation.

I searched her purse for the keys and opened the door. The handsome Scot deposited her gently on the bed. She curled up on her side and went straight to sleep, snoring quietly against the pillow.

Cal and I sighed at the same time. I giggled. "Holy shit, Cal. That was something."

He combed his fingers through his thick hair. "You can say that again. You were not the one being stripped in the back of a taxi."

"You loved it, admit it." He laughed and shook his head. "Sorry, Cal. She's a lot to handle. Always been."

Cal pulled out a chair and sat down, leaning on his thighs. "You've known each other since you were bairns?"

I nodded and sat on the edge of the bed, being careful not to touch Mia. "Since before we were in school." I threw a quick glance at the sleeping figure of my frenemy. "We never liked each other even as kids. Mia always seemed to have something nasty to say or do to me. Our parents knew each other—her father is an awesome man—and they all thought we were best friends." I made a gagging sound. "As if we could ever be friends. She spent most of her life trying to either make me miserable or take what was mine."

"Like Kyle?"

"He was her last and final stroke against me. Marrying my best friend was the cherry on her bitchy cake." I lowered my eyes. "She never loved him…."

Cal stood up and took a couple steps toward me. "He doesn't seem to like her much either. Why did he marry her?"

The real question was why Mia had married him. I knew Kyle had been bewitched by the persona she had put on for his benefit—a generous, sweet, and loving woman who just happened to be gorgeous and sexy too. But why had she wanted to marry him only to push him away immediately? It didn't make sense, not even for Mia. "I don't really know, Cal. He thought he was in love with her, but afterward, she just played with his emotions, I guess." My mind couldn't fathom how anyone could manipulate a man as smart and strong as Kyle.

Cal held my hands in his. "I heard of it before—emotional blackmail." I raised an eyebrow. "The blackmailer drops subtle reminders about whatever they want their victim to feel guilty about until he can't tell the lie from the truth. If Kyle is a stand-up guy, she may have used that against him."

I swallowed the bile that had risen to my mouth and tried to smile at him. "Go, Cal. The store is closed. I'll stay here until she wakes up. I need to talk to her."

My Scottish friend tried to talk me out of it, but in the end, I convinced him to go open the bookstore and leave me alone with my nemesis. It was time we had a serious conversation.

Damn Mia slept for the next two hours, curled up on her side like a child, her mouth half open. Grateful for my e-reader, I sat by the window reading a book and harbouring murderous thoughts about the gorgeous woman lying peacefully on that bed. When she finally began to stir, I stashed my reader away and settled back on the chair, watching her as she stretched and yawned, a wisp of spittle hanging from the corner of her mouth.

"Slept well, did you?"

Her head snapped up so fast, I thought I heard her bones pop like rice cereal in milk. "What are you doing here?"

"Cal and I brought you back here and saved you from making an even bigger fool of yourself." The part of me I wasn't very proud of was getting a kick out of seeing her so flummoxed. "We have to talk."

She sat up, pulling her legs under her and combing her hair with her hand. I hated that even in her drunken stupor she looked so put-together.

"I don't want to talk to you." Mia waved her hand at me, dismissing me as if I was nothing but an irritating fly. "Go away. Your face annoys me."

"Why? Why do you insist on keeping a man you so obviously don't love? I want to understand." I was done beating around the bush.

At first she seemed surprised—her eyes opening wide and her mouth slackening. But then she let out a loud guffaw and slammed her hand on the bed. "You really don't get it, do you? You've always been a dummy. A goody-two-shoes dum-dum."

The urge to slap her was strong, but I had a goal in view and wouldn't resort to childish actions—no matter how tempting it was. "What about you act like the grown-up you're supposed to be and we have a nice, adult conversation?"

She swung her legs over the edge of the bed, a furious scowl in her face. "Listen, you little bitch. I wanted to steal him away from you, so I did. Simple."

My blood boiled in my veins, and I could almost hear the rumble of my anger. "Why? Why must you have everything that's mine? You're rich, you're beautiful and sexy, and can have any man you want. I am nothing compared to you, and yet you still want what I have."

"You have and always had everything." She had my

attention now. I had *everything*?

I snorted. "I'm the only child of two middle-class parents who have never been to a five-star hotel or travelled abroad. I was an average student and a tomboy for most of my life. What can I possibly have that qualifies as 'everything'?"

Mia brushed her fingers through her hair and looked at her lap before raising her eyes to me. "You had parents that were there for you when you were a kid and not across the ocean while you scraped your knees in the playground. Your mom was there to hold you when you had your first period or your first broken heart."

I did remember her parents being away a lot. Mia's mom had been my mom's friend when we were kids, and she used to receive all these postcards from around the world. It never occurred to me then that that meant the little girl bullying everyone in school was going home to a babysitter every afternoon.

"I'm sorry you missed your parents when we were kids, but that doesn't make me the one who had everything, does it?" I hated that I was actually feeling sorry for the bitch. *Stop it! She doesn't deserve it.*

"Your parents came to every stupid school event, conference, even the horrible choir concerts." I remembered that well. It was the year I first came to the full realization I couldn't sing to save my life. "And you had all the friends."

"That's bullshit!" How could she even think that? She was constantly surrounded by people who idolized her and followed her around like puppies. "You were the one who had all the friends."

There was silence for a moment, and I thought I heard a sob. Was she crying? "Not one of those idiots who stuck to me like glue were my friends. If I was to lose all my money or become a geek overnight, none would remain my friend. You, on the other hand, had Kyle—always Kyle. Handsome, dependable, smart Kyle. I wanted him to be my friend, but I couldn't get him to pay any attention to me. It was like he was the only boy immune to my sexual magic."

My jaw dropped. "You wanted to be friends with Kyle?"

She stood up and stretched to her full height before me, a sneer on her face. "But now the tables are turned. I have the father who will do anything I ask him and your boyfriend." She planted her hands on her hips. "And I won't let him go, no matter what you say or do."

"But you agreed to the divorce," I said, fighting the urge to growl at her like I used to when we were kids. "Why did you change your mind?"

She cackled like the witch she was. "You're so fucking stupid, Liv. I was fine divorcing him knowing you had left the country and moved on. But then he decided to follow you to Scotland, the idiot. I couldn't let him go back to you, now could I? I won't let you have him."

There was no point trying to reason with Mia. She was batshit crazy. I jumped to my feet and turned my back to her, heading to the door. I heard her snort behind me, and I was tempted to swivel around and slap her. I kept going, rushing to get out of there before doing something I'd regret.

Slamming the door behind me, I didn't stop until I was down the driveway, far enough that her room was obscured by the trees. I got my phone out and called a taxi. My legs were wobbly beneath me. Why did I allow Mia to upset me this much?

***

Kyle

Playing house with Livie was an unexpected pleasure. Who would have thought I would like being so domesticated? I took the load of clothes from the washer and stuffed them in the tiny dryer. Was I hiding? Was that why something so unexciting felt so right? Reality was not pleasant, and my future didn't hold much promise right now. I was looking at a long wait and an expensive fight to get my freedom back from Mia. I was like an ostrich, sinking my head in the sand. Eventually I'd have to face Mia once and for all. Not today though.

I looked around, searching for something else to do, but Livie was a pretty simple girl. She didn't keep tons of clothes or other material possessions. Books were her only excess, and those were well organized and contained within the large back room she had turned into a library office. You would think being the co-owner of a book store would prevent her from having too many books at home, but she had a whole store-worth of books on her home shelves. I browsed for a while until I found one I thought I may enjoy. We had never had the same taste for books, even though we both loved fiction. I was more into mystery and thrillers; she was into fantasy and romance. However, I had steered her into reads that were not her usual cup of tea, and I liked to think I was one of the reasons she was such an eclectic reader.

I settled down by the giant bay window and had just begun reading when the phone rang. A landline was an oddity these days, and I stared at it for a while before picking up the receiver and answering the call.

"Mate, are you in the mood for a pint?" Jenny's poor imitation of an Aussie accent made me chuckle. "The boss has given me the green light to woo you with hops and barley. Are you in?"

As comfortable as I felt in my hidey-hole, I had to come out sooner or later. "Where?"

"I'm famished, and that pub across from the boss's place has a decent version of bangers and mash." Jenny made a few lip-smacking sounds and giggled. "Meet me there in twenty? I'll run as fast as my heels will allow me."

It was raining outside. "You're going to walk in heels in this weather?" I heard the muffled sound of voices in the background. "Jenny?"

"Sorry, conferring with boss-lady. She says I can drive the dinosaur." A high-spirited protest carried to my ear. Livie loved her old Rover. I smiled. "See you in ten then, if I get it to start right away." She hung up before I could say anything else.

A quick glance in the mirror told me I was dressed well enough to visit the local pub. My jeans and a black

T-shirt would do just fine, but my hair was another matter altogether—it stuck up in every direction as if it hadn't met a comb in a week. By the time I was finished taming my wild hair, it was time to go meet Jenny across the street.

The rain had turned into a persistent but weak drizzle. I scampered across the street, avoiding the puddles and the cars. Crossing the doorway into the pub, I adjusted my eyes to the semi-darkness of the interior and searched for the easy-to-spot figure of Livie's Scottish friend. It didn't take long to spot her red hair, standing by the bar and talking to another woman.

It wasn't until I was just a few steps away from her that I noticed who the other female was. I must have staggered and maybe even gasped out loud, because Jenny turned her face to me, her eyes widening.

"Kyle, what a surprise to see you here," she said, mouthing a silent *sorry*.

"Look who's here—my MIA husband." Mia's exquisite but unwelcome face lit up in a smile. How did she do that? How did she manage to look genuinely happy to see me? "Where have you been, sweetie? I missed you."

Before I could react, she had stepped forward and wrapped her fingers around the edge of my jacket to pull me toward her. I cringed, too flustered to pretend, and pulled away, avoiding her incoming lips. "What are you doing here, Mia?"

Taken aback, she hesitated for a moment. "Looking for you, of course. You've been a very hard man to find for the past few days."

I raked my hair with my fingers and took another step backward. Jenny seemed paralyzed, her gaze ping-ponging between the two of us. "I've been working, Mia. This was not a trip for pleasure." I had to keep up the pretence. "You shouldn't have come."

Mia threw her head back and laughed. "You are so silly sometimes. Where else should a wife be but with her beloved husband?" I choked at her words. Beloved? "Now that you're here, maybe we could have lunch together. What do you say?"

Speechless, I stood by the bar, my mouth agape like an idiot, not a squeak coming from it. *Say something. Say something.* Nothing.

"I called my doctor last night." Mia took a step toward me, her bombshell body moving sensually to the sound of her voice. "He needs to run some more tests, but he thinks I may be pregnant. We're going to have a baby, sweetheart." Anger filled me with toxic fumes. We hadn't had sex in months, and before that, I had always had the presence of mind to use a condom. She was lying again. "Aren't you excited?"

I lowered my voice and spoke through clenched teeth. "You are not pregnant, Mia, much less with my child. Stop coming up with more lies to try and hold me to this marriage. I won't go back to you."

Her fake smile turned into a frown. "Then you'll end up poor and lonely, my love." She hissed the words out. "I will take you for every penny you've got, and you'll be in debt for the rest of your life. See if Liv will want you penniless and ruined."

I couldn't. I just couldn't talk to her, be with her. The guilt she incited smothered me, suffocating me with its insidious fingers. I couldn't breathe. "I have to go," I managed to say before turning around and running out of the pub like a bat out of hell—the hellish flames she was able to evoke with her words.

Wanting to cool off before going back to Livie's, I walked around the block for a few minutes in the rain. When I finally went back, I was shivering, and despite being soaked, I felt dirty. Closing the door behind me, I went straight to the bathroom, filled up the bathtub, peeled my clothes off, and sank my frozen, aching body and soul into the steaming water. My body relaxed, the hot water washing away the kinks in my muscles. No water would ever be able to wash away the weight of my frustration and regret.

CHAPTER FOURTEEN
Uncovering Lies

"You really should read *Blind Magic* if you like romances that are a little different." Mrs. Fraser had come in for her weekly ration of romance novels, and I was trying to sell her on a slightly different story. I was one of those readers who got tired of reading the same type of thing over and over again, so I had made it my mission to convert every other reader who walked through my door. "It's a lot of fun." Mrs. Fraser seemed sceptical. I placed the book in her hands. "Here. Read a few pages and then let me know."

Jenny had walked into the store, dripping water all over the floors. "Oh my God, boss. You'll never guess."

Running to her with a towel, I tripped on the edge of a rug and almost fell. "What am I never going to guess?" She seemed frazzled. Something momentous must have happened.

She grabbed the towel and began drying her face and hair. "Can't tell you here. Let's go in the back."

I looked around for Cal, but he was nowhere in sight. "Where in heaven's name is Cal? For such a tall man, he sure can hide well."

As if on cue, the Scot came strolling from behind the shelves, arm in arm with an older customer. "Ms McKewen would like to order a book, boss."

Jenny jumped in. "Cal, you take care of it, will you? I need to have a serious talk with Livie." Cal opened his mouth to protest, but Jenny quieted him with an icy stare. "Now, Cal. Be a darling and take good care of the customers while the boss and I hide in the back."

Like I said before, sometimes I wondered who the boss was. I followed my Scottish friend into the back office, anxiety beginning to gnaw at my heels. What the hell was going on? She had gone to eat with Kyle, and now she was acting as if she had met with Deep Throat and uncovered some age-old mystery.

"You're making me nervous, girl." I followed her into the small office in the back, wiping my sweaty palms on my jeans. "What's going on?"

She waited until I was inside and closed the door. "Sit down. You're not going to believe the conversation I just had with Mia."

That caught my attention. I froze halfway to pulling out a chair and stared at Jenny. "You talked to the bitch? Why? Weren't you going to meet with Kyle?"

Jenny nodded enthusiastically and sat down on the edge of a stool. I sat down facing her. "When I got to the pub, she was already there. I had no time to warn Kyle." My mouth dropped open with a yelp. "Yes, the poor guy didn't know where to hide when he saw her."

Shit. I was hoping that a few days without any contact with her would heal Kyle's manipulated mind. This was not good. "What did he do?"

"He took off." Relief washed over me. Maybe the damage was not so bad. "But she stayed, and man, does she like the Scottish lager!"

For someone who so obviously liked to be in control, Mia sure drank a lot. I was still a little lost as to why Jenny looked like the cat that had eaten the canary. "And?"

"Apparently my face didn't trigger any sense of caution in her, because after a couple beers, she became very chummy with me." Jenny giggled. "Well, I may have helped her feel comfy by telling her I couldn't stand working with you. Anyway, she began revealing some things she probably shouldn't have."

"Like what?" My interest was piqued.

"Like the fact that she's on the pill."

"So what? Nothing weird there." I was not following. How was the fact that Mia didn't want a pregnancy amazing news?

"Think about it; she hasn't been with Kyle in a long time, so why does she need to take contraceptives?"

Jenny had finally lost it. Since when were divorced— or soon-to-be divorced—women not allowed to move on? Knowing Mia, she had moved on as soon as Kyle had moved out.

"Boss, sometimes you are very thick," Jenny said,

crossing her arms. "What did Kyle say his lawyer said about having something to hold over Mia's head?"

"That unless he had something, she could suck him dry in court." Which she was much looking forward to, I was sure. If anything, Mia was thorough in her cruelty.

"Right." She waited to see if I could connect the very random dots she was offering me. I couldn't. "Mia told me she's been rather generous with her sexual favours since and even before Kyle asked for the divorce. Let's just say, she's been spreading the love far and wide."

I literally heard the boom of a bomb being dropped in front of me. "How would the fact she's a slut help Kyle with the divorce?" I didn't want to get too excited about it.

"Shit, boss, will you get with the program?" Jenny pursed her lips comically. "If he could prove she was unfaithful to him, the divorce process would turn in Kyle's favour, wouldn't it?"

Could it be? Could Mia, in a lapse of caution, have just given Kyle a chance at winning? I needed to make a phone call to Australia. "If that's true, Jenny, I will nominate you woman of the year and double your wages."

"Really?"

I laughed. "Sorry, I can't. Not my decision. But I will be forever in your debt."

Cackling like a witch, she rubbed her hands together. "I've got you, my pretty!"

With a hug and a million thanks, I sent her back to the main store so I could call my mum. I looked at my watch, silently calculating the time difference. She should still be up. Mom was a night owl, staying up into the wee hours of the morning and sleeping in until noon most mornings. I punched in the number and tapped my nails on the desktop, anxiously waiting for her to pick up. *Come on, Mum. Get to the phone.*

"Hello?" My mum's nasal voice reached my ears like a kiss. I didn't realize how much I missed it until I heard it. "Who's this?"

"Mum, it's your favourite daughter. Livie."

"Olivia Marie, stop being silly. You're my only daughter." Mum could never get a joke. Her voice turned sour all of a sudden. "Is there something wrong?"

I caught myself shaking my head before I realized she couldn't see me. "No, Mum. There's nothing wrong. I just need you to do me a huge favour."

"Are you pregnant?" *Oh my God. Really?* "Dougal! Our little girl is in some kind of trouble," she yelled at my poor, unsuspecting father who was most likely fast asleep.

"Stop, Mum. I'm not pregnant and everything is fine." Talking to my mum was often like talking to a wall. Worse, because a wall didn't talk back. "Get me Maria Romano's phone number. Can you do that for me?" Maria had once been a friend of mine. Like most things in my life, Mia had managed to buy Maria to her side. For years now, my ex-friend had been Mia's closest sidekick. If anyone had any proof of Mia's indiscretions, it would be her.

For a moment there was silence on the other end, an extremely rare occurrence when talking to my mother. "What do you need her number for? Didn't you have a falling out some years ago?"

This was it. She was either going to go along with it no questions asked, or she was going to flip. I voted for the latter. "I need to ask her something about Mia. It's very important, Mum."

My mother laughed. "Why don't you just ask Mia? She's in Scotland, you know."

I sighed. Deeply. "I know, but I need to talk to Maria. Can you get me her number? You're still good friends with her parents, right?"

"Yes, we play canasta every week. You're not prying on Mia, are you?" This from a woman who held a membership to Gossipers Anonymous. I refrained from laughing hysterically.

"Mum, please. This is very important." I didn't want to give her too many details, but I couldn't leave her in total obscurity either. "Kyle's happiness is hanging in the balance, Mum. Please do this for him."

She didn't say anything for a while, and I could almost hear the gears in her head turning. "Okay, Olivia. I will call Jean and ask her for her daughter's phone number. Are you happy now?"

The grin on my face would have answered her question if she could see it. "Yes, Mum. Thank you so much."

After she hung up, I sat on the edge of my seat in that small office and smiled to myself. If I could get Maria to corroborate Mia's sexual adventures, Kyle may soon be free of the witch.

*** *

The jig was up. I had to return to Australia in the next few days. If I wanted this divorce to go forth, I had to start the litigation ball rolling. I had been dragging my feet because I wanted to stay as long as I could with my better half, but it seemed as if I was running out of excuses. Livie had looked shell-shocked when I told her, but she had composed herself remarkably fast. She had been acting weird and secretive for the past few days, constantly asking me if her mother had called every time she got home from work.

"I've never seen you this excited about getting a call from your mum." She had always avoided calls from her mother, who had the tendency to be a bit overbearing sometimes.

Livie smiled a Mona Lisa smile—enigmatic and pregnant with promise. "I may be expecting some good news."

Now, with my impending departure, her beautiful smile had faded. *Fuck. Why does life have to be so complicated?* Mia was ecstatic, of course. I hadn't talked to her since that day in the pub, and I was tempted to leave without telling her, but in the end, I called her at the hotel and told her. The thought of the long flight back home sitting next to her was hard to bear. *God, give me strength.* I needed to break all my ties with her. Again. And this time not leaving any margin for doubt. If I couldn't stand the idea of a few hours next to her, how could I have thought marrying her was the way to go? I must have been suffering from a bout of temporary insanity back then.

"The boss tells me you're leaving tomorrow." The tall Scot grinned at me, not even trying to pretend he was sad to see me gone. "Had enough of old Alba, had you?"

"Not my choice, Cal." *You fucking bastard.* Not exactly my idea to leave Livie at the mercy of this handsome devil. "My lawyer needs me back." I wanted to yell I'd be back, but I didn't know when I'd be able to.

He nodded toward Livie and Jenny who were by the coffee counter chatting. "You're leaving your girl here with me, then? Aren't you afraid I'll steal her away from you?"

The urge to punch him was overwhelming. "I trust Livie." *Even though I don't trust you.* "I'd trust her with my life." A frown escaped my control, betraying my displeasure.

Cal burst out laughing and clasped a hand on one of my shoulders, giving it a hard squeeze. "Mate, I'm just pulling your leg. You should see your face." He squeezed it again, and I cringed. "Livie is amazing, and I'd love nothing better than being her man, but she has eyes for you only. I hope you don't hurt her." His voice deepened with his last words.

I swallowed hard. I had no intention of hurting her, and yet we had a long, torturous road ahead of us still. "I'd never hurt her willingly."

Giving my shoulder a final squeeze, Cal tilted his head and smiled. "I know, but you have to be stronger than that. I don't know why you are still married to that woman, but Livie deserves better." He walked away, leaving me with the echo of his words resonating inside my head like the bells of a church.

The office phone rang, and I watched my girl run like a cheetah to pick it up, returning soon after with disappointment written all over her face. "I thought it was my mum. It wasn't."

I crossed the distance between us and drew her to me. "When did you become your mum's biggest fan?"

Livie chuckled against my chest, the heat from her breath crossing the shield of my cotton shirt onto my skin. I shivered. "I'm not. I'm just expecting some rather important news, that's all."

She grew quiet as she settled inside the shelter of my arms. I could feel her heart beating, a soothing rhythm I could not get enough of. I didn't want to leave her. Not now, not ever.

"Don't go." It was a tiny whisper, muffled by my clothes. My heart liquefied. "I don't want you to go, Kyle."

I pulled her away from me so I could look into her eyes. "I don't want to go either, Livie, but I have to." I bit my tongue so I wouldn't say the words I was thinking. *I'll be back soon.* I didn't want to promise anything I wasn't sure I could do.

"I know, but I hate it." She rose on her tiptoes and kissed me briefly. "I love you."

"I love you too."

"Will the two of you get a room already?" Jenny teetered on her high heels, her lower lip pinned between her teeth. "You should be enjoying your last hours together instead of hanging around here."

"What about the store?" I asked, holding my girl close.

"Cal and I will take care of the store while you lovebirds go get your freak on." Cal chuckled from the other side of the store. The guy had freakishly sharp hearing.

Livie hmphed and looked around, making sure no one else had heard Jenny. "Will you be quiet?"

In the end, we were pushed out of the store and found ourselves walking along High Street, cuddling against the cold air and heading toward Livie's flat. The full weight of knowing that in twenty-four hours I would have a couple of continents and an ocean between us settled in my stomach like a load of rocks. The temptation to postpone the meetings with my lawyer was strong. I could do my job digitally, so that was not a problem. But I had a bigger fish to fry. I needed to solve the Mia situation once and for all. My dad's voice rang in my head every minute of the day, reminding me I needed to take control of my life again, to make the right decision and stand by it no matter what cost. I just wasn't sure what it would take to do that.

"Kyle, what if we find some dirt on Mia? You could use it to sway the situation your way." We had stopped in front of her door, and I could hear the anxiety in her voice.

Livie leaned against the door, turning to face me. Her sweet breath seeped through her lips in puffs of whiteness, and I hesitated. Should I tell her what I was planning or refrain from making promises I may not be able to keep? "I'm not sure that's how I want to do it."

Her eyes widened. "What do you mean you're not sure? Why wouldn't you use all the weapons at your disposal?" Her voice held a sour note, not the usual tone I was used to.

Sometimes it's wiser not to say anything. Unfortunately, I wasn't that smart. "I don't want to hurt Mia."

I could almost see smoke wafting up from the top of her head and shards of glass in the look she gave me. Shit, why had I said that?

"Really? The bitch who has made you miserable? Are you telling me you are not going to use everything at your disposal to free yourself from this woman?" Her hands twisted between us just as her lips contorted into a frown. "Do I mean that little to you that you're not willing to do whatever it takes to be with me?"

"Livie, I didn't say I wasn't going to divorce her. I just meant—" She didn't let me finish. With a grunt, Livie pushed me away and opened the door to her flat. "Livie, wait."

Already halfway inside the building, she turned around. The wetness in her eyes made me stumble backward. "Goodbye, Kyle. My fault. I allowed myself to believe that you had finally come to your senses when you obviously have not. Stay out of my life."

She slammed the door behind her, and I was left staring at the forest green surface, still paralyzed in shock. What the fuck had just happened?

* * *

Livie

I gasped, unable to breathe deeply. I never made it up the first flight of stairs to my flat. My purse fell by my feet as I slumped onto one of the steps, my forehead against the carpet. What had I been thinking? I had never really believed Kyle would fight Mia, had I? *Yes, I did.* No matter how many times I told myself I would be okay if Kyle chose Mia over me, I knew I was just trying to convince myself of something I'd never be able to understand or accept.

My chest hurt, a massive pressure against my lungs and heart that left me breathless. My best friend was so far gone under Mia's psychotic control, not even our mutual love could pull him away from it. I had to face it—I was going to lose him. Who was I kidding? I had already lost him.

My phone buzzed in my coat pocket. It took me a few moments to acknowledge and bring it to my ear. "Hello." My voice was hoarse from unshed tears.

"Sweetheart, are you okay?" It was my mum, the voice I had been dying to hear for the past few days. "You sound terrible."

"Mum? I'm fine—I have a cold." It was easier to tell a white lie than explain why I sounded as if I had just cried my eyes out. "Why haven't you called me?"

"Jean had a small procedure done and has been under the weather. She just now called back." That explained the delay. I should have thought about it. "I asked her for Maria's number, Livie."

There was silence from the other end of the line. "And?" Not that it made a difference now, but I was still curious.

"It was weird. As soon as I asked her, Jean went off about

how Maria has been in a tiff over Mia's trip to Scotland," my mum said. "Apparently they had a falling out of sorts because Maria had told her it was not right that she had been cheating on Kyle ever since they got married." If I hadn't been sitting already, I most likely would have fallen on my butt.

"What did you say?"

Her mother made a clicking sound with her tongue. "Yes, very upsetting, right? I see now why you don't like her, Livie. Cheating on such a good man? And why?" The question reminded me that my best friend had just left, still determined to stay married to a woman he didn't love just because he didn't want to fight her in court. I loved him, and I knew he was only doing what he thought was the right thing, but it was too much. I had to let him go while I still had some self-respect left. This news was too little, too late. I wanted him to break those strange ties because he loved me more than he hated his fear of Mia's possible retaliation. He obviously didn't, so as much as it felt as if someone was yanking my heart from my chest, I was giving up on him. For good.

"It doesn't matter anymore, Mum. But thank you for doing this." I said my goodbyes and hung up.

Gathering strength I didn't have, I pulled myself off that step and up the stairs into the main level. Maybe I'd take a long hot bath and indulge in those dark chocolates Jenny had given me a while back. I had a bottle of chocolate wine in the fridge, and even though I rarely drank, it seemed like the perfect cure for my pain.

The phone buzzed again. It was Jenny. "What happened, boss? Kyle was just here to say goodbye." She paused for a moment. "He was kind of droopy. I thought you guys were going to make mad passionate love before he left tomorrow morning."

A sob escaped my throat. "Yes, that was the plan before I realized he has no intention of divorcing Mia." That name tasted like rotten milk on my tongue. All of this because of envy. A rich, beautiful, sexy, and well-loved woman who was insanely jealous of little old me—me, with my small boobs, vertically-challenged body, short straight hair, and freckled pale skin. Jealous enough to marry a man she didn't love just to stick it to me. What was wrong with her?

Jenny didn't say anything for a while. And when she spoke, her voice was quiet and hesitant. "Did he tell you that? That he wasn't going to divorce her?"

No, he hadn't said the actual words, but it was heavily implied. "I have to move on, Jenny. I tried. I thought he had broken away from her manipulation, but I was wrong." I could hear desperation in my own words. Defeat. Sadness beyond definition. "It's over, Jenny. It's all over."

"I'm coming over." As I was about to protest, I heard her yell out for Cal to close the store. "I'm on a rescue mission." Even in my state of hopelessness, she made me smile. "Hold your horses, boss. I'll be over in a few."

While I waited for my pseudo-rescuer, I washed up a bit and changed into my comfy clothes. I had just curled on the couch when the bell rang. Jenny was behind the door, a giant container of ice cream in her hands. "I brought backup," she said, the corners of her scarlet lips curving into a smile.

Uncharacteristically, I threw myself in her arms and burst into an ugly, sobbing, mascara-melting, hiccup-inducing cry. Jenny awkwardly patted me on the back, her hands so full with the ice cream container and her purse, she couldn't wrap them around me completely.

"I hate him," I yelled into her shoulder, fully aware I was full of shit. I wished I did hate him, but I knew too well I didn't. "How can he go back to the witch?"

"Come now, boss. You really don't know that." Jenny, the voice of wisdom. "He really didn't say that, did he?"

Prodded by my friend, I walked back upstairs to the living room. "It was the way he talked. He was protecting her."

We both sat down on the couch, and Jenny placed the ice cream container on the table in front of us. "Now, tell me exactly what he said."

For the next few minutes, I narrated the sad story of my last encounter with the love of my life. My patient Scottish friend sat, her back straight, nodding every so often to the deluge of words coming from my lips.

"And then I slammed the door in his face." Like a fat, final period in my love life. I sobbed again.

"I really can't say I heard him say he wasn't going to fight Mia." What did she mean? Was she deaf? "And he didn't protect her. He just stupidly decided to do the *right* thing at the wrong time."

What? Was she right? Had I overreacted? No, I was not the type to do that. Truth be told, I had been feeling a bit on edge—irritated, ready to burst into tears without any provocation. What was wrong with me?

"I think you really should talk to him before he leaves tomorrow, boss." How could a girl who looked like she was fifteen be so wise? "Give him a chance to explain himself. Then decide."

Of course, she was right. I had jumped to conclusions and had never let Kyle tell me what he was going to do once he went back to Australia. *Oh my God! What have I done?* "I have to go talk to him. Now!"

I tried to stand up, but Jenny held me still. "He said he was going to Aberdeen to take care of some things and wouldn't be back until after six. He's meeting with Cal and me at the pub afterward."

A deep sigh escaped my lips, as if all the pressure I'd been holding inside was finally allowed to release. There was still time to make amends if need be. I would meet with him at the pub and talk things over. Maybe, just maybe, there was still hope for the two of us.

"Go get spoons, Jenny. We have a giant container of delicious *gelato* to work on, and I have a sudden and overwhelming craving for something cold and sweet."

CHAPTER FIFTEEN
Final Decisions

Kyle

Not sure how to feel or how to react, I had chosen to give Livie some space. Allow her time to calm down, to decompress; maybe she would realize that at no time in our conversation had I said I wasn't going to fight Mia for a divorce. Maybe my sudden need to return to Australia was not sitting well with her—she'd been acting a little on edge lately. And who could blame her? I had been such a weakling, always postponing the one thing I knew in my heart I must do, the fear of doing the morally wrong thing holding me hostage. But I had decided—I was going to do whatever it took to get Mia to sign the divorce papers.

My soon-to-be ex-wife had gone to spend the day in Aberdeen. "I'm going to pamper myself away from this hole in the wall," she had said the night before. "I have a spa appointment and reservations in a five-star hotel. I'm sick of that dump you chose to stay in." The hotel we were staying in was far from a dump, but Mia was used to the luxuries that only certain establishments could provide.

I was going to go to her hotel in Aberdeen and insist on a signature. Anxiety had made me stop off the road twice already to catch my breath, holding my forehead to the rental car's cold steering wheel and muttering under my breath, "I can do this. I can do this."

After I left Livie—or Livie left me—I had gone straight from the hotel to the rental car place, picked up a Mini Cooper, and begun my drive to the city. I didn't want to allow myself any time for hesitations, but worry was getting to me. I drove in spurts of high velocity and turtle-like crawling, an accurate reflection of what was going on in my head.

I got to Aberdeen faster than I thought possible, and before my cold feet had gone any colder. By the time I was standing in front of her door, divorce papers in hand, I was shaking as if an earthquake was working its way through my body. I took a deep breath, counted to ten—and then ten more—and knocked on the door. A few minutes later, I knocked again. Footsteps made their way toward me, and with a loud click, the door slid ajar.

A bearded face stared at me through the opening. "Can I help you?" Who the hell was that?

"I'm looking for Mia."

The hairy, half-naked man turned around and called, "Mia, there's someone here for you."

When my future ex-wife showed up at the door, dressed in a revealing negligee and her arm sensually draped over the man's shoulders, my heart dropped. Not that I cared she was sleeping around—fuck, I had been doing the same—but to know she had been holding me to my promise when she obviously did not love me stung.

Fortunately, for once I didn't let my emotions cloud my actions. I took the phone from my pocket and snapped a quick picture of the two. Mia blinked and scowled at me.

"What are you doing here, Kyle?" Mia didn't even bother to look embarrassed at being caught with her pants down.

I swallowed the acid that had collected on my tongue. "I need to talk to you." She opened her mouth to protest, but I was done with her. "Now!"

For the first time since I'd met her, Mia hesitated, blinking furiously for a few moments and licking her lips. "Down in the bar," she managed to say before disappearing behind the door.

The elevator was hot and claustrophobic. I shrugged off my coat, small beads of sweat collecting on my forehead. This was it. It was now or never.

I ordered a cold beer at the bar and settled at a corner booth, waiting for Mia to show up. It didn't take long. When she walked in the hotel bar, every male eye turned to her. She didn't seem real at times. How could anyone be that perfect? At least on the surface.

She sat down across from me, a sneer on her lips. "Sorry. I forgot to tell you my cousin was visiting."

I exploded in bitter laughter. "For God's sake, Mia. Do you really think I'm that stupid?" With a wave of her hand, Mia called the barman and asked him for her favourite drink. "Let's be serious for a moment. I really don't care who you're sleeping with. I think you know that. I don't love you and you don't love me. Period."

Mia wrinkled her nose as if she had smelled something bad. "So why did you follow me here then?"

I slapped my hand on the papers I had placed on the table. "So you'd sign our divorce papers." It had slipped out so easily, so naturally I barely noticed it. But it felt good, as if a weight had been lifted from my chest.

That surprised her—her eyes bulged, and her mouth slacked open. "Sign the papers? After what you did to me?"

So she was not done with the blame game.

I brushed a hand across my face, tired all of a sudden. "I didn't do anything to you, Mia. Our marriage didn't work, nothing more, nothing less."

Was it my imagination or had her face turned a deeper tone of red? "Because of *you*." She huffed and took a sip of her drink. "Remember that."

"Fuck, Mia. How could I forget? You would never allow me to forget, would you? You take special pains to remind me every time you have a chance."

She was positively scarlet by then, her lips pursed and her hands playing nervously with the glass. "Because you left me after being married for less than a year."

Guilt pangs reverberated inside of me as usual, but this time it was different. I couldn't even explain how or why. Maybe seeing her in that room with another man gave me the courage to do it. She had no lack of male interest, so why did she need me?

"Did you want to marry me just to spite Livie?" I had never

thought of that, maybe because it sounded so outrageous. "Is that what this whole thing has been about?"

I struck a chord. From bright red, she turned pale as a ghost. Hard as it was to believe, I had just hit the nail on the head.

"Shit. I am *that* stupid after all. I never saw it." I shook my head, disgusted with myself as much as with her. "I flattered myself thinking that maybe you did need me, maybe even love me a little at one time. What an idiot. You love no one but yourself."

"I did love you, but you didn't...." Tears erupted in her eyes on cue.

"You have a choice, Mia. You either sign these papers right now or I'll send this picture to the press in Australia." Now that I had committed to it, the words were flowing easy. I showed her the half-naked picture of her and her lover. "You will be in every tabloid in the country as the unfaithful wife that you are. Is that what you want?" She opened her mouth to say something, but I cut her off. "And don't try to threaten me by using my father. I know that's just a scare tactic. We're done, Mia."

I pushed the papers in front of her and offered her a pen. Mia seemed as if she was about to have a conniption fit. After a moment of hesitation, she took the pen and signed the papers, her hand shaking violently. "Are you happy now?" she asked in a choked voice, her eyes suspiciously wet.

"I don't wish you any harm, Mia," I told her as I collected the papers and slid off the seat to my feet. "In fact, I hope you find someone who will love you and make you happy. But that won't be me."

Without further ado, I turned on my heels and left the hotel. With each step I took, my soul felt lighter, freer. I could breathe easily again, and the fog that had clouded my mind for so long lifted. I drove away with a smile on my face. I was free.

***

Livie

The thump-thump of my heart echoed in my ears as I scurried from the store to the pub where Kyle was to meet with Jenny later. My future was riding on this encounter. Had I scared him permanently out of my life and pushed him into Mia's lap with my rash assumption? God, I hoped not, because I was eager to make amends and let him know how much I truly loved him.

The pub was buzzing with the sounds of humanity, bodies crammed against each other, the smell of beer and sweat scenting the air. I scanned the room, looking for Jenny, who had left the store earlier, and spotted her in our favourite table in a corner. Neglecting to get myself a drink, I made my way toward her, weaving through the entangled strands of people.

"Is he here yet?" I sat down next to her in the booth. Jenny was cradling a beer glass in her hands. "I came as fast as I could."

Jenny shook her head, a strand of her hair coming loose from her bun. "He texted me saying he's running a little behind. He had something important to do in Aberdeen."

I let out a long and loud sigh, releasing the anxiety that had been collecting in my chest. Good, I still had a chance, however minimal. "Do you think he's going to accept my apology?"

"Are you kidding me? Of course he will." Jenny opened her eyes in surprise. "The man is crazy about you. He doesn't have eyes for anyone else but you."

Brushing my hair with my fingers, I bit my lower lip. "I hope you're right, Jenny."

The hands on my watch had just hit ten o'clock when I saw him. Standing close to the front door, his gorgeous slanted eyes setting him apart from all the other men in the pub, Kyle scanned the crowd. My stomach somersaulted.

Please, God, give me this.

I waited, my heart in my throat, for his eyes to meet mine. Suddenly the room went quiet, the sounds of voices fading into the background and reaching my ears as if from a distance. His onyx eyes met mine, and I swore I heard the fanfare of angels playing their brass horns. At first, I clenched my fingers into a fist, afraid of seeing coldness in his gaze, but my anxiety washed away when his eyes softened and his lips curved into a smile.

At that moment, I felt I should run to him in slow motion like in the movies, but the room was too crowded for such a thing. Instead, I jumped off my seat and we inched our way to each other through the mass of people standing between us. It seemed to take forever, but soon we had thrown ourselves into each other's arms and melded our lips in a ferocious kiss. Nothing in the world tasted quite as good as Kyle. I may have swooned slightly, because Kyle had to support me with his hands when my knees gave out beneath me.

When our lips came unglued, I couldn't take my eyes from his. "I love you," I whispered.

The room exploded in applause, snapping us from our reverie. I glanced around and was surprised to see the pub's customers clapping and staring at us. Kyle laughed. "Take a bow. It looks like we were the stars of the show tonight."

Following his lead, I bowed deeply, an amused smile stretching across my lips. "Thank you ever so much." I brought a fist to my chest and bent my head like I had seen many actresses do when receiving an Oscar. The crowd laughed and in seconds, everything had gone back to normal and my sweet Kyle was still by my side, his hand holding mine as if afraid I would run away.

"Do you want to go to my place?" I knew Jenny wouldn't mind. In fact, I was pretty sure she would totally endorse it. "We need to talk."

Kyle lowered his lips to the crook of my neck and kissed me. Shivers rippled up and down my spine, shooting little shudders to all my extremities.

"After we make love."

He didn't have to say more. I shoved my way through the mob, dragging Kyle behind. The cold air slapped me so hard, my eyes filled with tears. I realized I had forgotten my coat inside, but it didn't matter—my flat was right across the street from The Witch's Heid. Kyle sheltered me within his warm arms, heat replacing the chills. We slowed our pace, enjoying each other's warmth as we crossed the street. I pulled the key from my pocket and unlocked the door to the building. Barely inside the foyer and drowned in darkness, Kyle drew me into his arms and kissed the spot right behind my ear, turning me into liquid.

"I choose you, Livie." His voice was so soft I was not sure I'd understood correctly. He spoke a little louder, his lips still wreaking havoc with my sensitive skin. "I love you, and I want to be by your side for the rest of my life. I choose you."

"But you're leaving tomorrow." It was a weak but heartfelt complaint. I hung from his shoulders, my legs turned into jelly under my weight. Kyle's lips were magical.

Kyle stopped, and I whimpered in disappointment. "I'm not leaving. Mia signed the papers, and I will mail them tomorrow to my lawyer. I called my boss, and I will be sending him my articles by email. I want to stay here with you." He was finally free. I wanted to jump for joy, but he pulled away from me. My eyes, now adjusted to the darkness, searched his. "If you want me to."

I yelped and tightened my hold around his neck. "You fool. I want nothing else."

He chuckled into the side of my face. "Do you know what I want more than anything else right now?"

"A plate of chicken salt chips?" I raised an eyebrow.

"Well, that too." I laughed, and he slid his hands around my waist and flattened his hands against my back. "I want to take you up to that big room of yours and make love until the sun comes up. Maybe even a little later."

"What are we waiting for?"

I punched the light switch as we made our way up the stairs, tripping over each other, desire rushing through my veins like liquid fire. We stumbled inside the flat, stripping off our clothes as we moved up the last flight of stairs, our lips finding their way to each other's time and time again.

I fell on the bed already half naked. Kyle studied me from under half-closed lids before removing my panties, the only item of clothing standing between us. "You're beautiful, Livie."

He pressed his naked body against mine, and I moaned. When his lips latched around my breast, I saw stars—a constellation that swirled and twinkled in my eyes as waves of pleasure ran through my body. No man had ever made me feel like this, so light I might float away into the sky.

When his lips found their way to mine, I was so high on his touch I could barely form a coherent thought. All I could think about was his taste, the heady feeling of his hands on my body, his intoxicating scent. Kyle wedged a knee between my thighs and gently pulled them apart while his hand skirted down my belly to caress the part of me that yearned for his touch the most. I sobbed, somewhere between agony and ecstasy, bringing my lips up to his shoulder. Driven by the intense sensation his fingers were conjuring, I sank my teeth into his shoulder.

Kyle yelped and stopped his sweet ministrations. "Fuck, Livie. What the hell?" He stared at me, a wicked smile belying his words.

"Sorry. Got carried away." I chuckled, not too repentant. "That's what you get for leaving me on the ledge for so long."

A passing cloud shadowed his eyes for a moment. "You're right. I deserve it."

No, no. The last thing I wanted to do was make him feel guilty. He had had enough emotional blackmailing from Mia. I wanted to make him feel loved, not indebted. "Kyle, you don't deserve it. I was just fooling around. You deserve the best, and that's just what I'm going to give you." I paused to study his face, making sure that cloud had faded. "On one condition though."

The smile was back on his delicious, sexy lips. "What's that?"

"You have to give me your best too."

With a loud chuckle, he nodded. "Sweetheart, you have no idea what I can do with these lips. Only the best for my girl."

He was not kidding. The things that man did with his mouth and tongue would melt an iceberg. My body was on fire. Every inch of me was begging for release, but he was relentless. "For all that's sacred, Kyle. Will you just get on with it?"

Breathing heavily, Kyle raised himself on his arms to look teasingly into my eyes. "I'm not sure I'm ready yet." The devil had a smile stretched across his lips.

I couldn't handle it anymore. In a swift move, I grabbed him by the waist and pushed him down on the bed, rolling over him. "You know what they say; if you want it done right you must do it yourself."

I spread my hands on his chest and raised myself for a moment before coming down on him. Trembling as he filled me, pleasure ran through me in electrifying waves. I yelled out in sheer bliss when he drove himself deeper inside me. I rode him, first slowly and then frantically, meeting each thrust of his hips with mine, getting closer and closer to the edge. And then the galaxy exploded, sending hundreds of supernovas adrift in my body. Gasping, I pressed myself down, wanting to be even closer to him before collapsing over his chest, spent.

"Don't you ever leave me again," I whispered against his skin. "I love you, Kyle."

His voice startled me. I thought he hadn't heard me. "I'm here to stay, Livie. Forever won't be long enough."

***

Kyle

We had been lying in bed for hours, legs entwined, both reluctant to move too far from that nest of pleasure and comfort. The knowledge that I was free from Mia's hold made my yearning for Livie's body so much more intense. I couldn't get enough of her, and I showed her how I felt many times over that night. In the morning, we rested in each other's arms, bleary-eyed but happy.

"Will you ever forgive me, Livie?" Doubt still gnawed at me, taking tiny bites of my self-confidence.

She lifted her face toward me and swiped a hand over my chest in a caress. "There's nothing to forgive. You were doing what your conscience told you was the right thing— what Mia made you believe was the right thing. I'm so glad you had the strength to break the ties."

"I still feel guilty." I did. Not enough to go back to her, but enough to leave a sour taste in my mouth. "I was an idiot, whether I like it or not."

With a jerk, Livie sat up, the sight of her nakedness making me hard again. "Shit! In all the excitement, I forgot to tell you."

I couldn't help it; my hand moved of its own accord to caress her breast, and she smiled. "What did you forget to tell me? That I am by far the most amazing lover you've ever had?" I fondled her further, and her body reacted to my touch.

A deep red tint rose and spread to her cheeks. "Stop that, Kyle. Keep doing that and I won't be able to tell you this."

Reluctantly, I dropped my hand and fake-pouted. "Okay, okay. What is it?"

Livie wiggled on the bed, positioning herself better to face me. "My mom talked to Maria's mother. You know, Mia's friend." Not a name I wanted to hear while in bed with Livie. "She told her Mia had been cheating on you from day one."

My jaw dropped, and my heart might have stopped for a second. "What do you mean?" My thoughts were so muddled I couldn't make sense of any of it.

"Mia had been sleeping around since the moment she married you." Processing that information, my throat went drier than the Mojave Desert.

I covered my mouth with a hand to smother a sob that threatened to leave my lips—in disbelief or anger, I was not sure which. "She had been lying to me from the beginning? I can't say I'm surprised now that I have had a good taste of her real nature."

Livie nodded, her pixie face clouded by worry. I must have looked angry; my neck, cheeks, and eyes burned uncontrollably.

"I must be stupid." Shame was quickly replacing my anger—embarrassment filled my mouth with bile. What did that say about me? That I would believe a lie without question? "I was going to destroy my life for a lie? How dumb can I be?"

Livie caressed my face, her eyes frantically seeking mine. "Don't say that. You're not stupid. Mia is a master of manipulation. She's always been. It was not you. It was all her."

I rubbed my forehead, trying to iron out a ghost of a headache. "You must think I'm weak and pathetic, Livie." I wanted to be her hero, not someone in need of being rescued. "I'm a fucking joke."

With a ferocious kiss, Livie shut me up. Those lips could make me forget anything. My muscles relaxed, and I could breathe normally again.

"You're my hero, Kyle. You've always been." She was no damsel in distress, my sweet and wild friend. "The fact that you were able to break away from her even as she pulled every trick in the book says a lot for your strength and courage." She ran a finger gently over my lower lip, sending shivers rushing through my body. "And the fact that you felt so guilty about using her own dalliances against her speaks volumes about your kind soul. That kindness made me fall in love with you in the first place."

"But I stuck worms down your shirt." I chuckled at the memory. "Not very kind."

Livie laughed. "Maybe so, but you helped me clean up afterward and offered me your biscuit at lunch. You rocked my world from that moment on."

The magic in her words chased the shame away, the humiliation of having been manipulated for so long. Livie could bring out the sun on the rainiest day. I smiled and pulled her face down until her lips were touching mine. "I love you so much, Livie," I whispered over her mouth. "Nothing in the world could ruin this moment."

We lingered in bed for a couple more hours, napping in each other's arms, but soon it was time to face the reality of the new day—Livie needed to go open her store, and I needed to call my editor. We took a long shower together, got dressed, and stepped into the chilly morning hand in hand.

After we picked up the pastries from Mrs. Bailey's bakery, Livie told me to use her office so I could speak to my editor privately while she prepared everything for the day. From my seat in the office, I could see her move around the store, setting the fresh rowies under the glass dome on the counter, stacking cups and saucers on the shelves of the coffee bar, shelving books and tucking in chairs under the tables. I couldn't stop the smile that crept to my lips, a feeling of utter satisfaction warming my belly and chest, bubbling up my throat and spilling out with my breath. I was happy. I hardly recognized the feeling, it had been so long since I had felt it fully. Free of my guilt and free of a woman I didn't love, I could finally breathe easily and thrive in mindless, complete happiness.

I joined Livie at the bar just as Jenny walked in, turning the Open sign at the door. It still blew my mind how she could walk on those high heels and never once stumble.

"Look, the lovebirds are here," she exclaimed, shrugging off her coat and throwing it on top of a chair behind the counter. "All rested and ready to start a new life together?" Livie blushed and Jenny whooped. "Didn't get that much rest after all, did you? A night of wild abandon and hopefully a little debauchery, then."

If Livie blushed any more her head would boil with the heat. I came to her rescue. "I'm staying in Scotland."

Her attention effectively diverted, Jenny clapped her hands with great enthusiasm. "Oh, I'm so glad. You both deserve a fairy-tale ending."

"I'm hardly a Prince Charming." If anything, I was a frog in need of a magic kiss.

Jenny's eyebrows rose in perfect arches. "Who said

anything about you being Prince Charming? I think in this fairy tale, Livie is the prince and you're Cinderella."

She was not wrong, and after a moment of silence, I burst out laughing. Livie threw her arms around Jenny's neck and hugged her. "I love you, my little Scottish friend."

The first customers arrived before Cal strolled in, his eyes studying the scene as if he sensed something had changed since the night before.

"Isn't the Aussie reporter supposed to be on his way back to Australia?" He nodded toward me.

"He's not going anywhere," Livie said, stuffing her mouth with a rowie. "Make yourself useful, Cal, and go fetch me some ice cream from the corner store, will you? I'm craving something icy and sweet."

"It's fucking four degrees outside." Cal looked positively shocked and outraged. "Why would you want something cold?"

Livie pursed her lips and crossed her arms. "Do I need to remind you I'm the boss? And if I want ice cream, you shouldn't question it." Her quivering lips betrayed a smile.

Cal dropped his arms alongside his body in mock dejection. "As you wish, lady boss. I'll go get the bloody ice cream."

I snickered a little, watching this scene from my seat at a nearby table. A customer approached the counter, and Livie stepped up to serve him coffee. Jenny sat beside me, pulling her chair closer to mine.

"I'm very happy for the two of you." She bent down in my direction, lowering her voice to a near whisper. "For a while I thought Livie would have to do it alone."

I stared at her, not understanding. "Do what alone?" Was she talking about the bookstore?

"I could be wrong, Kyle, but I think you're both going to have a baby."

I held on to the edge of the table as the world suddenly spun around me. What was she talking about? What baby?

"Haven't you noticed her cravings? How she gets tired easily?" I shook my head stupidly. No, I hadn't noticed. But then again, I had been so self-involved in my own misery, it was possible I had missed the signs. "She's pregnant, Kyle."

In my chest, my heart was swelling with overwhelming joy. I was going to be a father. Was that possible? We hadn't planned it, but much to my surprise the idea was settling pleasantly within my heart. *I am going to be a father.* I wanted to run and sweep Livie off her feet, swing her up in the air, and then kiss her until our lips were swollen and red. Livie was going to have my child, living proof of our love.

I had always hated surprises, but this one was the best thing that had ever happened to me. I sprung off the chair and ran behind the counter to envelop Livie in my arms. I could feel the warmth of her breath caressing my lips as I let out a burst of laughter. "You're having my baby?"

Startled at first, a smile soon replaced Livie's grimace. "*Our* baby," she corrected me. "It's not official yet, but I do think I'm pregnant. How did you find out?"

"Jenny."

Livie laughed, her gentle perfume wafting up to my nose. "It figures she'd know even before I did. Are you okay with it?"

"Okay?" I lifted her up a few inches off the ground and grinned. "It's the best news ever."

I brought her back down slowly, her face tantalizingly close to mine. "I'm a little scared," she confessed, "but super excited too."

I covered her mouth with mine, awed by how amazing she tasted and how familiar. I groaned. "Damn, you got me hard again." I didn't think I would ever get enough of her. "What are we going to do now?"

"We settle here in Scotland and have us a wee Scottish bairn." Her Scottish accent was not the best, but the words sounded like the best story ever written. "And do the best to prove to ourselves that our love is not fictional."

Brushing my fingers across her freckled cheek, I shook my head, a smile dancing on my lips. "Well, it sounds kind of fictional-ish, doesn't it?"

Her smiling face turned serious, her eyes softening as she pressed her cheek against my hand. "Yes, Kyle. Ours is a love for the books."

Thanks for reading *Fictional-ish*. I do hope you enjoyed Livie's and Kyle's story. I appreciate your help in spreading the word, including telling a friend. Before you go, it would mean so much to me if you would take a few minutes to write a review and share how you feel about my story so others may find my work. Reviews really do help readers find books. Please leave a review on your favorite book site.

Don't miss out on New Releases, Exclusive Giveaways and much more!

Join my newsletter:
http://bit.ly/reisnewsletter

Like me on Facebook:
http://bit.ly/FBNatalina

Join my reader group:
http://bit.ly/RebelsOutcasts

Follow me on Twitter:
www.twitter.com/TichaB

Follow me on Pinterest:
www.pinterest.com/lisboeta62

Acknowledgements

I have to begin by apologizing to both Australians and Scots for the liberties I took with your countries and your customs (including the divorce process). The setting I created is rather an anachronistic Scotland, not the real thing. I took what I knew of the country I lived in many, many years ago and mixed it up with some more current information and voila! Livie's and Kyle's Scotland was born, *fictional-ish* like the title claims.

I want to thank my friend Leslie in bonnie Scotland for being my eyes and ears in today's Scottish life, my British friend Anne for her help with some questions I had about lager (alas, I don't drink), Rebecca Thomson who volunteered to beta this book in its early stage and helped me with some Australian details, and Google Earth that allowed me to revisit Scotland without leaving my house.

Jenny Walker, if you read this, I want you to know I named one of the characters after you as a thank you for having been such a good friend to me in Scotland. I'm so sorry we lost touch.

To Nessie, the million castles, and the cairns of Scotland a heartfelt thank you for feeding my imagination with seeds for wonderful stories. And to Scotland, of course, for providing me with four of the happiest adult years of my life.

I'm so grateful for Becky, my publisher, and Olivia, my editor, for being what Kate Bush once called "them heavy people" and challenging me to write a better story (even if it practically drove me bonkers). Thank you so much for your support and guidance.

The Hot Tree team, from betas to editors and proofreaders to other writers, you guys rock!

Thank you, Tracey, of Soxsational Cover Art, for the gorgeous cover for *Fictional-ish*. I love it to bits.

I have to thank my critique group, the Writing Room, for all the support and suggestions. David, Karen, Nicole, Anne-Marie, Brad, and Arlene thank you for all your input. It was priceless.

To my husband and my kids, sorry for the laundry that went unwashed, the meals that were not cooked, and the messy house that went uncleaned. Thank you for putting up with my creative craziness and my crankiness anytime the muse was not speaking to me.

My sprinting partners who motivated me to keep going even when the muse had abandoned me. Thank you, Sara, Alisha, and Marianne. Here's to many more sprints.

Thank you, Mom and Dad, for encouraging me to follow my dreams, and my sister for always being my best friend even oceans apart.

And a very special thank you to my aunt and namesake, Natalina, for nurturing my love for the arts. I know you're somewhere in heaven, looking down and smiling at the fact that your goddaughter is now writing the stories you so enjoyed reading. Here's to you, Tia Natalina!

About the Publisher

Hot Tree Publishing opened its doors in 2015 with an aspiration to bring quality fiction to the world of readers. With the initial focus on romance and a wide spread of romance subgenres, Hot Tree Publishing have since opened their first imprint, Tangled Tree Publishing, specializing in crime, mystery, suspense, and thriller.

Firmly seated in the industry as a leading editing provider to independent authors and small publishing houses, Hot Tree Publishing is the sister company to Hot Tree Editing, founded in 2012. Having established in-house editing and promotions, plus having a well-respected market presence, Hot Tree Publishing endeavors to be a leader in bringing quality stories to the world of readers.

Interested in discovering more amazing reads brought to you by Hot Tree Publishing? Head over to the website for information:

WWW.HOTTREEPUBLISHING.COM